All Roads Lead to Rome

Other Books by Yamile Saied Méndez

Twice a Quinceañera
Love of My Lives

All Roads Lead to Rome

YAMILE SAIED MÉNDEZ

kensingtonbooks.com

Content warning: death or dying, infant death, teen pregnancy/
childbirth, SIDS-related death of an infant, suicidal ideation.

KENSINGTON BOOKS are published by

Kensington Publishing Corp.
900 Third Avenue
New York, NY 10022

Copyright © 2025 by Yamile Saied Méndez

All rights reserved. No part of this book may be reproduced in any
form or by any means without the prior written consent of the Publisher, excepting brief quotes used in reviews.

All Kensington titles, imprints, and distributed lines are available at
special quantity discounts for bulk purchases for sales promotion,
premiums, fund-raising, educational, or institutional use.

This book is a work of fiction. Names, characters, businesses, organizations, places, events, and incidents either are the product of the
author's imagination or are used fictitiously. Any resemblance to actual persons, living or dead, events, or locales is entirely coincidental.

To the extent that the image or images on the cover of this book de-
pict a person or persons, such person or persons are merely models,
and are not intended to portray any character or characters featured
in the book.

Special book excerpts or customized printings can also be created to
fit specific needs. For details, write or phone the office of the Kensington
Sales Manager: Kensington Publishing Corp., 900 Third Avenue, New
York, NY 10022. Attn. Sales Department. Phone: 1-800-221-2647.

Kensington and the K logo Reg. U.S. Pat. & TM Off.

ISBN: 978-1-4967-3710-6 (ebook)

ISBN: 978-1-4967-3709-0

First Kensington Trade Paperback Printing: July 2025

10 9 8 7 6 5 4 3 2 1

Printed in the United States of America

The authorized representative in the EU for product safety and compliance
is eucomply OU, Parnu mnt 139b-14, Apt 123
Tallinn, Berlin 11317, hello@eucompliancepartner.com

To Karina and Anedia, amigas forever

Chapter 1

The wedding was set to start at six o'clock sharp. If Stephanie Marie Choi—Stevie to her friends—didn't hurry, she'd be late. In her defense, she had only gone to bed not even six hours before, and the jet lag had hit her like an anvil, but she'd promised everyone she'd be there, so she had no choice but to show up. She already felt a bit guilty for having slept away most of the day while in Rome. This was, after all, her first time in the Eternal City, and she was delighted at everything her eyes had landed on. It was just like in the movies. Even in the wintertime, Rome was purely magical. It was far more romantic than Paris, which she had already visited multiple times in her twenty-seven years of life.

Brady MacLean's argument of starting a new life with the girl of his dreams on the first day of the year—for good luck—had made sense back in August when he first proposed. But now it seemed ridiculous. It was as bad an idea as Valentine's Day. Some stubborn people, aka Brady, hadn't even considered that future anniversaries could suck forever if anything went wrong.

2 • *Yamile Saied Méndez*

Way to ruin the holidays forever if this marriage didn't work out.

Besides the jet lag, Stevie was still hung over from the New Year celebrations/bachelor/bachelorette party that had taken place the night before. A jet-lagged, hungover, moody Stevie wasn't for the weak of heart, but duty called.

As she was getting ready for the wedding ceremony, Stevie remembered that one of her best friends, Madi, had said Rome was the perfect place to seal your destiny with one's true love. Then again, Madi's life seemed to be charmed and seeped in magic. Of course she'd see everything through rose-colored glasses. Stevie swept her hair up in a high ponytail to show off the new fairy tattoo on her shoulder. She reapplied some of the red lipstick she'd "borrowed" from her other best friend, Nadia, on Christmas Day. Then she blew a kiss to the mirror and left for the wedding.

Although Brady's mom had been adamant that the wedding should run on a tight and precise schedule, by the time Stevie ran into the small ancient church shivering from the cold, only a handful of people had arrived—all were on the groom's side. When Brady saw her walk in, he shot her a radiant smile. If Stevie had ever stopped to consider that perhaps there was a soulmate waiting for her in spite of who she was, maybe she'd be the bride today.

Once upon a time, when she was barely eighteen and Brady was twenty, they had a short fling. They'd both been door-to-door rookie reps, selling alarm systems in Lubbock, Texas. Maybe it had been the heat of the South, or the boredom of working hard every day like a hamster on a wheel. It could have been that Brady's smile really was that charming and his blue eyes so trusting and kind. Whatever it was, Stevie had let her defenses down, and one afternoon, she'd kissed him spontaneously. It wasn't her first kiss by any means, but it seared her heart just the same.

As amazing as the kiss had been, it wasn't enough to tie her

All Roads Lead to Rome • 3

down, though, mainly because she *really* liked Brady and she had no intention of ruining his life. She was a bad apple, according to every authority figure in her life, from teachers to nosy aunts, and even her own mother. Stevie didn't want to make his life miserable like hers, so she decided to friend-zone him.

Now Brady was getting married to Céline, a beautiful, sweet French girl who was kind but, in Stevie's opinion, too vanilla, too accommodating, and too predictable. Maybe that's why Brady had decided to settle for her. Céline and Stevie were opposites of each other in every sense of the word. Céline was tall and statuesque, whereas Stevie was short and stocky. Céline was blonde and fair-skinned. She resembled one of those elves you'd see in an epic fantasy movie. Stevie's skin wasn't as dark as her friend Nadia's, but she was definitely on the darker olive-colored side, and her black hair had natural blue tints if the light hit her just right. Céline was refined and well-spoken. Stevie swore like a trucker and was like one of the boys. She felt like one of them, too, which was why she felt quite comfortable when she was in the midst of a group of guys. She took great pride in outdrinking, outswearing, outearning them.

"Stephanie," Brady said in that breathy way of his when she reached him. "Now that you're here, I'm not so nervous anymore."

Stevie's insides tingled. Of course, she didn't have feelings for her best guy friend, like at all. She hated to admit it, but the way he insisted on calling her by her proper name always got to her.

"Brady," she said, while kissing him on the cheek. His skin felt so soft against hers, and she closed her eyes to savor the moment. She didn't have romantic feelings for Brady, nor did she ever sexually fantasize about him, but she was undeniably hungry for human touch. It was ridiculous how much she craved it. Stevie had been on her own for ages, and if she were being honest with herself, it was easy for her to overestimate how much resilience she really had to spend the holidays all on her own.

"Mom thought you wouldn't dare show up," he remarked.

4 • *Yamile Saied Méndez*

Stevie glanced toward Brady's mom, who was sitting on the first row. The reigning Mrs. MacLean was furiously texting. "Why?" Stevie asked, wondering if something had happened the previous night during the pre-wedding festivities. As hard as she tried, Stevie couldn't remember.

Brady shrugged. "She's old-school. I don't think she believes a man and a woman can be friends. You know what I mean?"

She knew what he meant, and the thought made her feel dirty, somehow. "Céline's not here yet?" she asked, trying to change the subject and looking around as if expecting the magnificent bride to pop up from her hiding spot in the wooden pews or behind a pillar.

Brady's mom was now resolutely keeping her gaze on the crucifix on top of the altar with a horrified expression on her face. Brady's family were all Mormons, although he was inactive. He wasn't even religious, and neither was Céline. She said she liked the aesthetic of the church, which had been perfect since this winter was supposedly the coldest in decades. It was much too cold for an outdoor, nondenominational wedding.

"She won't be here for a while. They're French," Brady said, chuckling. "I don't know what Mom was expecting."

"And people are still recovering from the holiday festivities. After all, it's the first day of January, you know," Stevie said, gently elbowing him in the ribs; but being a full foot shorter than him, she hit him in the lower stomach.

"Ouch," he whispered, doubling over. "So close to the family jewels! I need the equipment to work on my wedding night, woman!"

Stevie smiled, but her eyes went all misty, so she avoided looking at his face. Not that she'd ever go Julia Roberts in *My Best Friend's Wedding* on him, but she didn't want to even have to deal with the temptation. The regret that would one-hundred-percent follow wasn't worth the risk.

"Maybe it was dumb for me to choose today, but remember

All Roads Lead to Rome • 5

when you told me to start the year how I want it to go?" Brady asked. "Well, I mean to spend the rest of my life with Céline, so I better start the year right."

Stevie scratched the back of her head to distract herself from the pain in her heart that she felt upon noting the tone of voice of a man deeply in love. "You could at least have chosen a place in a warm location. I don't know, the Caribbean or South America. Australia, even. It's summertime there, and you loved it last time we visited," she teased.

"Other than the pictures on social media, I have no memories of it. I was out the whole time, and I never want to end a year and start the next like that again," he said. His eyes crinkled in the corners when he smiled. Brady made a gesture of brushing his hair, but he must have remembered he couldn't mess it up, because he changed his mind as his fingers touched the top of his head. "Besides, she wanted Rome in the winter. Who am I to deny the queen of my life?"

Stevie smiled through another pang, this one even sharper and deeper than the first. It wasn't exactly a pang of regret, because she knew that if she and Brady had been a thing, it wouldn't have ended like this—in a fancy church wedding. Instead, it would've ended with one of them filing a restraining order against the other. Most likely, him against her. There was no denying the pang of envy was real, because she would never have a man speak of her this way. She wasn't the kind of woman men leave everything for or give their hearts to on a silver platter.

Irrationally, Stevie wanted total devotion or nothing at all. Once upon a time, she'd once had it. Then, in what seemed like a blink of an eye, she lost it all.

"You don't deserve so much love," her mom had told her once. More than a cruel statement, it had become a curse that Stevie just knew would follow her for the rest of her life. It was also a lesson she'd never forget.

6 • *Yamile Saied Méndez*

Ever since Stevie had heard those words, she'd been no one's first choice—ever. She had tried to change and earn that kind of devotion, but she'd failed miserably.

Never again would she set herself up for this kind of disappointment.

Granted, she wasn't even thirty yet, but in her soul, Stevie felt ancient, jaded, and cynical—when it came to love, at least.

Next to her, Brady wrung his hands. She patted his shoulder. "You said you weren't nervous. Having cold feet?"

He shrugged. "What? No! I'm just excited. People think only girls dream of this day, but I've been fantasizing about my wedding all my life. I'm so lucky! I don't know what I did to deserve her."

The smile on this gentle giant melted Stevie's frozen heart, even though it was pierced with unintended arrows. "She's the lucky one," she replied. "And no one ever has to earn the privilege of being loved. It's a right everyone should have."

Of course she didn't believe this, but her words made him smile again, and that's all she'd been shooting for.

While they waited for the bride, they talked about happy and funny days in the past. For the last five years, during the summers, they had co-managed a home alarm sales office in South Texas. Besides earning more money than a young person with no other skills but selling pitches and managing a group of rowdy guys, they'd formed a friendship Stevie hoped would last forever. Now, after becoming aware of his mom's opinion of platonic friendships between men and women, she hoped that their partnership would survive his marriage.

Soon, the church filled up with people from the bride's side, and an hour and a half after the planned start time, Brady's mom stepped up to him with a dazzling smile on her face and said, "She's here!" Then she shot Stevie a warning look that froze her. It happened so fast that it seemed as though it never happened.

Brady's eyes immediately flew to Stevie's. This wasn't the

All Roads Lead to Rome • 7

time or place to ask his mom why she was being a witch. Stevie nodded at Brady, letting him know everything would turn out perfectly.

And it did.

Lined up next to the rest of the groom's party, standing in as the best man, Stevie watched Céline enter the church and draw the attention of every set of eyes. She was a vision in her vintage Valentino gown, her victorious smile glowing behind the thin veil. She took Stevie's breath away.

Next to her, Brady was having an epiphany. Without waiting for a cue, Stevie handed him a handkerchief, and he dabbed at his eyes with zero self-consciousness. She was proud of him for showing his emotions. She'd taught him well. But she kept hers tightly reined in. Stevie would fulfill the role of being his best man, but she had no intention of playing the heartbroken best friend crying at the side of the altar.

She smiled at Céline, but the bride didn't return the gesture. To make matters worse, Chloe, the matron of honor, one of Céline's best friends and now sister-in-law, shoved Stevie aside and smirked at her instead of apologizing. She was married to Andrew, one of Brady's brothers and the other best man, and she didn't hide the fact that she didn't want Stevie to be part of the wedding party.

Obviously, people whispered and gossiped about her and Brady's friendship, and she wasn't going to be the freak show everyone came to see. She lowered her head and tried to blend in, somehow hoping to become invisible. The ceremony started, and Stevie fought hard to stay present in the moment instead of disassociating like she did when things got too overwhelming to process.

When the Italian priest asked in flawless English, "Does anyone object to this union? Speak up now or be silent forever," Andrew, on Stevie's left, playfully elbowed her.

Everyone in the church seemed to be looking at her. Everyone but Céline. Stevie swallowed her discomfort. It sounded like a

8 • *Yamile Saied Méndez*

gulp, which echoed throughout the church, louder than she'd intended. A ripple of contained laughter swept through the attendants. With her face burning with humiliation, Stevie made a dismissing gesture with her hand, as if to indicate the priest could continue.

"Thanks," Brady mouthed at her.

"Asshole," she whispered back. Stevie rolled her eyes to hide the tears prickling. They surprised her, because she had never even considered making a great gesture like in the movies, not even a tiny one, to be honest, and she wondered if Céline had arrived so late to give her a last chance. One she never thought she had and now had lost forever.

"I now declare you, husband and wife," the priest pronounced.

Bride and groom kissed, and the audience exploded in applause. At least, Céline's family did. Brady's, who was used to more solemn religious meetings, followed demurely with a few seconds' delay.

Andrew gently pressed Stevie's hand. "Are you okay?"

She didn't dare look at him, because his wife, Chloe, was practically drilling a hole into Stevie with her stare. "Perfect. Happiest day of my life now that I'm not in charge of this fool anymore."

Dismissing her feelings with cheap humor, pulling her hand back, and wiping it on her dress as if she felt dirty was a typical Stevie move. But she managed to keep her fake smile on when the two families waited outside to throw rice at the newlyweds, although she was freezing in her pink dress. She'd worn the exact color Céline had assigned to the bridesmaids and her, but of course, Stevie had chosen the skimpiest one she could find, and she'd left her faux fur coat inside the church. She was paying for it now. She had to tiptoe on the cobblestones to save the heels of her brand-new Christian Louboutin stilettos, but never once lost her balance.

All Roads Lead to Rome • 9

As the best man, she rode with Andrew and Chloe to the reception and was subjected to being a first-row witness of their bickering as the matron of honor bashed him for having held Stevie's hand.

"He didn't . . . it wasn't," Stevie started to say, but Chloe cut her off.

"Please stop. Everyone saw it," Chloe insisted.

"Saw what?" Stevie asked, her blood boiling.

"Please, Stephanie," Andrew begged. "Stay out of this. You're making it worse."

Stevie balled her fists to stop herself from punching him. "Don't call me Stephanie ever again, you idiot."

"Don't call my husband an idiot, you slut," Chloe shot back, grabbing her husband's hand.

Stevie scoffed at how quickly the two of them had turned on her when she was the innocent bystander to their dysfunctional relationship. These two had been married for less than six months. Céline and Brady had met at their wedding, after all.

"You shouldn't have come, Stevie," Andrew muttered.

Stevie's eyes prickled, and she had to look out the window.

"Aw," Chloe said in a mocking voice. "Are you going to cry, bitch?"

If it weren't for the fact that the action would've certainly made the front page of the worst tabloids, if not the social media accounts of Céline's throngs of influencer friends, Stevie would have jumped from the car. She tried to breathe like Madi had taught her while Chloe and Andrew argued again. The poor driver looked at the three of them through the rearview mirror. Finally, they arrived at the reception venue in the middle of Rome. Stevie regretted that she had to give the toast and couldn't run away back to the safety of her hotel room. She had no one to blame but her own stupid self.

It was obvious now that she'd lost Brady to marriage. What a tragedy. More than good friends, they'd been excellent business

10 • *Yamile Saied Méndez*

partners. By the time she made it inside the venue, she was fuming with anger. The seething kind of anger that can't be hidden and is usually mistaken for something else, like jealousy.

And she wasn't jealous!

Céline and Chloe and the rest could keep their stupid husbands, for all she cared. Stevie had never even had a crumb of interest in any of them. Why would she try to *steal* them, now that they were married, when she could've had them before? It didn't make sense. But she wasn't going to try to reason with these idiot girls.

Her mood didn't improve at the actual reception. Whoever had planned the seating had assigned her to the farthest table from the happy couple, tucked away from everyone else. Still, as much as she could—or as much as Céline's friends let her—Stevie performed her best man duties to the best of her ability. She avoided all alcohol, just in case. She played with the nieces and nephews and the other random kids who for some reason came up to chat with her. She talked to the older aunts and distant acquaintances. But the whole time, Stevie wondered what she was doing in a place where she was certainly not wanted.

After dessert, Andrew gave his best man speech. Stevie tried not to roll her eyes or yawn at the cringe words that came out of his mouth. When Andrew announced that Stevie would be speaking next, she truly wished she'd followed her gut and left before the other girls in the bridal party had a chance to humiliate her even more.

Aware that every eye was on her, she gave the short and sweet toast celebrating the happy couple that she'd prepared, making an effort to speak of the two of them as a unit, just in case. Céline must have found no fault with it, because she gave her a small smile while Brady beamed at Stevie. Chloe and Andrew were bickering again.

Ignoring them, Stevie stood in the small group of single ladies waiting to catch the bouquet. Most women in the party, even the young ones like her, were either engaged or married. So

All Roads Lead to Rome • 11

Stevie stood next to the tween girls and the divorced middle-aged aunts who were eager to get a sign from the universe that a second chance was right around the corner.

Stevie didn't need any signs. She already knew there would be no second chances for her, because it was her choice not to have one, damn it! Still, the bouquet fell on her head, and out of a reflex, her arm shot out to grab it. She caught it like a pro. It must have been muscle memory from her years of high school softball.

Stevie held the flowers against her chest like she was in a Miss Universe pageant, to the absolute hilarity of Brady, Andrew, and the rest of the boys. Céline winked at her, and Stevie replied with a curtsy, hoping to smash any wrong ideas she may still have about her partnership with Brady.

"Please, let's get ready for the bride and groom's first dance!" the DJ announced, as the first chords of Ed Sheeran's "Perfect" rang through the room.

Stevie glanced at Brady, who shrugged, as if waiting to be scolded in front of his family. He'd dedicated this song to her once, when he was still trying to make them a thing. It was cheesy, but she'd always thought this was their song, and now he played it at his wedding for another. But she took it in stride and smiled. When the rest of the attendants took to the floor, she smoothly made her way to the back of the room, like one of the wallflowers of the movies she secretly loved to watch. She thought she blended perfectly with the shadows as she retreated behind a curtain, only to find she wasn't alone.

Chapter 2

Standing behind the see-through curtains, a tall blond guy was looking at the dance floor as if the couples were characters out of a zombie movie. When Stevie bumped into him, he was so startled that he spilled his wine on her.

"Oh my God!" he said in heavy accented English. "Sorry about that!" He proceeded to yank the handkerchief from his jacket pocket and dab at the front of her dress, muttering something in Spanish.

Her family was from Peru, but Stevie didn't speak Spanish, although her friends Nadia and Madi had taught her the essentials, namely swear words. This man was swearing like a sailor in the most perfect Argentine accent she'd ever heard as he carefully tried to blot out the red wine from her pink silk dress.

"It's okay! Leave it!" she said, laughing. Stevie wished she spoke a language other than English to at least have some moment of privacy from her internal nightmare.

He stopped then, and when he looked at her, time stood still, and not in a good way. It was all so ridiculous. From the bright-

All Roads Lead to Rome • 13

ness of his sparkling blue eyes to the way she got so nervous to finally being in front of the one guy Brady had ever been jealous of, Cristian Alvarez.

"Oh, shit!" she gasped.

"Oh, shit indeed," he said, with a crooked smile that sent sirens wailing in her mind. "Nice to finally meet you, Stephanie. I've heard a lot about you."

"And I've heard a lot about you, Cristian," she replied, her skin prickling like it was warning her about a predator.

It wasn't an exaggeration. All she'd ever heard about Cristian Alvarez from Brady was problematic. He was a self-centered prick who left a string of broken hearts behind him and ruined reputations. One of the summer sales guys had promised to kill him for taking his sister's virginity, as if virginity were a jewel and they lived in the dark ages.

Stevie's body went cold all over. Had she fallen into a trap? Had Céline and her posse sent him to torture her? She was already emotionally frail, and if this guy wanted to mess with her, he was going to have a rude awakening. Somehow, she'd never been in the vicinity of his exploits. Why had Brady invited him when he hated him so much?

He must have read the question in Stevie's eyes and rushed to reply, "Céline invited me. Her grandpa and my grandma are neighbors . . . of sorts. Ross, my grandma, doesn't travel anymore, and since I was in Europe already, she asked me to come and represent the family. I didn't expect to see you here, honestly."

"Why not?" she asked, in the most cutting tone she could muster.

Cristian pressed his lips as if he didn't want to say what he was thinking, but his eyes darted toward the bride and groom on the other side of the room.

Stevie sighed. "Because Céline hates me."

Cristian shrugged one shoulder. "She doesn't hate you. She knows that if it weren't for you, Brady would still be living in

14 • *Yamile Saied Méndez*

his parents' basement. Now he's on the straight and narrow. She thinks she can take it from here."

Stevie had known all this, but it was nice to have the validation of someone else, a stranger, confirming her suspicions. "Just for the record, Brady is intimidated by you."

Cristian laughed explosively, throwing his head back. Then he said something, but she wasn't sure if it was English or Italian.

Stevie felt in her marrow that she should be stepping back, away from him, as far as possible. But he had a magnetism she couldn't seem to resist. Maybe it was the accent that made her lean toward him instead. "What? I don't know what you're saying."

His eyes were still shining with laughter when he said, "My bad. Brady said you were Spanish, and I assumed from Spain."

Stevie rolled her eyes. "I'm an American, via Peru, and before that, Japan and Korea."

"Ah," he said, tapping the side of his head as if he were committing this information to memory. "Makes sense now."

"Where are you from?" she asked. "Brady never mentioned it."

He narrowed his eyes at her. "Really? What *did* he say about me?" Cristian tried to act all offended, but he was certainly flattered that Brady spent so much time bashing him.

Stevie wasn't going to fuel this guy's ego, for all his charm and cuteness. She wasn't going to tell him all the trash Brady said about him, either. But she'd give him something. After all, she was mad at Brady for asking her to be the best man when he knew Céline wouldn't like to see her on her wedding day, much less have her be a part of the party.

"Just that you were the typical bad boy. A jock," Stevie said.

"A joke?" Now his face hardened. "He was making fun of me?"

Now Stevie was the one trying to contain her laughter. "Not a joke. A jock. Like . . . an athlete."

All Roads Lead to Rome • 15

Cristian clicked his tongue. "Ah . . . yes. I'm a goalie. Or at least I was. I just got to the end of my last season."

"A goalie?"

"For fútbol? I guess you Americans call it soccer."

"My family is proudly South American, and we call it fútbol, thank you very much." Stevie's cheeks were flaming like every time anyone questioned her Latinidad. She and her dad had bonded over watching the Peru national team games on TV, and when Peru didn't make the World Cup, they'd cheered for Argentina.

Cristian placed a hand over his heart and said, "Ooh. I see that's a touchy subject for you. Fútbol, then. The Peruvian people are brothers and sisters to Argentines. Argentina, that's where I'm from."

Stevie suddenly understood why Brady hated Cristian so much. Argentines had a reputation for being conceited. But Nadia was from Argentina, and she wasn't prideful like people said, and neither was her family. Still, Cristian kind of fit the mold for the stereotypical Argentine of European descent, a fútbol player, and a womanizer. He was the last thing Stevie needed now. Her reputation was already in shambles.

There was a loud sound, and Stevie looked at the dance floor over his shoulder to see what was happening. Brady and some of the other guys from the office were dancing around Céline and her posh European friends.

"Why aren't you with them?" Cristian asked.

She swallowed her longing. Stevie wanted nothing more than to feel like she truly belonged here, but she wasn't going to say it to this guy. "Because I don't want to ruin Céline's day. And Brady's, for that matter. After today our friendship might be over, but we're business partners. And you?"

"Because I only know Céline, and I don't want to ruin Brady's day. And Céline's, for that matter."

"You didn't bring a plus-one?" Stevie asked him.

"Did you?"

16 • *Yamile Saied Méndez*

Under any other circumstances, Stevie hated playing question Ping-Pong, but maybe she was lonely. She had to acknowledge she was enjoying this challenge. "I'm complete as I am," she said, making a hand gesture to show off her figure.

In spite of his reputation as a hummingbird, the kind that feasts from every flower, Cristian didn't fall into her trap. He didn't gaze at her body like other men would, taking the chance she'd given him to gawk. The band started playing a classical version of a Karol G song. It was one of Stevie's favorites, but in violin and piano. Cristian must have read her bodily reaction and sent her *the look*.

Her fast reflexes kicked in. "No," she said.

"Why not?" he asked, his hand over his heart again.

"Because I don't want people to get the wrong idea about me." This was one of the truest things she'd ever told a stranger. Stevie didn't know why she blurted that out.

"Céline already warned me you're off limits," Cristian revealed.

Something flared inside her. Why was Céline meddling in her life when she didn't want Stevie to be part of hers? Did Brady have anything to do with it? To his defense, there had been several scary occasions with the summer guys, both reps and installers, who got too friendly, and Brady had to intervene. But now they were far from the office. What if she wanted to meet someone? She didn't do one-night stands, but she had the right to make her own choices.

"It's just a dance." Cristian extended a hand to her. "I'm not looking to hook up, either," he added, as if he'd read her mind.

If there was anything she had to work on, it was on not being so trusting. Stevie was a horrible reader of people. Still, she couldn't depend on her friends Nadia and Madi to vet guys for her, or Brady, not if she didn't want Céline to stab her in the eye with a fork one day. Somehow, Stevie would have to learn who to trust, not based on appearances. She'd have to learn how to listen to herself. It was just a dance. What could it hurt?

She took his hand, and he led her to the dance floor, but they

All Roads Lead to Rome • 17

stayed on the outer edges, away from the newlyweds. Cristian placed a hand on the small of her back, and she placed hers on his shoulder. This song had a waltzy rhythm, and it was easy to follow the *one, two, three*. He was so much taller than her, even in her four-inch stilettos. Stevie didn't dare raise her head to look at him. At the same time, she didn't want to close her eyes and get dizzy, so she fixed her gaze on his shoulder and noticed how nice his suit was. Nice, like in *expensive*. Being a goalie must be very profitable, indeed.

"So, you said this is your last season as a goalie. What will you do now? Stay in Rome?"

Instead of answering her, he *tsk*ed.

"What?" She looked at him and saw he was smiling. He had such lush and long eyelashes. They softened the sharpness of his blue eyes.

"Your Americanness is showing again. First you ask where I'm from, and then what I do for a living. What are you going to ask me next, how old I am?"

"Maybe?"

He smiled again, and his cheeks blushed a soft pink.

They danced for a minute, and then she asked, "So? Where in Argentina are you from? What will you do for work now that you're done being a professional athlete, and how old are you?"

Stevie smiled when a soft chuckle resonated in his chest. She wanted to lay her head on it, but she resisted.

"I'm not going to tell you all my secrets when I don't even know you," he said.

"What are you afraid of? You can't be that old."

"I'm twenty-seven," he said.

"Same," she replied. "My birthday was December first."

"Mine was October thirteenth!"

She tried to channel her inner Madi and calculated his zodiac sign. He was a Libra sun. Was that compatible to her sun in Sagittarius? Not that she was planning on ending up with a self-confessed player, but she'd have to check with her friend later.

18 • *Yamile Saied Méndez*

"See? It wasn't that hard. Now, where are you from, and what will you do for a living?"

He laughed. "I'm from Rosario, which is considered to be the cradle of fútbol, and my grandma wants me to join the family oil business," Cristian disclosed.

She pulled back to look at him better.

"Oil? Like in . . . petroleum?"

"Oil like in essential," he said, giving her a twirl. When he caught her in his arms again, he added, "I guess I'll be a nepo baby."

Stevie laughed and shook her head. It took a player to know another one, and she had to admit he was good at his game.

"Were you a nepo baby on the fútbol team? Does your family own it?"

Now he laughed. "Nope. That was all me. I've been playing for a team here in Rome since I was eighteen, but they didn't renew my contract."

He said this matter-of-factly, with no self-pity in his voice, but still, Stevie felt a pang of sympathy for him in her heart.

"What? Why?" she asked. "I'm sure you were fantastic."

"And how would you know?"

With her puckered lips, Stevie pointed to the hand that was holding hers. "You have such big hands. And you know what people say about big hands."

That wicked light glinted in his eyes again. "What do they say?"

Stevie blushed. She never blushed. She was famous for blurting out the most uncomfortable truths and making people cringe. But this time, she'd fallen into her own trap. She'd turned into such a workaholic that she was losing her edge. She looked down and said, "Big feet. If you have big hands, you have big feet. And goalies need both to catch all the balls." She bit her lip. *Catch all the balls?* It was a good thing the song ended before she kept blabbering.

"I guess my time is up," Cristian said. "I don't know much

All Roads Lead to Rome • 19

about etiquette, but all the movies say that dancing more than one song would be considered improper, so . . . bye?"

Céline and Brady were ready to start cutting the cakes, the fancy one and the groom one that was a *Star Wars* ship. Stevie had called dozens of bakeries in Rome until one agreed to make it exactly as Brady had requested it. He'd been delighted when he saw it, and that had been enough to make all the effort worth it. Even the humiliation of Céline, Chloe, and the rest ignoring her. Her job here was done.

If she left now, no one would miss her. Even though she hadn't liked being the center of attention before, now that she was ignored, she felt like she was suffocating. She needed air. But she didn't want to be alone. "Do you want to head out?"

"Like, ditch the party?" Cristian sounded relieved. He looked around the room.

"Exactly," she said, hoping she could find an Uber or a taxi.

"Let's go," he said, grabbing his jacket that he'd draped on the chair.

Stevie grabbed her faux fur coat and relished the luxurious feeling of the silk interior against the naked skin on her shoulders. Her feet complained at having been constrained to the prison of these impractical shoes for so long, but she had brought nothing to change into. Still, Stevie held her head high like a queen as she nodded goodbye at Brady. Not because she needed his permission to leave, but because she wanted him not to hold a grudge that could potentially sour his honeymoon. Céline would never forgive her.

Stevie hugged the bouquet close to her heart, and a thorn pricked the tender skin above her breast. She pretended it didn't hurt like hell but loosened her grip on the flowers.

Brady's eyes burned a hole on Stevie's back as she and Cristian left through a back door.

Chapter 3

Outside, the freezing air of Rome hit her face and quickly brought her back to her senses. She was holding a stranger's arm in a strange city. Even though she'd lived on her own since she was seventeen, Stevie was still very much a country mouse from Orem, Utah. Or *Borem*, as she and her friends called it.

"It's way colder than I thought," Cristian said.

"It is." Stevie's teeth started chattering.

A heavy silence followed, just for a second.

"I can walk you to your hotel and then leave like a gentleman," Cristian said in a soft voice, sensing she might be feeling uncomfortable.

Stevie pursed her lips and shook her head a little. Now that she knew he thought she was nervous, it was easy to get her armor back on and pretend to be impervious to lesser mortals' fears like strangers and big ancient cities. "I'm okay. I just need a moment to get used to this hellish temperature," she said, shivering right on cue.

All Roads Lead to Rome • 21

A cat that was rummaging through a pile of garbage bags hissed at them, as if they'd been trying to steal its treasure.

"So, you don't like the cold," he said, as if collecting facts about her like puzzle pieces to form the picture Céline had painted of who she was.

"I like the cold all right," she said. "It's the cold that doesn't like me."

"That's impossible," he said. "I don't see how anything, even cold weather, could not like you."

She chuckled. "Empty flattery won't work with me," she said. To prove her point, she showed him her hands. They were covered with angry pinpricks. "See?"

He stopped in the middle of the street to examine her skin. "What happened? It looks like you got stung by ants."

"It's cold rash."

He looked at her like she was a mythological creature. "You're allergic to cold! Oh my God! Why are you here in Rome in January?"

She pulled her hand from his and continued walking. "My best guy friend was getting married. Besides, the weather app reported mild temperatures, and I believed it."

He caught up with her, and as if they'd practiced it before, Cristian placed her hand in the crook of his arm and covered it with his. Stevie held on to him for warmth, or so she told herself as she tucked her other hand inside a pocket of her coat. Once, she'd told her friends that in her opinion, walking arm in arm was a way more intimate gesture than holding hands. Every time she'd seen old couples walking like this, she felt an envy she couldn't contain.

"Are you sure you don't want to head back to your hotel?" Cristian offered again.

She smiled warmly. "I don't want to go back yet. It's still so early. Besides, I need to get souvenirs for my friends. Maybe even a Christmas present for my mom. I kept putting it off, and I know I won't have time to shop tomorrow."

22 • *Yamile Saied Méndez*

"There's always the airport," he said, as if he'd been in that exact situation before.

"I think the girls and my mom already have everything you might want from an airport. Besides, after the new year, the last thing you want to receive is another Kinder chocolate egg."

"You're right," he said, right before pointing at a tourist trap and exclaiming, "Look! I bet you can find something there. I need to get something, too, before I go home."

The sensible thing for Stevie to do would be to cave in and get some gift cards so her mom and the girls could buy whatever they wanted and then head back to the hotel. She could take a hot shower and have something to eat—on her own. But she was lonely. If Stevie was being honest, she had to admit she was sick and tired of being lonely. Knowing herself as well as she did, the temptation to ask Cristian to come up to the room with her would be too great. She also knew that this kind of situation never ended well, at least not for her.

What made it even more risqué was that she didn't know anything about Cristian other than the cautionary whispers she'd heard about him. Stevie didn't want to taint her memories of Brady's wedding night by sleeping with this beautiful guy, whom she'd only end up hating the morning after. She didn't want to hate him. More importantly, she didn't want him to hate or dislike her. Given her past experiences, it was only a matter of time before he would.

Still hesitating, she followed Cristian into the store, which was bigger than she'd expected it to be, and he immediately lost himself in the aisles. This was maybe Stevie's last chance to leave before she had time to prove all the rumors about her were true. She was cruel. She was a bitch. She was cunning and flaky.

Stevie turned around to leave. Before making her exit, right there on a shelf, she spotted a pair of gloves in a shade of blue so perfect, she could've sworn they'd been made just for her. The gloves were the color of deep oceans and nighttime skies. She picked them up and sighed at the softness and warmth of

All Roads Lead to Rome • 23

such thin fibers. She had expected them to be itchy and scratchy, but they were anything but. Madi and Nadia would love them. Without the slightest hesitation, she picked up a pair for each of her friends, and another for her mom.

What would Ana María Choi be doing right now? Stevie checked her watch and did the mental math. *Let's see, it's almost midnight in Salt Lake City. Right about now, she'd be throwing a lavish party for the whole neighborhood.* If there was anything that Ana María Choi craved more than air, it was people around her. In spite of everything, mother and daughter had that in common. They needed people around them, just not each other.

During the last year, Stevie had thought of calling her mom many times, but something always came up, and she ended up not calling or texting. Before she knew it, months had gone by without speaking with her. The more time that went by between checking in with her, the harder it became to initiate a conversation. Stevie didn't consider herself a bad person, but she had to admit she'd been a terrible daughter.

As shame and guilt burned inside her, Stevie felt the weight of someone's stare. She looked up and saw that Cristian was looking at her intently.

How long had he been observing her in silence? She got all self-conscious and nervous. "What?"

Cristian blinked like he was coming back to reality. "I found something you might like." He was holding a pair of gloves just like the ones Stevie had cradled in her arms.

"This color is just screaming Stevie," he said, slowly helping her put a glove on, finger by finger. Sometime in the process, she'd left the other pairs on a shelf.

"What's this fiber?" she asked softly, rubbing the weave between two fingers.

Cristian shrugged. "I'm just a footballer. I don't know anything about anything. I have good taste, though, so if I like it, it's most likely something expensive."

24 • *Yamile Saied Méndez*

Stevie chuckled. She was the same way. "Wool usually makes me itchy. But this is lovely."

"I know what you mean, but I think it will be more helpful to get something else besides gloves to venture out into the streets of Rome," he said, wiggling his eyebrows like a dork.

She playfully slapped his arm, and a couple of the gloves he had picked up fell and rolled on the floor.

Cristian promptly knelt down to gather them up again. Then he handed them to her one by one.

Stevie said, "As much as some people would love to see me wearing only gloves, you should know that the yellow pair is for Madi, and the red for Nadia, who's a lawyer and only wears señora colors now, but inside, she has a wild personality."

"And Madi? Why yellow?" he asked, grabbing a pink pair.

Wondering whom he might be buying them for, Stevie replied, "Because she's a human explosion of sunshine."

"She sounds incredible," Cristian said. "Maybe you could introduce us." He gave her a crooked smile.

Stevie sent him a sharp look, and his smile widened. "Number one, you're so not her type. She's not into blonds, and number two, you might not have the right initials."

"Initials? What do you mean?"

"Like, what's your full name?"

He leaned against a shelf and crossed his arms. "Hmm, I see your technique to gather information is getting better. The first thing you should've asked for is my name, though."

She rolled her eyes.

"It's Cristian Exequiel Alvarez."

His accent sounded as yummy as a piece of decadent chocolate. She could tell how he used it to seduce people of the female persuasion. She shrugged one shoulder. "I was right. You don't have the right initials."

"You keep saying that. What does it mean?"

Stevie couldn't believe the size of this man's ego. He looked

All Roads Lead to Rome • 25

so offended that he didn't qualify as a possible love interest for her friend because of his name.

She smirked. "When she was like eleven, Madi dreamed that the love of her lives—notice the plural, as in many—had the initials J.R."

"Really?"

"Really. You won't believe the stupid guys she's dated over the years just because of their initials."

They continued walking deeper into the store, toward the shoe section. One of the store attendants, a man in his late thirties with dark shadows under his eyes, politely nodded his head at them. He said something in Italian that Stevie couldn't understand.

Cristian nodded back, and replied in Italian, still clutching the pink gloves to his chest. He asked something, and the man pointed to another display.

"*Grazie,*" Cristian said, grabbing a plaid scarf and a beanie from the shelf. Then he turned to Stevie, who was studying his every move, and said, "At least your friend Madi knows what she wants. What about you? Do you also vet people by their initials?"

"Initials? No. I don't care what people's initials are."

"But you know what you want?"

"I know what I don't want," she shot back.

"Do you believe in eternal soulmates, like Madi?"

Stevie wanted to laugh out loud and make a snide remark, but her now-deceased son Tristan's face flashed in her mind, and she couldn't. There's no way she could tell a stranger that she'd already met and lost the love of her life. That her heart was broken beyond repair, and for this reason, she'd never risk hurting it again.

She shrugged. "I don't know. If you haven't noticed, or if Brady didn't tell you, I'm more of a down-to-earth, tangible things, practical person. I don't know if there's fate or destiny.

26 • Yamile Saied Méndez

I just believe in consequences. I don't know if we were alive in some shape or form before, or if there's anything else after. We just have the now, but we pay for the now forever."

They stopped walking and stood in front of a small corner by the dressing rooms. He looked at her like she was a puzzle he couldn't figure out. Standing there next to him, Stevie tried to pretend she wasn't a walking and talking contradiction, but she was failing miserably. As they had walked, she'd grabbed random things from the shelves: pants, a sweatshirt, a pair of socks, and fluffy slippers.

"I don't believe in eternal soulmates, either," he said, taking things from her hands. This time, nothing fell to the ground. "I refuse to believe in destiny. If everything is pre-written, then what does it all mean? But I believe that sometimes things happen for a reason."

Uninvited, Stevie's mom's voice echoed in her mind. *Everything happens for a reason. Everything happens for a reason.* Hatred surged inside her. "That's bullshit," she said, horrified to realize her voice was all shaky. "For some things, there's no reason. None at all."

It was as if the chill of the night had snaked its way inside the toasty store. But Cristian was intuitive enough not to contradict her. He just looked at her and said, "I respect that opinion. But also, sometimes there is a reason, and we just don't know what it is yet."

Stevie shrugged stubbornly, but he didn't double down to make her see things from his point of view. Something must have told him that no matter how hard he tried, she never would.

"Let's go," she said abruptly, as if to prove that some things were irrational, that there didn't need to be an agenda. Maybe guessing her intention, Cristian followed her.

They paid for their items, and then the store attendant led them to the changing rooms. When they emerged wearing the most touristy outfits ever, the attendant also shared an espresso with them. The coffee was rich, strong, smooth, and invigorating.

All Roads Lead to Rome • 27

When they left the store, Stevie's every nerve was tingling with possibility. Snuggled in her fur coat, she said, "That coffee was something else! Galaxies are being born in my mind."

Cristian laughed. It was a goofy laugh that sounded like a braying donkey. It made them laugh even more. "I feel like I could run ten miles in fifteen minutes. What was in that coffee?" In a swift move, he grabbed the bag that Stevie held, the one where she carried the gloves she intended to give to her friends and mom. He put it inside the bigger bag that contained Stevie's dress, stilettos, and the bouquet of flowers that had already started to wither. But he kept the small gift bag with the pink gloves separate.

"Who did you get that for?" Stevie asked him point-blank. It wasn't that she was trying to figure out if he had a girlfriend. Unless he was a total psycho, it didn't seem like he had a significant other. She was dying to know whom the gloves were for.

"My grandma, Nonna Ross," he said. "She's from Italy."

"From here?"

"Not Rome. She's from this tiny island off the Amalfi Coast."

"Capri?"

"Ischia," he replied. "Have you ever been there?"

Stevie had been all over the Mediterranean, but not Ischia. She shook her head. "You?"

His smile was immaculate. A gullible woman could easily lose her mind for a smile like that.

"The first real vacation I had, I flew my Nonna to Italy and took her to visit her island. It's one of my core memories."

The love for his grandmother resonated in his voice, and Stevie had to look away before he saw the envy rising inside her. She loved her grandma Yolanda, who'd always sided with her, but since the breakup with her mom, Stevie had also kept her grandma at bay. At that moment, Stevie realized just how much she missed her. "Tell me more about her," Stevie said.

By then, they were walking down a cobbled street, and although she was warm in her coat, Stevie leaned into him as if

28 • *Yamile Saied Méndez*

he were a campfire. In her boots, she was several inches shorter than him.

Cristian leaned into her. "I love that you said your friend Nadia dresses like a señora. Well, that was my grandma her whole life. She's a señora to the letter, but as a young girl and woman, she was a true tomboy. In in her old age—her words, not mine—she found her softer feminine side. She's reverted to being a child inside, but not in a creepy way. She doesn't dress like a young girl or play with dolls. She just laughs more and does things for fun. She has also admitted to me that she loves the color pink. No one in the family, except for me, believed her when she said she was going to buy a pink car. Ten years later, she's still driving her Barbie car all over Las Vegas. I always make a point of giving her something pink when I visit. It's our thing."

If this sweet talk wasn't coming from Cristian Alvarez, her ovaries might have exploded. There was no way she was going to let him seduce her by masquerading as an angel. Although he wasn't an angel, he totally looked like one.

"That's sweet," she said, realizing she'd just been following his lead. "So, where are we going?"

"Where do you want to go?"

Stevie looked at her watch. It wasn't even nine. She regretted that other than the airport, hotel, church, and the wedding venue, she'd hadn't seen much else of the Eternal City. "If a person only has one night to spend in Rome, where would they go?" she asked, afraid she'd lost the chance to get to see the sights and take a few shots for her Instagram. How else would her mom know she was having a great time?

"That depends on many factors," he said, after thinking for a few seconds. "Like who you're with. What you like to do. And how hungry you are, if at all."

He had her at *hungry*. She put her hand up, and right on cue, her stomach gurgled. "What if one is beyond hungry? But I checked my app, and everything's closed."

All Roads Lead to Rome • 29

"Well, it's January first, darling," Cristian reminded her.

"Well, I'm starving," she said, stomping her foot clad in Ugg knockoffs. It was an extreme reaction, but she had to do something to hide how much she'd loved that he called her *darling*. It might be a clutch word of his, an affectation. *Darling* meant treasured one, favorite, beloved. And no one had called her any of those things in a long time.

"Let me think . . ." he said, scratching his head and messing up his blond curls.

Her hand itched to tuck his hair behind his ear, but she held herself still while he looked around, probably trying to figure out where to take her.

"I know!" he said, taking her hand in his. "Now, let's hope they're open."

"Can you check on an app? Call?"

He chuckled. "It's not an app type of place. They've never even had a landline. For all I know, they've been open since the days of Romulus Augustus."

She stared at him. "The last emperor?"

"That one," he said.

"You know? No one ever said that about you."

"Said what?" he asked, a corner of his mouth hitching.

"That you're a nerd."

He laughed. "I love that you think so. Because I am. Now, let's also hope they have room for us."

"Don't they take reservations?"

He snorted. "They're the not the type of restaurants that take reservations, either."

"Let's hope," she replied, trying to match his stride, which wasn't easy, considering she was two heads shorter than him.

Stevie not only hoped this mysterious place was open, but that it also had room, and was clean. She'd had nothing to eat but a small piece of bread she made herself eat at the reception. She'd been so nervous about the toast that she hadn't had an appetite. Since she was in charge of the toast and was going to be

30 • *Yamile Saied Méndez*

drinking at least that one flute of champagne, she hadn't wanted to take any chances.

Now that small nibble was a distant memory. They walked past the Colosseum, which was all lit up and magnificent.

"Too bad it's closed today," he said. "You know, the Colosseum?"

She hesitated for a second while her future was split in a million possibilities. In the likeliest one, the reference would go over his head, and he'd think she was weird. But there was one small chance he'd get it and the night would have a magical ending, depending on his reaction. She took the plunge, and in a deep, dramatic voice recited, "My name is Maximus Decimus Meridius. . . ."

She glanced at him.

The corner of his mouth twitched again, but he didn't laugh at her, nor did he look at her like she'd grown antlers. Instead, he picked up where she'd left off, and quoted the rest of the famous phrase from *Gladiator*, in which the former commander of the emperor's army swears to take revenge on his murdered wife and son, in this life or beyond.

Cristian held her hand and shuddered as she yelled, "Chills!"

"Every time."

Her eyes were prickly with tears like every time she remembered that scene from the movie. She'd watch it with the guys on her first sales trip, and it had become her favorite, even though it was so old. Now she was filled with regret that she hadn't given herself the time to explore this magical city—eternal Rome.

"Did you see how amazing it looks inside? The renovation has taken years, but it's jaw-dropping," he said.

She ducked, and his eyes widened in shock. "No! You can't tell me you haven't been inside the Colosseum yet."

She sucked air though her teeth. "Didn't get to, unfortunately. I arrived just in time for the bachelor party. You weren't there, by the way."

All Roads Lead to Rome • 31

"I'm not a fan of those things," he admitted. "I've never been much of a partier. I'm a nerd, remember?"

"So, you're not like most footballers."

"I'm exactly like most footballers," he said, chuckling. "By the time we're in our late twenties, our bodies are broken beyond repair. If we eat too much of the wrong thing or drink, we pay for it. We play video games and watch movies. You get used to the quiet lifestyle," he said.

They were about to cross a busy intersection when Cristian stopped her, even though they had the right of way. "Careful," he said, "you don't want to start the year being run over."

They made way for a caravan of Vespas to go by as they honked enthusiastically. At the front of the line was a newlywed couple. The bride was smiling so widely, she looked like a painting of what happiness was supposed to look like. Envy flared inside Stevie again.

"I wish I met you earlier," Cristian said, with longing in his voice, as they crossed the street. "I would've taken you all over Rome."

"I wish that, too," Stevie said softly. A voice in her head blared that she should be careful. She was vulnerable and lonely. She shouldn't fall for the first guy who offered her tenderness and protection. This guy least of all.

"Here we are," he announced, pointing at a row of houses that looked centuries old. There were no signs of businesses anywhere, much less of a restaurant.

"Where?"

"Maria's Kitchen is one of Rome's best-kept secrets. You're in for a treat."

"Kept from whom?"

"Tourists. Americans," he said in that infuriating, provocative tone.

She shot him another cutting look. It was becoming a ritual with him now. "You keep saying *Americans* like it's a bad thing."

"I guess they're not all that bad, are they?" He knocked on the door, and without waiting for an answer, he turned the doorknob, and walked into "the house."

"Depends on your definition of bad," she muttered, and then inhaled deeply. The scent of fresh bread and tomato sauce made her taste buds salivate. "If it tastes as good as it smells, then I guess I am in for a treat."

"Just you wait," he said, giddy, leading her toward the only light she could see.

"Ciao, Cristian," the hostess said from behind the podium at the entrance. She was a young girl with a pretty beauty mark that made her face unforgettable. She added something else in Italian, and Cristian replied, smiling as he glanced at Stevie.

Guessing he was asking for a table for two, she returned a tight smile.

The girl made a sign for them to follow. The only illumination came from a few candles burning on a table. Cristian took hold of Stevie's hand, and they followed the girl to the dining area of a kitchen. There were about ten tables, but only a couple of them were open. The hostess sat them by a window from which Rome looked majestic.

"Buon appetito," the girl said, and she left with a conspiratorial smile.

Cristian helped Stevie into her seat, and then sat beside her.

"Wow, this is quite the view," she said, impressed with his gentlemanly gestures.

Cristian gazed at the city. "It's like a dream that never gets old."

A server stepped in to pour them water, and he brought a basket of assorted breads and olive oil. Stevie tried a piece, and the bite dissolved on her tongue. If the rest of the menu was as scrumptious as the bread, then she had no complaints.

"What's the best dish here? Oh, the hostess didn't leave a menu," Stevie said, looking around to ask for one.

Cristian smiled and said, "No menu. We eat what Maria cooks for her family."

All Roads Lead to Rome • 33

Stevie had heard of places like this, but she'd never been to one. She looked at Cristian suspiciously.

"Trust me," he said, and held out a hand for her to grasp, like he was Aladdin.

This guy . . . he was a dork.

She chuckled and shook her head. "Famous last words that can only announce disaster."

He was ready to reply when the first course arrived, and they both turned their attention to the most important thing at hand: the food.

Two hours later, Stevie groaned, "This was the best meal I've ever had." She leaned back on the chair, grateful to be wearing cheap stretchy pants. "But I'm stuffed! I swear I won't eat ever again."

Cristian laughed. "Ow! My pants are too tight now! I can't breathe."

"I hope you left room for dessert," the waiter said in English, as he placed two servings of chocolate cake and two cups of espresso in front of them.

Even though they'd just sworn they were too full, a few minutes later, their dessert plates were clean.

"Did you like it?" Cristian said, eyeing Stevie carefully as they walked out of the restaurant.

She got ahold of his arm again. "I think I just gained ten pounds, but I'm not going to complain about it. That's how much I loved it."

"Calories don't count during vacations," he said, patting her hand with his as they walked back out into the night.

The temperature had dropped considerably, and the cobbled streets looked shiny with frost. But there were still people walking about the city.

"Should we get a taxi? He can drop you off first," Cristian suggested.

During their spare conversation over dinner, they'd found out their hotels were across the street from each other. Stevie didn't want this night to end yet. She also didn't want to reach the moment she'd have to decide if she was going to invite him to her room or not. She'd been the most at peace with him than she'd been with a guy in ages. Cristian was finally someone she could talk to without masks, pretending, or having to impress.

"I think we need a walk after that dinner," she said. "Calories might not count, but I'm bursting."

Looking relieved, he smiled and said, "Let's walk, then." Then he wrapped her arm in the crook of his elbow again, and off they went.

Chapter 4

She'd only had a glass of wine with her dinner, but it was the whole combination of delectable food and a sense of being home that loosened her tongue. One by one, the barriers Stevie put between her and the world suddenly came tumbling down. Cristian looked more comfortable, too.

They talked the whole time. About her friends, about his. About their families and dreams for the future. Cristian wanted to coach little kids. Teach at a public school. Volunteer with organizations that helped people overcome traumatic events.

"Why do you want to do that?" she asked, glancing up at him.

He bit his lower lip as if considering how much to share with her. "When I was seventeen, I was recruited by Roma, FC."

"Seventeen?" At seventeen, she was going through a life-changing event of her own, one only her closest family and friends knew about. One that was seared in her soul.

Cristian continued, "I felt like I had touched Heaven with my fingertips. That night, my whole family went to celebrate. It was my parents, my sister Jorgelina, my girlfriend of three years—her name was Micaela—and me. On the way back, we were hit by a drunk driver."

They stopped on the corner to cross the street, and Cristian paused as if he needed movement to tell his story. The beeping of the crossing signal from behind her echoed how Stevie's heart thundered in her ears.

The light turned; they walked, and he continued. "No one but me survived."

Stevie felt like the air had vanished from her lungs. She pressed his hand tightly and said, "I'm sorry."

He gave her a sad smile. His eyes were so dark, they looked black. "I was in a coma for three weeks, and when I woke up, Ross, as everyone calls my Nonna Rossana, was sitting beside me. When I recovered, I had to decide if I was going to move with her to the United States, come to Rome—the team still wanted me—or stay in Argentina." He sighed as if the weight of that decision still pressed down on him.

Stevie knew from experience that even when a terrible challenge has passed, its ghost can keep coming back over and over again to inflict pain.

His mouth twitched in that tiny smile that dimpled the corner of his mouth. "I came to Rome, of course. That's what my family had wanted. That's what they had died for." Stevie was going to say something, and he rushed to add, "I know, intellectually, that they didn't die because of that. They died because of one person's bad decision and just plain bad luck, but that's how I felt, you know? That's how I still feel. Ross traveled to see my debut. I made my mark on the team, and even had a few appearances in the national team. The Argentine team, of course, champions of the world." Now his smile was dazzling. "But there's an injury on my shoulder that just won't heal. It's time to retire."

"And work in the family oil business?" she asked, tying back to the conversation they had started while they danced at the

All Roads Lead to Rome • 37

wedding. Had that been tonight? It felt like the wedding had taken place another lifetime ago. Suddenly, she sniffled.

In a swift move, he handed her a handkerchief. A real one made of fabric, not tissue paper.

"It's the cold air," she said, dabbing her nose. He nodded, agreeing to the lie to spare them both.

Stevie held on to the handkerchief, but she didn't know what to do with it. It's not like she could wash it and give it back to him. She'd worry about that later. "So?" she asked, wanting to pick up their conversation where he left off.

"Maybe I'll work in the family oil business," he said, and swallowed. "But I need to go home to make my peace with some things."

"Home as in Argentina?"

"Correct."

Argentina was literally at the other end of the world from her.

As if he needed to justify his decision, he said, "I left too soon. I only ever went back when we had games, so I never really had time to . . . I don't know, grieve. Put a final period to the story."

"And you can be a part of the family business from Argentina?"

He gave her a curious look, and this time, instead of averting her eyes, she held his gaze. It was a pity she and Cristian had just met. They had so much in common: love for travel, food, and the same dark and silly sense of humor. Once she saw past the layers that years of rumors had painted about him, Cristian felt like a friend she'd met in another life. Madi would say it was fated. And Stevie hated the concept of fate. It only ever brought her heartache and tears that burned. Fate played the worst jokes on her by giving her the best things, only at the worst possible time, and once she made her peace with it, it took everything away.

It wasn't like she was going to open up her heart and tell him all this, but she was trying to put her thoughts in order when they reached a water fountain.

38 • *Yamile Saied Méndez*

"Is that . . . ?" She stopped in her tracks. She didn't know the name, but she'd seen it in pictures and movies, of course.

"La Fontana di Trevi!" Cristian said. "And let me guess, it's your first time visiting it, too."

She rolled her eyes at him. "What if it is my first time?"

He put his hands in his pockets and said, "Then, you must throw three coins and ask for three wishes." When he pulled his hand out of one of his pockets, he showed her a bunch of coins. "Go on, help yourself."

She bit her lip, hesitating. But she gave in and picked three coins from his open palm. Before returning the rest to his pocket, he picked three coins for himself.

"How does this work? You throw them all at once?"

"No, no, no," he said, gently holding her hand so she wouldn't throw all the coins in one go. "You do one at a time."

"And why three?" she asked, suspicious.

"It's tradition, isn't it? You throw one to come back to Rome. Two to fall in love. And three to get married."

Stevie stepped back from the fountain. "Get married?"

"Scary, isn't it?" asked Cristian, chuckling.

"Terrifying," she said, but she didn't really mean it.

Her whole life, all Stevie had ever wanted was a family of her own. A man who adored her. A cozy home. And maybe, even kids who loved her unconditionally. The problem was that all her life, she'd been told she didn't deserve those dreams. Worse, she had actually come to believe it.

She'd fallen in love plenty. But marriage? What did marriage even mean? It was a piece of paper—a contract. Today's ceremony wouldn't make Brady and Céline love each other more. But as a saleswoman who knew the binding power of a contract, she knew that once a person signed that piece of paper, a commitment carried more weight. It had value it didn't have before. She turned away and sat on the edge of the fountain. A few feet away, a man was proposing to another, and a group of friends were videoing the whole thing and cheering them on.

All Roads Lead to Rome • 39

Cristian sat next to her. "What's wrong, Estefanía?"

The way he'd said her name . . . only her dad had ever called her Estefanía. Instead of correcting him, she leaned on him and, as if she'd done it a million times, tucked her head in the crook of his neck. They fit perfectly.

"Do you think you'll ever settle down?" she asked.

"Settle like marry?"

She nodded.

"See, I feel like settling down and marrying are two different things. My parents married young, and they moved around a lot. Just when they started putting down roots . . . time ran out on them." A darkness came over his eyes.

Stevie swallowed the knot in her throat. She grabbed his hand and pressed it hard. Societal rules and good etiquette said in these moments, one should say empty phrases like, *They're in a better place,* or *They're angels watching over you now,* or *God needed them on the other side of the veil.*

She knew the people who recited those words were well-meaning. But she also knew how horrible it was to be on the receiving end. How cold those phrases could land. How they were a way for the person suffering to know the other party was uncomfortable, and it was better to change the subject. Her heart started beating harder as she internally battled with the idea of telling Cristian about the young son she had lost, Tristan. After all, he'd shared something dark and personal with her.

Cristian cut the emotional tension in the air by saying, "Part of the reason I need to go back to Argentina is so Ross can marry her secret lover."

Stevie sat up and looked at him. "Secret lover?"

He shrugged, smiling. "He works in the company, but wants to retire, which is code for finally living with the love of his life."

"If this is your attempt to cheer me up, you're failing. Even grandparents have more romantic lives than I do."

Cristian laughed. "His name is Armando and he's this little old man. He and Ross were neighbors all their lives when they were younger, and then, when they had their families. You know, in some countries, homes are passed from generation to generation. When my grandfather died and she was left with three kids to raise, he helped her out. He was a recent widower, too."

"They've been lovers since?"

He cringed. "I . . . don't think so. I believe their love grew with the years."

"But why is their love secret? Or not-so-secret. I imagine you're not the only one who knows about it."

"You know how prejudices are." Cristian scratched his head, but he must have forgotten he was wearing a beanie. The way his hair curled around the edge of the dark wool was adorable. He continued, "They lived in a little town outside of Rosario, in Argentina. Ross says, 'Small town, big inferno.' I think they're afraid of what people will say if they admit they've been to-gether all this time, but I also think the thrill of doing some-thing forbidden has kept them going."

Stevie couldn't sustain the intensity of his eyes. She was afraid that he'd see how much she loved stories of love and redemption.

"Do they still live in that town?" she asked.

He looked down at his feet and said, "Armando does. The oil company has fields of lavender and chamomile they export for their oils. You should see them. It's all blue and yellow as far as the eye can see. But the company's headquarters are in Nevada. That's where my whole family lived for a while. I was actually born in Las Vegas."

"No way!" she said. "You are an American, too, and you've been teasing me all night?" She playfully slapped his arm, which made her realize, once again, how buff he was.

"Shhhh," Cristian said, and then grinned. "Don't tell any-one. In all the things that matter, I'm an Argentine. After all, the whole family lived there once upon a time. My uncle Juan Domingo and his family settled in Nevada, as well as my aunt Rita and her family. But my parents never loved it there, and we

All Roads Lead to Rome • 41

all went back to Argentina. Ross has lived with one foot in one place and the other in another for years."

"Pining for her impossible love, Armando?"

"No, it's not like that. My grandparents loved each other very much. And Armando loved his wife. Ross and Armando were best friends all their lives, and when they were both alone, their friendship blossomed into something incredible. I think it's time they have a chance. They've waited long enough. A love that grows from friendship is the ultimate goal, don't you think?"

She thought of Brady and Céline. They were in love, but they didn't have a deep friendship yet. How would their relationship progress? With all her heart, she wished that their marriage worked. She wanted to believe that even if it didn't work for her, it worked for others, that it existed. That a love that was constructed over time was real.

But what about her? She had no one that she knew from a young age who could become that legendary love for her.

"We haven't thrown our coins into the fountain yet, and it's late and cold," Cristian said, shuddering and rubbing his hands. The streetlights bounced on his beanie, which glistened with dew. There were still people around them, but the proposal party had already left.

"Oh, you're right," Stevie replied, but she didn't stand up. "I have questions about the tradition, though. Do the events happen in order?"

"That's a good point," he said, laughing. "Maybe people marry, then fall in love and come back to Rome to celebrate? I don't know how the magic works. But you can't come to Rome and not make a wish."

"But it's scary. . . . Did you throw your coins knowing what you were in for?"

"I was eighteen and heartbroken," he said, averting his eyes from hers.

"Did you?"

He turned toward her. "Yes."

42 • *Yamile Saied Méndez*

"But your reputation. . . ."

"What about it?"

She shrugged. "It doesn't really show you want to be a family man." She shivered. Her feet were starting to become two blocks of ice, even in the fake Uggs.

"Really? Who says my reputation started because of a misunderstanding? Or because people don't really know me?" he asked, and there was a sadness in his eyes. He sighed. "Anyway, to answer your question, yes. I threw the coins. But marriage is not for me. At least not yet."

"When, then?"

The corner of his mouth quirked, again. "Why? Are you interested in this?" He made a sweeping motion over himself. He was such a dork.

At least he made her laugh. "Not now."

"When?"

"I don't know," she mumbled, throwing her hands in the air. "When we're older? How old are Ross and Armando?"

"Seventy-something?" he said, narrowing his eyes as he looked in the distance, as if the seventies were so far in the distance, he could hardly see that far.

"It's settled, then," she said, jumping to her feet.

He cocked his head to the side, curious. "What's settled?"

Stevie still wasn't that much taller than him sitting down. She realized what a dangerous position this was, especially for what she was about to say, but she said it anyway. "If by the time we're in our seventies we're alone, we'll marry each other." She left the words bouncing and then made a *ta-da!* gesture with her hands.

He laughed. "Well . . . how did you come to that grand idea? Why do you think you'd want to marry me when I'm that old?"

She grabbed his face in her hands and studied it like it was a famous painting. "I think you'll age gracefully. And I'll still be beautiful. I look like my grandma Yolanda, and she's still gorgeous."

"Brady said you were dangerous, but I thought it was a description and not a disclaimer, a warning."

The words fell hard on Stevie, and she dropped her hands from his face, as if the contact burned her. He'd been laughing, but she didn't want the people she loved to describe her as dangerous.

"I don't mean it in a bad way," he said. "In fact, I think that you make a great point. If we're going to marry as old people, it might as well be someone who knew us in our prime?"

"And we can become better friends through the years."

"That's actually a good idea," he whispered. He narrowed his eyes again, and nodded, as if the faint glimpse of them in the future wasn't that bad after all.

"I mean, it's stupid. We're not in a movie," she said, looking away from him. The way the golden moonlight touched the cupolas of the city took her breath away. The air tingled around them. She looked at him, and he'd been staring at her.

"Okay, so, what are the terms?" she asked, to remind both of them that they were talking long-term, not now. Not tonight. "When we're seventy, if we're not in a committed relationship, we'll marry each other so we can have a fun travel companion?"

He pursed his lips and then smiled. "Do we get to talk or see each other before then?"

She slapped his arm. "Of course! Otherwise, how are we going to become the best friends the world has ever created?"

Cristian nodded with a pensive look, but he avoided her eyes.

"You're wondering if this will be a friends-with-benefits situation?" Stevie ventured to ask.

He looked at her then, and the corner of his mouth twitched. "What do you prefer?" Maybe he didn't intend for his voice to be all seductive. Maybe it was raspy because it was cold, and they'd been talking for hours, but still, it seemed like an invitation.

"Maybe that part of the deal can change as needed?" she asked.

44 • *Yamile Saied Méndez*

"Won't sex ruin the friendship?"

"Maybe it will spice it up," Stevie said. "We won't know until we know."

"Do you have sex with all your friends-in-progress?"

She was taken aback and slapped his arm. "Of course not. I've never slept with Madi or Nadia."

He laughed, but when he spoke again, his voice was serious. "I don't do one-night stands."

"Why not? Is that like a personal vow?"

He paused, as if he were trying to find the words. Finally, he said, "I'm the product of a night stand, believe it or not. My mom adopted me when I was two."

Stevie didn't know what to say, which was okay, because he continued, "It's not that I was saving myself for marriage." He made a funny face, and Stevie chuckled. "I mean, for me, being intimate with someone is a serious thing. My mom used to say it's an exchange of energy."

"Madi says that, too," Stevie added.

"I get . . . what's the word in English?" he asked, making a motion with his hand for Stevie to help him out. She really wished she spoke Spanish more fluently. His accent in English got thicker and thicker the more tired he became, and she knew there were so many things she was losing in translation.

"Protective?" she suggested.

He shook his head. "Territorial."

"Ah," she said. "You're a jealous type of guy?"

"I wouldn't say I'm jealous. I . . . maybe I am. I don't know. I just get attached too quickly, and then have a hard time letting go."

"Okay," she said, understanding. She was the same way. After spending time with a person, that way, she carried a part of their soul with her forever, but that was too creepy to say, even tonight, to him who had been as non-judgy as a guy could be.

All Roads Lead to Rome • 45

"But," he said, taking off a ring from his pinky finger, "if we're promising to get married in the future, that makes us . . . compromised?"

Stevie knew what he was saying, and that it was all a joke, pretend. Still, her heart started hammering so hard she could hardly breathe. "Engaged?"

He laughed. "Yes. Even if it's a symbol, I want to give you proof of my commitment to our vow." He slipped the ring on her ring finger, but on the right hand.

"Well, then, if I have to wear one, you'll have to wear one, too." She took off a ring she kept on her thumb. It was a simple gold band she'd bought in Florida for spring break once.

"Here," she said, placing it on his right-hand ring finger. "Now we're engaged." Still holding his hand, she looked up. Her breath left her in a sigh. His lips were parted and his sleepy eyes so soft.

"Now a kiss to seal the deal?" she asked softly.

Without a word, he closed his eyes and tilted his head up to hers. Before their lips met, she inhaled again. The water in the fountain rumbled, and their kiss deepened and deepened. Stevie got dizzy and grabbed the front of his coat to steady herself. Cristian placed a hand on the back of her neck and pulled her closer to him. When they came up for air, they stayed looking into each other's eyes.

Stevie wished she could take all her words back. That she could also make it so he took his, too, especially the part about not ruining a friendship with sex.

"Do you still want to make that wish?" he asked.

She nodded and grabbed the coins she'd put in her pocket. He stood up, and facing the fountain, he said, "At the count of three."

They counted together, she in English and he in Spanish. At three, they both threw their coins into the fountain. The water rippled, and when it settled, she saw the coins were side by side.

"Do you want me to walk you to your hotel now? Or call you a taxi?"

"Let's walk together. It's just around the block, right?"

His smile flickered again. Now she could see that the blue was speckled with gold.

His eyes widened. "We didn't take a picture! Let's take a selfie."

"But don't post it!" she said, leaning into him and smiling for the picture.

Once they arrived at her hotel, they stood on the sidewalk as around them, tourists arrived with bleary eyes. The magic was wearing off, and inside Stevie, something screamed at her not to be so stupid, not to invite him up to her room. His kiss had been just too perfect. She already felt a Cristian-shaped hole in her. But if he did come up, she'd ruin everything.

"I don't have your phone, fiancée," he said, trying to sound nonchalant. "Should we at least exchange numbers?"

She took out her phone, but the battery had run out long ago.

"It's okay. I'll give you my number. You send me yours. We can keep in touch from our corners of the world?" Cristian suggested.

But his phone was dead, too.

"Maybe it's a sign," she said, her enthusiasm deflated. "Maybe we should let fate take us, and if we meet again, then we'll know the deal wasn't stupid."

Suddenly, she realized the whole thing seemed so silly. The moment had been like a burst of purity and beauty in a ripple of time, outside the universe and the order of things. A glimpse of how her life would have been if she were the kind of person who deserved someone like Cristian, bad reputation or not. At least she never said a word about Tristan. At least that part of her life was still sacred to her.

Neither one seemed to want to say goodbye, so she took the first step. "It was great to meet you, Cristian. See you soon."

All Roads Lead to Rome • 47

She kissed him on the cheek. The scent on his skin made goose bumps explode in her.

"Be safe and be happy, Estefanía," he said. "See you soon?"

They still held hands, and she took a step back but didn't let go of his. Their arms stretched until only their fingertips touched. She wanted to tell him to be safe and happy, too, but not too happy without her, which only proved how selfish she was. How much better than her he deserved.

In that moment, Brady came out of the hotel, looking haggard and red-eyed. When he saw them, his face was a storm. "Seriously?" he said.

"What are you doing here?" Stevie asked, worried. "You skipped your reception? Don't wedding parties in Europe go all night?"

"Oh, the Europeans are still partying. Céline wasn't feeling too well, so we came back so she could sleep a little before we left for our honeymoon." Brady sighed. "Then I found out our flight was delayed, so I came back to my room to get something from my dad. Leaving now."

He looked Stevie up and down, and she could totally imagine the narrative he'd constructed in his mind. She was wearing clothes that were obviously not her style. Cristian's lips were so red, they looked like they'd been kissing for hours. She wished. And most incriminating of all, they were holding hands.

"Have a good time on your honeymoon, Brady. Take care of Céline," Cristian said. "Bye, Stevie. Great to meet you."

His voice still sounded friendly, but it didn't have the warmth that had kept Stevie clinging to him all night. Besides, he'd called her Stevie. He turned around, crossed the street, and went into his hotel. Stevie stood on the sidewalk, looking at him like the last ship from Planet Earth was taking off and a giant meteor was rushing to hit the planet.

"Poor guy," Brady said. "I guess it happens to the best and the worst of us."

48 • *Yamile Saied Méndez*

"What do you mean the best and worst?" she asked, whipping around to look at him. No one was going to talk about her (pretend) fiancé like that.

Brady shrugged. "Another guy you just destroyed, Stevie."

He laughed, but she didn't think he was funny. Brady's comments had soiled the beauty of the night.

"Have a great honeymoon," she said. "Tell Céline congrats from me again." And she headed to her room.

Chapter 5

Ten Years Before

If Stevie got pulled over, she would not only get a ticket, but she'd be grounded forever. If what she suspected were real, she'd be worse than grounded. She went inside the house, hoping to make it to her room unnoticed. Fate had other plans, though. Stevie's mom was waiting in the kitchen. Her brother, Max, who was the epitome of the perfect, ideal son, patted their mom's shoulder.

Stevie had seen her mom angry, disappointed, scared, and sad. But she'd never seen her mom cry. Ana María Choi never took down her armor in front of her daughter like she did for her son. Stevie had long suspected her mom and brother had a different relationship from the one she had with Stevie. Mother and son were so different, and yet, they got along. Max was only three years older than Stevie, but he'd accomplished so much more. He was the dream child, and Stevie was the changeling evil fairies had left.

"Good night," she said when she stepped into the kitchen. She clutched her tote bag against her body for support. Her

50 • *Yamile Saied Méndez*

trademark beaming smile wouldn't keep her out of trouble this time.

"Good night, Stevie," Max said with a sad expression.

It wasn't that Stevie couldn't understand her brother's dilemma. She did. Here he was, nineteen years old, and instead of being with his roommates up in Salt Lake, he was home, on a Saturday night, comforting their mother.

Because Stevie had been gone since the day before. She'd turned off the app that tracked her location. She hadn't even answered her phone at first when her mom called, then later her brother, and finally her grandmother. For her mom to include Stevie's grandma Yoli, things were dire and desperate. She had felt guilty all day long. Of course she had. She was reckless, but not heartless. But it had been worth it. The telling-off she had coming her way would be worth it, she told herself.

It was Liam's birthday, his eighteenth, and she'd planned a whole romantic day before he went off to college after the summer. She hoped they'd get to celebrate many, many birthdays together, but she didn't believe in sacrificing today for the sake of the future. The future may never come.

She'd learned the hard way after her dad had died of a freak heart attack while hiking to Timpanogos Cave, like he and Ana María did once a week once the weather turned nice. That had been two years ago. She never had a party for her *quinces*, of course. No one was in the right frame of mind to celebrate a wayward daughter when a perfect father who overlooked all her flaws was gone. His absence was like a missing front tooth.

Ana María Choi turned to look at Stevie, eyes red-rimmed with tears that had since dried. "I really don't know what to say, Stephanie."

"Let's not say anything, then," Stevie said, stepping toward her mom, thinking of giving her a hug.

Maybe this time, she'd get off easy. Maybe this time, she and her mom would spare each other from saying the hateful words they never really meant but which cut like glass and left infected

All Roads Lead to Rome • 51

wounds neither one would recover from. Before she could place a hand on her mom's shoulder, Ana María stood up so abruptly, the chair fell.

Max looked at Stevie like it had been her fault that the chair fell. Like it had been her fault their mom looked all withered like a dry flower.

"It's not going to be so easy," her mom said, louder this time, as if the sound of the chair falling had turned up the intensity of their argument. "Where were you? What were you thinking? Don't you care that I was afraid to death for you?"

"We were about to report you missing," Max said. The accusation in his voice shamed Stevie into averting her eyes.

"It's the summertime, and I'm home by curfew, which is midnight, by the way," she said, raising her chin in defiance. She'd done nothing wrong.

"It's the summer for you because you have no responsibilities," her mom said. "It's easy to drive in a car that your father left and spend the money he gave his life to earn."

"Papi didn't die working," she said. As soon as the words flew out of her mouth, she wanted to bring them back. Because she and her mom thought the opposite about practically everything, but in this, they agreed: Federico Choi had worked himself to death and died doing the only thing he enjoyed besides providing for his children. How unfair life was.

"Your brother is taking summer semester so he can graduate early and be responsible, taking care of himself. That's all I ask. For you two to be independent—"

"I *am* independent," Stevie shot back with pride.

Her mom scoffed. "That's not independence, hija. You're spending money on stupid things like a fancy dinner, outings in Park City for your boyfriend—"

"That's not stupid," she said.

"When he tosses you aside, you'll realize that you invested in the wrong person."

"Relationships aren't business transactions, Mamá," Stevie

52 • *Yamile Saied Méndez*

said. "Love is not a transaction. I'm not investing in Liam. He's my boyfriend. He loves me. I love him. Why can't you be happy for me?" She stopped talking, because her voice cracked.

Max had sent her a warning look.

Tears didn't solve anything.

"I see you running toward a cliff. It's my obligation to warn you," Ana María said.

"Why? What is it to you?"

"Stevie, how can you say that?" Max said, shaking his head.

Ana María put a hand up and said, "No, let her. Let her think her actions don't bring consequences for all of us. It's my obligation and my business to warn you because I'm your mother." Ana María swallowed but didn't add the words Stevie was craving.

How hard could a simple *te quiero* be?

"This lifestyle you lead can't end well," Ana María finally said.

"I like my lifestyle. I like my life. What's so wrong with it?"

"Stephanie, once the summer's over, what do you want to do? Think five years from now. Seven years from now. Where do you see yourself?"

The image flashed in Stevie's mind unbidden, because it was always right there in the background. It made her happy, so she revisited it often. In five years? In seven? She saw herself in a house, modern chic with a baby boy, cooking for Liam for when he'd be back from his finance job. She saw herself as an influencer, writing posts about traveling while making a home for your family, so your husband wants to come home to you instead of spending endless hours in the office.

But she couldn't say this.

Number one, although she and her mom were vicious to each other, Stevie loved her. She couldn't hurt her even more than she already had. And number two, self-protection. She couldn't tell her mom this dream. Because all she'd ever hammered into Stevie was the need to be independent from a man—that is, never depend upon his income. She needed to have her own career. She always encouraged Stevie to attain independence, freedom, education, and opportunities. That's why their ancestors had left Korea for Japan. That's why a branch of the Choi family tree had sought these opportunities in Peru. And why eventually Stevie's parents had left Peru for the United States, where Maximo and Stephanie had been born.

How was she going to throw so much sacrifice away? How was she going to be so selfish? After all, even if she said she wanted to go to culinary school and be a chef, her mom would freak out. Or she'd insist on Stevie being the kind of chef that collects Michelin stars and maybe gets a reality TV show. All Stevie wanted was to cook for people. At home. For fun. For love. That wouldn't be enough for Ana María, though. Stevie knew that from experience.

Her nerves were already frayed, and by now, it was best to go through the motions. "I want to graduate and go to business school. I already told my advisor." She had almost said, "I already told *you*," but it was late, and she didn't want the fight to extend for hours.

"You say that you want to graduate and go to college, but last term your grades were dismal. How in the world are you going to get into college with those grades?"

Stevie sighed. "I'll work harder, Mamá."

She lowered her head and pretended to be defeated.

Her mom wasn't fooled, but Max was.

"Okay, I'm glad you're back safe and sound. I'll call Abuela so she can go to sleep, and we can start with a clean slate tomorrow. Okay?"

He looked at Stevie, who nodded and then said, "Okay."

Her brother was giving her an out, and she really appreciated the gesture. She looked at her mom. Ana María had aged exponentially these last couple of years. The grief from her husband's death and the heartache she got from her daughter were destroying her. Stevie could see it, and she felt bad. She really did. But she wasn't going to sacrifice her life to try to make her mom happy.

"Okay," she said. "Tell Abuela Yoli that I'll call her tomorrow. No, better yet, tell her I'll come over." She leaned in to kiss Max and turned around to head to her room without even a glance at Stevie, whose heart felt like it was crumbling.

She swallowed her tears and looked at her brother.

Max shrugged. He was blushing as if he was embarrassed to be the tool their mom used to punish Stevie. Because she was so affectionate with him, so lavish with her praise, Stevie knew her mom was capable of this kind of love. But why not with her?

"What did you expect, Steve?" he said, calling her the childhood nickname that never failed to make her smile. Even now that she'd finally let the tears fall. "Come here," he said, and hugged her.

She cried silently like she'd done all her life, and he just held her. He sniffed her hair and said, "You smell like campfire."

"We were up at the canyon," she said.

"You were with Liam all day, then?"

She shrugged, but he gently pushed her away to look at her face. He looked so worried. But he didn't need to be. She knew how to take care of herself.

"I hope you're being careful. I hope he's nice to you," he said, so dramatically, which made Stevie mad.

"What do you mean by that? Of course he's nice to me."

Max rolled his eyes. "He doesn't have the best reputation. Or he didn't when I was still in school."

"Exactly. He didn't have the best reputation. But those were all rumors. He's the best kid. He loves me."

He made a gesture for her to calm down, to lower her voice. She hadn't realized she'd been yelling. "Sorry," she said.

Max whispered, "Please, be careful, or I'll kill him."

She rolled her eyes and laughed. He laughed, too. Max couldn't even kill a fly—literally. He'd told her off once when she had killed a spider that he'd ask her to take out of his room.

All Roads Lead to Rome • 55

"I mean it," he said, baring his teeth.

He might be in college, but he was still a goof.

"Good night, Maxi. Thanks for helping me out."

"You owe me! Do the same for me next time," he said. This time, she laughed for real, as if he'd ever need her help rescuing him from a sticky situation.

Stevie headed to her room and went straight to the en suite bathroom. She had to pee so hard, but before she did, she checked her underwear. No period yet. Hesitating, she took out the pregnancy test from her tote bag. She'd had close calls before, and she was usually prepared, but she didn't keep the tests at home anymore. Once, the cleaning lady had found it and asked her about it. Without hesitation, Madi had said it belonged to her. Poor Madi, to be thrown under the bus like this, but her lie had worked, because Asunción had kept quiet about it. Now Madi carried all the incriminating evidence with her.

Earlier in the day, she'd almost taken the test at the campsite, thinking that if the worst-case scenario happened, she'd surprise Liam with it. But something told her that wasn't a good idea. So she took the test now. She peed in a cup that she kept under the sink, put the stick in, and then set it on the counter while she did her skincare routine.

That was another thing the Choi women had in common, an obsession with keeping their skin clear, no matter what. Unlike most of the girls in her friend group, she'd never had acne in her life.

The timer on her phone went off and startled her. But the feeling was nothing compared to what she felt when she glanced at the stick.

Two pink lines.

Liam didn't reply to her texts, but he picked up on the first ring. "What does that mean?" he asked, sounding like he'd already been sound asleep.

She let out a breath to steady her voice. "It means it's positive. It's mean we're pregnant."

56 • *Yamile Saied Méndez*

Liam chuckled. "What? You're pregnant?"

The silence that followed was so heavy, she almost collapsed with the weight of it. What was he thinking? Liam was smart and so mature for his age. She'd always loved that about him, but now, what was he thinking?

"Why are you telling me now, Stevie? Now I'm not going to be able to sleep, and I have a game tomorrow."

She bit her lip. Always, always his baseball was first. She'd never been jealous until now.

"If I'm going to be up all night, then, I think you should know why. It takes two, Liam."

Another pause.

"But you said it was impossible this time of the month? Like, it can't happen during the full moon, right?" Liam questioned.

He was smart, but he knew nothing about how babies were made, or how women's cycles worked. To be fair, she hadn't known either, until Madi's grandma Alina had taught Madi, Nadia, and Stevie how to calculate their cycles with a chart and all.

"It's not like I did it on purpose. I told you it was safer to use a condom," she said.

He made a sound she couldn't understand. "I can't deal with this shit right now, Stevie. We had such a perfect day, and then you had to ruin it like this? Why do you pull this kind of thing?"

"Me, ruin the day? What about how my life could be ruined? Did you . . . did you stop to think about me for a second?"

Another sigh. "Of course I think of you. Listen." He took a deep breath. "There's nothing we can do now."

Now that his tone of voice had softened, she felt like crying.

"Try to get some sleep, and then if tomorrow the test is still positive, we can figure out how to eliminate this problem."

Of course the test would still be positive the next morning. But she was so relieved he was talking in plural. Neither one wanted a baby right now. She wanted to tell him she wasn't planning on going through with the pregnancy, but she'd been so scared he'd think badly of her. And now he'd said, *eliminate this problem*. They were obviously thinking along the same lines.

"I promise on the moon and all the stars that everything will be all right," Liam whispered in that way that gave her goose bumps, even if they were miles apart. She could imagine his breath tickling her ear. "And we'll be more careful next time, okay?"

He could promise on the moon and all the stars until the sky went dark, but the next day, Liam didn't answer her calls. When she tried to contact him on social media, he was gone. It was like he never existed. She was too embarrassed to call Nadia and Madi. They'd been friends forever, they were sisters of the heart, but she knew they'd be heartbroken for her, and right now she couldn't deal even with the thought of knowing she had let them down. Desperate, she called Laurie, a girl from school.

"He's still online," Laurie told her. "He's ghosting you, babe. He blocked you; that's why you can't see him."

She spent all day at home. She'd told her mom she was sick. And she was, because maybe it was the anxiety of keeping her secret, or the dread over Liam not answering her calls, or maybe just one of the symptoms of her condition, but she was nauseated all morning. She even threw up once when she smelled the chicken her mom was boiling for soup.

When her mom brought her soup to bed, Stevie was so happy and relieved. She couldn't tell her mom yet, not until she figured out what she was going to do, but she savored the moment of being coddled more than she did the soup. She noticed the way the vegetables were all cut up small, with love and care, and that her mom had left celery out, since Stevie didn't like it. Although the smell had made her nauseated, the taste was like liquid love, warming all her insides. She closed her eyes to savor each flavor, each note of saffron and paprika, the hints of basil and lemon, while the whole time she was aware of her mom, going around

58 • *Yamile Saied Méndez*

the room picking things up, throwing others away, and maybe looking for a clue that would tell her the cause of Stevie's illness.

This was Ana María's way of showing love, and when Stevie was done with her food, they watched a soap opera on the old TV in her room, a Turkish one with people who looked like the Kardashians. The next day, when Stevie felt worse and even threw up the 7 Up she'd been given by her mom, Ana María insisted they go to the emergency room.

"I've heard meningitis is going around the community," Ana María said. "I don't want to take any risks."

Stevie could've told her mom then and saved herself the drama at the ER. But she didn't know how to tell her mom the truth. Now that her worst fears had come true, that Liam had tossed her aside like her mom had predicted, like her brother had warned her about, she didn't know what to do. She felt like she was on a roller-coaster ride and her seat belt had come undone. She wanted to get off, but no matter what, she'd get hurt, and others would also be hurt in the process. But would her mom ever forgive her?

Unable to refuse going to the hospital, Stevie let her mom walk her to the car and lovingly fasten her seat belt and tuck a blanket around her. "Medicine now can do wonders," Ana María muttered, as if she were talking to herself. "Don't you worry, my sweet. You'll be okay soon."

The doctor confirmed her words, but not in the way Ana María had expected. "She'll be okay once we treat the symptoms of her pregnancy, ma'am," the ER doctor said. She had bags under her eyes that belied her youth. "We'll put in an IV, and I'll write her a prescription for an anti-nausea medicine. Her OB-GYN can take over after the weekend."

Ana María's face had the color of melted wax, and the ER doctor realized what she'd just done. She glanced at Stevie apologetically and said, "I'll give you some privacy to discuss." She started walking away, but then looked at Ana María and said,

All Roads Lead to Rome • 59

"There are options, though. The pregnancy is still early enough that it would be a simple procedure."

Ana María turned her back to the doctor, disgusted. The doctor glanced at Stevie and left.

"She's right," Stevie said after a few seconds of silence.

"About the pregnancy? I don't doubt it. I wondered that night that you came in late. I noticed you looked chunkier than usual."

Stevie pressed her lips and took the jab. Well, the stab, really. She deserved it. She deserved everything her mom had to say about her, because Ana María had warned her, and here they were. "Also, about the procedure. I don't want to have . . . I don't want it to continue," Stevie said, twisting the sheet around her index finger until it hurt.

"It's too late for that, señorita," Ana María said. "You should've thought about that before you gave yourself to that boy. Because it is that boy, the baseball player, right? Liam?"

Stevie nodded. "Who else would it be?"

She'd never had another boyfriend.

Ana María's square jaw was severe. "I wouldn't know, now, would I? Where is he? I'm going to call him right now."

Before Stevie could stop her, Ana María dialed Liam's number. She'd had it because she had insisted on saving it when Stevie and Liam started dating. But of course, Liam had blocked Ana María, too.

The nurse came back with an IV, and maybe it was her imagination, but the cold feeling in her veins had just surprised her when Stevie started feeling better immediately. "Thanks," she said.

The nurse smiled with compassion and pity. Stevie wanted to disappear.

"Get used to those looks," Ana María said. "That'll be our life from now on."

"Nobody will know," Stevie replied. "I'm not telling anyone."

60 • *Yamile Saied Méndez*

"It will be obvious soon, Stephanie."

"What?" Stevie said, panic rising in her. "I'm not going through with it. You can't make me."

Ana María didn't even raise her voice. She just walked right up to Stevie's face and said, "You will do what I say."

"Mamá, don't make me."

"You can only plead like this because I gave you the chance to be alive."

Here it comes, thought Stevie. At least they were in a semi-public place. Her mom had never been physically violent, but she'd slapped Stevie once. She could put up with the words, but not with being slapped. She knew not everyone was like that. She lowered her head and took the heat.

"That baby, yes, small as it is, it's a baby, Stephanie. He or she didn't ask to be born. You brought this upon yourself being so terribly irresponsible. You're going through with it, and you'll be responsible for once and for all."

"I'm not ready to be a mom," Stevie cried.

"Of course you're not. But you're not going to kill an innocent being. You'll have the baby for a respectable family to raise as their own. It's the least you can do."

"What if Liam comes around? Can we go talk to him and his parents?"

Ana María's eyes lit up. She hadn't considered that Liam could change his mind. Once he saw Stevie, he'd regret having blocked and ignored her. It was a natural reaction, to run from a situation like this. Stevie would forgive him. They'd put all this behind them.

Ana María headed to Liam's, hoping to talk some sense into him, or get his parents' support. "He's as guilty as you are of this." This was the last time she mentioned the fact that Stevie hadn't gotten pregnant on her own.

Two hours later, mother and daughter were driving back home. Stevie was so dehydrated, even after the two bags of flu-

All Roads Lead to Rome • 61

ids that she'd had at the hospital, that although her breath came up in jabbed sobs, no more tears fell from her eyes.

"That good-for-nothing," Ana María kept mumbling every few seconds. "Such a coward. I want to kill him. I want to kill them all."

Stevie didn't want to defend Liam—she couldn't, not anymore—but she didn't want her mom to go to jail. Still, Ana María was right. He was a coward. His whole family was a bunch of cowards. When she and her mom had shown up at the house, his father had come to the door and sent them away, threatening to call the police.

"That baby could be anybody's. Liam has a bright future ahead of him, and it's only natural that girls like your daughter will only come up with any kind of lies to get a piece of his money. Our money. But you won't succeed, missy," he'd yelled in Stevie's face while Liam's mom watched them with horrified eyes from the kitchen. Liam's little sister, Sally, was hiding under the table. The fear and hurt in them broke Stevie's heart.

Liam had never showed his face. Yes, he was a coward.

"We can insist on a paternity test. Maybe you won't even have to wait until the baby is born," Ana María said, sounding unhinged by now.

"What for, Mamá? There's nothing I can do."

"Maybe you can say he forced you to . . . you know?"

Stevie dry-heaved and placed the paper bag to catch her vomit just in time. "I'm not going to say that. He didn't make me. It wasn't like that."

Ana María sent her a disappointed look.

Did her mom really prefer that she'd been forced to have sex? She couldn't even think the R-word. Would that make this nightmare better?

The pregnancy was easy to forget during the summer vacation, and even into the fall. Stevie had always been small, but after years of gymnastics and softball, she was muscular. Besides,

62 • *Yamile Saied Méndez*

she'd been so sick that it was a miracle she could eat grilled chicken and strawberry milkshakes. The little weight she gained was lost in the big hoodies and pants that luckily were in style. No one noticed anything. For several weeks, she could hide it, even from her friends.

Nadia and Madi thought that Liam had broken up with her because he'd gone away to college in California. But when Madi showed her a picture on social media of Liam with a famous model in LA, Stevie lost it and told them the whole story.

"Wait. . . ." said Nadia, looking green. "You're pregnant? Like, right now?"

Stevie had no more tears to shed. She lifted her top and revealed a tiny bump, but a bump nonetheless.

Nadia and Madi exchanged a look of shock. And hurt.

"Why didn't you tell us before?" Nadia asked, kneeling in front of Stevie, and holding her hands. "We would've helped you."

"How, Nadia? How can you help?"

Madi bit her lip. "By holding the emotional load, Stevie. That's how. We're best friends. Moments like this are what best friends are for."

But her friends didn't understand. They were like little girls, still watching *Gone with the Wind,* dreaming for their "Ashley" and making binders with plans for their dream weddings. Stevie would never have a great love like that or a wedding. Who'd want her with a baby?

"My mom wants me to place it for adoption," she said.

She couldn't talk about the baby like it was a person. It was an *it*—a thing growing inside her. Moving. Making her sick. Making her body change. Placing one more barrier between her and her mom. And now between her and her friends.

"Maybe that's for the best," Nadia said, but her voice sounded doubtful.

"How am I going to raise it?"

"We'll help you," Madi said. "My mom was a single mom. She'll help. She's been through this."

All Roads Lead to Rome • 63

Stevie wasn't so sure, but at least she didn't feel so desperate anymore. She couldn't even talk freely with her mom. Every time they spoke, Ana María would bring up the topic of finding an adoptive family, and Stevie couldn't even open the binders the social worker sent her.

"The young couple from England? Think about it? They'll give the baby a family and spoil him with love. Isn't that what you want?"

When Stevie didn't reply in the correct way, according to the invisible script that she never knew existed, but her mom expected her to follow, Ana María would get so angry. She'd give her the silent treatment for days.

"If not, there are the two women who also applied with the private agency. One of them is Asian. At least the baby would look like one of them. Think about it," she said the next time for breakfast. It was the first time Stevie had been able to eat bread, but she later threw it up.

Her grandma Yolanda was on Stevie's side, but her mom didn't bring her around to the house anymore, and without a car, Stevie couldn't visit her.

Max never declared on whose side he was, but there was no need to. He, perfect son Max, was going to agree with anything Ana María said.

Stevie didn't even know what to think. Finally, she decided that if the baby looked like Liam, she'd place it for adoption. If the baby looked like her, though, she didn't know what she'd do. She had time, though. Three weeks before her due date, her water broke, in English class, and all her resolutions went down the drain.

Chapter 6

One moment she'd been writing an essay on the dangers of social media, and the next, she was being life-flighted to the hospital in Salt Lake. The doctor announced Stevie needed a C-section.

It all happened so quickly; she didn't have time to process anything. She only remembered waking up and seeing Max's face, swollen with crying so much.

"Hi, Steve," he finally said. "You finally woke up. Perfect timing, because the nurse brought someone to meet you. Want to meet your son?"

Stevie almost said no. But she was alive, and she didn't know what had happened to her or why this was happening to her. "Okay," she tried to whisper, but could only move her lips.

Her brother placed something beside her. "Look."

Heart hammering, she closed her eyes. The heart monitor chimed with an alarm. After a deep breath, she turned to look, and saw him for the first time.

All Roads Lead to Rome • 65

He was perfect.

He was beautiful.

And he was hers.

She started crying, and Max cried, too, as he caressed her hair.

"Where's Mami?" she asked. Her throat hurt so much. Later she learned it was because of the ventilator she'd been hooked on for three days.

"Mami went to get something to eat."

Later, she also found out that when she was unconscious, Liam had come by the hospital, late at night when only Max was allowed in the room. At first, Max had to pull himself back so he wouldn't kill the coward who'd left his sister to fend for herself. But when Liam had cried, Max knew it was a good thing this whole thing hadn't happened fifty years ago, when parents forced people to get married to keep up with the appearances. Stevie wasn't alone, though, and being yoked with the lead ball that was Liam would be a life sentence Stevie didn't deserve.

As the days passed and she recovered, Stevie also learned that the couple from England had changed their mind when they saw the baby had inherited the Asian genes from his mom and not the blue eyes of his father. She didn't know how they'd heard that Liam was a blue-eyed blond, but she imagined that Ana María had showed them a picture, the one from junior prom where she looked beautiful, and he looked so handsome.

In any case, the lesbian couple said they were more excited than ever to make a home for the baby, that they'd be willing to make it an open adoption, if that helped Stevie feel better about her decision. But the baby was hers. She couldn't imagine being torn apart from him.

"I'm keeping him," she declared the day before she got the okay from the doctors to leave the hospital. "And I'm naming him Tristan."

66 • *Yamile Saied Méndez*

Mrs. Boer, the social worker who had been trying to make sure Stevie understood all her options, said, "You're his mother. No one can make you place him for adoption."

A flare of hope blurred in Stevie's heart. But she braced herself for the next words she knew were coming. "Your love hormones are at an all-time high right now. I mean, it's how nature works, but who can blame you? He's the most beautiful baby boy I've ever seen," Mrs. Boer declared.

"I'd love him even if he were ugly." Stevie's whole being lit up at the compliment. Beautiful was an understatement. He was glorious. She clutched Tristan closer to her. He kept nursing hungrily. The nighttime nurse said that it was a miracle her milk had come in even though she'd been in a coma for three days. He never missed the bottle, and Stevie's love was incandescent.

"I know you'd love him no matter what. But—"

There it was. Stevie held her breath. "The Schustermanns wish you the best and want you to know that should you change your mind, they'll take him."

The Schustermanns were the lesbian couple, and Stevie was grateful for the sentiment, but she said, "I won't change my mind."

Her mother eyed her from the corner. Stevie knew her well enough to see she was angry beyond measure. But she wouldn't confront Stevie in front of strangers, even Mrs. Boer, who had been kind and respectful.

The social worker nodded patiently and patted Stevie's hand. "It's still good to have options, Stevie," she said softly. Then, she stood up and caught Ana María's eye. "Can I talk with you for a second?" Mrs. Boer asked in a cold tone of voice.

"Of course," Ana María said, and followed her outside.

Tristan's suckles slowed. The maternity websites had said babies don't smile until they're at least one month old or so. That the gestures they make are the product of gas. But Stevie was sure he smiled at her. She counted his fingers over and over. She

All Roads Lead to Rome • 67

studied his face, memorizing every feature. He was absolutely perfect.

Voices raised outside, and she came out of her baby daze to pay attention.

"She does have options," Mrs. Boer was saying in a strained voice.

"But she's not giving the baby any," Ana María replied. "I'm too busy to help out with him. I won't swoop in to rescue her because next year, the same thing will happen, and I'll end up raising a bunch of grandchildren. I did my share. Not very well with her, Heaven knows why, because I swear to God I raised her and Max the same."

There was a soft shushing sound.

"Don't shush me," Ana María snapped. "Don't be condescending."

Stevie's heart pounded hard. She didn't know what the social worker had said to get her mom so incensed, but she was happy that Mrs. Boer seemed to be on her side.

"It's your prerogative, Mrs. Choi. You can kick her out and lose a daughter. Or you can help and support her in this, perhaps the most difficult time in her life, and gain a relationship not only with her, but also her son."

A heavy silence followed, and although Stevie heard her mom's muffled voice, she didn't hear what she was saying. A few minutes later, the door opened, and Ana María walked into the room.

She met Stevie's eyes. Stevie held Tristan closer.

"You can't make me give my baby away," Stevie said, shaking.

Ana María sighed, defeated. "I'm not going to make you do anything. Don't you think if I knew how, I would have done it way earlier than this?"

Stevie's ears rang. "Ma, I want to raise him." She had never begged for anything in her life, but she'd beg for Tristan if she

68 • *Yamile Saied Méndez*

had to. She'd do anything for him. Anything. Even give her heart out. Even trample on her pride.

Ana María started crying. "I didn't want your life to be so difficult." Stevie's heart broke at seeing her mom cry. But at the same time, it was healing her to have this connection with her mom. "I want him to be happy, more than anything. I love you, Stevie, even if I'm so hard. I'm hard because you're my stronger child. Because you're so capable of ruling the world if you set your mind to it. I just didn't want you to ruin your life. This is the worst that I could've imagined."

There were plenty of worse things that Stevie could imagine. But she was alive, and while there was life, anything was possible. "Maybe it's not the worst that could happen. Mamá, I'm not the first girl to have a baby at age seventeen."

Ana María shook her head and chuckled. "My mom had me at seventeen, you know?"

"Abuela?" Stevie asked, and the world as she knew it came crashing down. Her grandma was the most devout evangelical woman she knew. Stevie had never even heard her say a bad word. She was the kind of person who left money on the floor if she found it.

Ana María shrugged. "This doesn't mean I'm happy that you're going through this, but I'm your mother. And you're mine. We're getting through this together no matter what."

Chapter 7

Alone or with the support of her family, Stevie found that everything was harder than what she had ever expected. What had she thought? That life would give her a break? That her mistakes would all be forgiven? No, on the daily, her mother reminded her how much Stevie's mistake had cost not only her but the whole family. Ana María's light sleep was impacted to the point that she needed sleep medicine to get a few hours of rest before going to her job at the flower shop.

Max's girlfriend dropped him. She didn't like that he sometimes babysat Tristan so that Stevie could help out at their mom's flower shop. Abuela's friends from church brought back to the surface the fact that in her youth, Yolanda had been *wild*, having a baby at seventeen. It was time to pay the balance of her sins.

"I don't care what those snakes say," Abuela Yolanda said in Spanish, while feeding Tristan his bottle. "I was young, and I don't regret having Ana María. Whatever they say, she's not a sin, and little Tristan isn't one, either. You're el papito de mi

70 • *Yamile Saied Méndez*

corazón," she whispered, and kissed his forehead. "You smell so good!" She glanced at Stevie, and pride shone in her eyes. "You turned out into a good little mama, in spite of everything."

Ana María rolled her eyes, but she didn't contradict her own mother, which was a reprieve for Stevie, who took even more pride in doing a good job for her son. Even if it was hard. Her mother forgot that Stevie paid for her mistake more than anyone else, of course.

In the summer, she didn't mind waking up before the sun to take care of Tristan. He was, after all, her everything, and she loved watching and taking care of him. She was adamant that he nurse as much as he wanted, and when he was ready for solid foods, she made everything from scratch. Stevie had always loved feeding people, and now that love bloomed into a passion. She delighted in preparing him the best little meals. She started posting her results online, using Tristan as her model.

One morning, she woke up with a request from a rich lady from Park City to make food for her twin baby girls. Stevie was delighted with the offer. She wrote a reply and asked Nadia to proofread her message before she sent it off. She wanted to sound as professional as possible. The woman replied with an even bigger order that made Stevie dream with the possibilities.

She'd gone shopping for groceries, spending almost to the last of her savings from last year's birthday. When her mom arrived from work, she was in a bad mood. But when she saw Tristan, a smile replaced the frown lines. They came back when Stevie took the chance to start working.

"What's all this, Stephanie? Tristan won't eat all that even in a week. He'll get sick. It will all get spoiled."

Stevie had wanted to share this opportunity with her mom, and at the chance, she couldn't help smiling. "I got an order from an influencer in Park City, Mamá. She saw one of my videos on social media and wants to try some foods for her daughters."

Ana María didn't reply for a few seconds. Tristan was playing with her hair. Then she dropped the bomb. "I don't see how

All Roads Lead to Rome • 71

this will be a good idea. What if her daughters get sick and she blames you?"

Stevie hadn't thought about that. She was so careful with how she cooked. She obsessed not only about the quality of the ingredients, but the hygiene of the process. She took pride in how immaculate she kept the kitchen. How she sanitized everything Tristan touched or put into his mouth, which was the same thing. A year ago, her room had been a mess. Now it was spotless because of Tristan.

Ana María must have seen how her words had affected Stevie, because she added, "Sorry for always finding the one negative thing in every situation. Sorry. I didn't mean to burst your bubble, but that's the way I am, hija."

What a change from a few months ago, when Ana María would've never apologized. The words still hurt, but Stevie was grateful after all that her mom was looking out for her—in her own way.

"Thanks, Mami. Maybe this will help me earn money from home."

"Cooking?"

"Yes," Stevie said, shrugging. "What's wrong with that?"

Ana María looked away but didn't say anything else.

Stevie set out to work, being extra careful with how she packed the little meals. It was a plentiful summer. Squash, carrots, sweet peas, and all kinds of fruits. She tested each recipe and had Nadia and Madi try them.

"It's the most delicious thing ever," Madi declared after trying the all-organic-and-sugar-free strawberry-and-yogurt parfaits.

"Gerber better watch out," said Nadia. "If I had a baby, I'd order from you."

"You can reshare on your accounts," Stevie said. "Maybe your sister and her friends would want to try them?"

She glanced up just in time to see conflict flash in Nadia's face.

Stevie knew her friends supported her no matter what. But being among the few Latine kids at their giant high school, they already dealt with a lot of shit from classmates and teachers. Nadia was brilliant, but she had to work three times as hard as the white kids for her teachers to notice her. And Madi? She could pass as a white kid, with her lighter skin color and the bubbly personality of a future yoga teacher, but most people just discounted her brains because she was so pretty. It was enough that their friend was a teenage mom; if they started promoting her products, everyone in their super conservative community would think they were next in line to have a baby out of wedlock.

Trying not to show that she knew what the two of them were thinking, Stevie said, "Or maybe Isabella can share? I'll send some samples for Olivia."

Nadia's sister had a little girl and lots of friends who were into natural parenting.

"I'll tell Isa to share widely," Nadia said. "She already loves everything you make."

"Speaking of which," Madi added, "you haven't cooked for us in forever. And I don't mean baby food. I mean, real people food."

"Babies are real people!" Stevie laughed.

In her family, love wasn't always expressed in words. It was only through food, and although she was lavish in telling her friends she loved them, she mostly liked to show it in treats she made for them.

Finally, she had the order complete for the lady in Park City. The drive was about an hour from Orem. Back and forth, it would be two hours. Abuela Yolanda offered to watch Tristan so Stevie could meet her customer. Stevie was delighted. She'd get to drive on her own for the first time since Tristan had been born. She never complained that he was glued to her twenty-four seven, but she missed her alone time.

All Roads Lead to Rome • 73

"Thanks, Abuela," she said, and kissed her grandma on the cheek. "This means a lot to me."

Abuela Yolanda smiled at her. They looked into each other's eyes, and Stevie wondered what the old lady was thinking, but she didn't want to ruin the moment in case she didn't like the answer.

Stevie took off in her mom's car. With the money she got from this order, she'd fill up her gas tank. She'd also immediately invest in more containers, and maybe pay for ads that would get her more visibility. Maybe next year, she could sell her baby foods at the summer festivals. It was too late now to get all the licenses and permits, but next year . . . next year Tristan would be a toddler. Maybe . . . maybe things would look up. Maybe her dad was watching over her from Heaven, and her life would only get better. Her life and Tristan's. She was now a person in two bodies.

Feeling giddy with the possibilities unfolding in her mind, after a couple of wrong turns, Stevie arrived at the house. Now, she hadn't grown up in poverty. Her parents were firmly middle class and had always tried to give her everything she needed and most of the things she wanted. In fact, and not that it was a competition, compared to Nadia and Madi, she had a lot of things her friends never had: a designer purse for her fifteenth birthday, her own car when she turned sixteen, even a small allowance and the use of a credit card.

However, in seeing how Mrs. Llewellyn lived, Stevie suddenly craved more—for her son. Wasn't that how life was? She hadn't given him a father, but she was determined to work twice as hard as a mom so that Tristan never felt the absence of a father figure in his life. If only Stevie's dad hadn't died! Their lives would be much, much different.

She got out of the car, and carefully unloaded the order of baby food. Trying to channel all the confidence she'd had as a kid, she walked to the front door and rang the bell. A musical

74 • *Yamile Saied Méndez*

chime echoed inside, and far away, a little dog barked. It was the yappy kind that, more than a pet, was an accessory. She bit her lip, worried that she was going to wake the twins she'd cooked two days for.

A few seconds later, when she was debating whether to ring the bell again, a woman opened the door. She was the typical beautiful Utah mom, a mixture of California blonde and Scandinavian height. Her eyelashes were so long, dark, and thick that Stevie knew they were not real.

"Hi," Stevie said, flashing her winningest smile. "I have the baby food delivery." The woman paused long enough for Stevie to panic that she'd gone to the wrong house. "Oh! The Tristan's Treat order?"

"Yes, that one," Stevie said, pleased with how easy the name of her business rolled off of the woman's lips. She imagined one day the brand would be as famous as Annie's or Wendy's. Was there a brand inspired by a son? And a son of a teen mom, at that? She'd have to look that up to feature it in her social media.

Shop local from a single mom inspired by her infant son!

"Come in," the woman said. "I'm Elise Llewellyn, by the way."

"I'm Stevie," she said. "Nice to meet you."

The house seemed the floor model of a designer company. Marble, white hardwood floors, and natural textiles everywhere. It had that elusive expensive hotel lobby scent no Yankee Candle could touch, a mix of basil and something citrusy.

Stevie couldn't believe her luck. Of all the people who could have been her first big order, it had to be someone who was obviously really well off, not to say wealthy. Stevie had never paid attention to what her parents learned at sales seminars they attended to become better small business owners. She'd never thought about money or networking before, but she knew enough to guess that someone with this kind of house would have a lot of connections.

All Roads Lead to Rome • 75

"You can put everything here," the woman said, pointing at a black stone counter.

"Oh, this is beautiful," Stevie said. "What kind of material is it?"

"What? This old counter? It's concrete! Can you believe it?"

"It's gorgeous," Stevie said. "Would you like me to unpack and tell you what each thing is?"

"Sure," the woman said. She was dressed in all neutrals and was so tall that Stevie felt dwarfed next to her.

Carefully, Stevie took out each container she'd lovingly packed and labeled. It had all looked so cute at home, with the logo of a silhouette of Tristan's profile. But the plastic containers looked kind of out of place in this beautiful kitchen. She'd try glass jars next. She told Mrs. Llewellyn, Elise, what each thing was.

"Do you have like a label with instructions or something?" Mrs. Llewellyn asked.

"I don't have a hard copy. For the environment, you know? But I'll text you the digital versions. You'll find all the info there for your peace of mind."

She didn't have digital versions per se, either. She had her recipes that she'd typed in her school Google Docs account. She'd add the logo and share that. Next time, she'd prepare postcards. It was a learning curve, but she hoped she'd been prompt enough so it didn't look like she was pulling words out of thin air.

"Since you're all digital, is it okay to send a payment directly to your bank? I haven't done paper checks in like forever, and I only do cash when I go to a third-world country. You know what I mean?"

Stevie swallowed words that had crowded in her mouth and nodded, hoping her smile seemed genuine. "Of course."

The woman looked confused. "You mean you don't have to consult with your boss?"

"My boss?"

76 • *Yamile Saied Méndez*

"Yes, Stevie from the invoice." Then the woman's eyes lit up, as if she'd finally heard Stevie's introduction from minutes ago. "You're Stevie! But you're so young. How old are you?"

Stevie hesitated for a second. She was tempted to say twenty-one. Some college guys had told her she looked older, and she knew that now that she was nursing Tristan, she looked older than Nadia and Madi with her fuller shape. But she wasn't embarrassed by who she was.

"I'm seventeen," she said. "I'm my own boss. I mean, it's my company."

Mrs. Llewellyn's eyes widened. "Oh, my! At seventeen, I still didn't know how credit cards worked, and here you are, a whole entrepreneur!"

Stevie blushed at the compliment. She was about bursting with pride.

"What gave you the inspiration? I mean, baby food prep? It's brilliant! Are you the oldest of one of those Mormon families that have seven or eight kids?"

Stevie scrambled to find the right words, and the woman must have confused this as awkwardness.

"I mean, I am Mormon, too, you know? Not that practicing. I like to wear tank tops, and I need my morning coffee. With twin girls, how could I not? All I'm trying to say is that I understand the Mormon dynamic."

Stevie sighed. "I've never been Mormon, but I'm familiar with church. I mean, I live in Orem. How could I not?" she said, mirroring the woman's words. "I was inspired by my baby, Tristan."

"Oh, sweetheart!" the woman exclaimed, looking horrified. "You're too young to be married."

Stevie should have nodded and made a quick exit, but she was starved for conversation with someone who wasn't a direct member of her family. True, Nadia and Madi visited as much as they could, but they were in such different stages in life, they didn't have that much in common anymore. She craved conver-

All Roads Lead to Rome • 77

sation with other people who knew what it was like to raise a little baby, and she didn't have the opportunities, really.

So, she said, "I'm not married. I mean, Tristan's dad isn't a part of our lives. I dropped out of school and started this business. My mom is supportive, but I wanted to have my own thing. For my son."

Mrs. Llewellyn's eyes became teary and intense. "Of course. Of course. Wow. I'm so impressed. Sit down, Stevie. I'm so intrigued by your story. Tell me, how did you come up with the recipes?"

Stevie told her everything. How she'd been bored out of her mind. Not because she had nothing to do, because Tristan required constant care. She'd had to drop out of school for now, but she had missed the intellectual challenge of school. She'd created this hoping it could be something she could be proud of. To show her mom she wasn't a failure.

Stevie, who never allowed herself to be vulnerable, bared her soul to this virtual stranger, who listened without judgment. Suddenly, she felt her breasts getting fuller and fuller. Tristan's face flashed in her mind, and the milk flowed from her breasts. She looked down and was relieved to see that the dampness wasn't visible in the black fabric of her T-shirt.

"You're an inspiration," Elise said, probably confusing the pause in Stevie's words for emotion or something. "I'm so proud of you, a young girl. I mean, I feel like if you put your mind to it, you could rule the world."

Stevie smiled, gratefully. Her mom said that, but in Ana María's mouth, the words had a double-edged-sword feel to them. They were a compliment that just showcased all the lost potential. In Elise's mouth, there was only admiration and approval.

"Thank you. Thanks for everything, really," she said, standing up. "I have to go. My baby will be hungry soon. I pumped, but I'm dying, you know what I mean?"

Elise gave her a questioning look, and then glanced at Stevie's

78 • *Yamile Saied Méndez*

chest. She couldn't have seen that she was dripping milk just saying her baby's name, but she must have guessed.

"I never breastfed them. I mean, imagine. Twins. But yes, get going, and I'll make an order for next week. Are you going to offer all the same things, or will you expand?"

Stevie hadn't even thought of expanding. But she wasn't going to say that. "I'm actually adding more savory recipes for dinner and fruit options for dessert."

"Fantastic," Elise said. "Expect an order from me."

Stevie drove home in a daze of happiness. She took Abuela Yolanda on a quick ice-cream run to celebrate. She walked on clouds all week long. She didn't receive any orders from any other customers, but when she was starting to despair, Elise sent her a text listing a huge order.

Who cared if Elise was her only customer for now? She had said she'd gift the extra jars to a few close friends to spread the word. Stevie spent her last savings in buying glass jars; she printed the recipes and ingredients on nice paper, and she added some freebies.

The next weekend, she brought Tristan along on his first long drive, to drop off the order. Too bad; this time, Elise wasn't home. A woman who introduced herself as the housekeeper received the tote and closed the door without offering Stevie even a cup of water. Oh, well. Rich people like this were busy. Everything would be worth it in the end.

Tristan didn't love the drive, although the canyon in the fall was the best. He was six months old, but lately he'd been so colicky. Abuela Yolanda said he might be teething, so Stevie stopped twice on the drive from Park City to Orem to feed him. If there was one piece of online advice she didn't intend to follow, it was letting her baby cry it out. The sound of Tristan's sadness was a knife to her heart.

She knew her friends were getting ready for senior year, but going to a classroom for hours seemed like such a waste of time. While she nursed Tristan in the back seat of her car, she scrolled

All Roads Lead to Rome • 79

on her phone, researching what she needed to get the GED. She was glad that it didn't seem like it would be too complicated. She was over sixteen, so she didn't need her mom's permission. Once she passed the test and had the degree, she'd be able to attend business classes at the community college.

Even though Tristan kept crying, she had stars in her eyes. Maybe that's why she didn't notice it was so late. Ana María wasn't happy, and like always, she wasn't shy in letting Stevie know. "Next time you have such a long drive, let me know," she said. "I could've come with you. Poor baby. He's been crying so much. You have to think about him, Stephanie."

Stevie would've never taken her mom along. She'd been looking forward to speaking with Elise Llewellyn. Now she was tired, hungry, and cranky. Her patience was dregs on the bottom of a cup. "He's okay. I'm his mom. I know what I'm doing," she said, taking Tristan from her mom's arms.

That night, Tristan was so fussy that she had a hard time settling him down. She wondered if he'd eaten something that hadn't agreed with his stomach. She longed for a full night of rest, for sleeping past seven in the morning. Tristan was perfect, and she never complained about him, but in that moment, the only thing she wished for was a few minutes of peace and quiet.

When she went to the bathroom, she was frustrated to see the stain on her underwear. Her first post-partum period. She felt cheated. Some websites said that some women didn't get a period until the baby turned one or stopped nursing. To make matters worse, when she returned to the room she shared with Tristan, she found that he was awake. Again.

Abuela Yolanda was right. He was teething, and when Stevie dozed off, he clamped his teeth in the delicate nipple. She exclaimed as she tried to pull him away from her breast. It was the first time since he'd been born, that she felt something else for him that wasn't adoration. He must have felt the change in her mood, because he broke into disconsolate tears.

She tried to comfort him, but a few minutes later, her mom

80 • *Yamile Saied Méndez*

knocked on the door. "Everything okay? He never cries so much."

Stevie was trying her best. It still wasn't enough. "He's fine. He just bit me, and when I pulled him away, he didn't like it."

Ana María shook her head.

"What, Mami? I'm trying, okay? Don't try to make me feel worse because it's not going to work!"

Tristan cried harder.

Ana María took a step back. "I was going to offer help, but I guess you don't need me."

"You're right. We don't need you. LEAVE!" she yelled.

Stevie knew she was being irrational. It wasn't just the fussy baby that upset her. It was the fact that Elise still hadn't paid for two weeks' worth of baby food prep, and Stevie had no money to buy food for the coming week.

Maybe for Elise, the money wasn't a big deal, but for Stevie, it was. Tristan was running out of diapers, and now she was back on her period and needed tampons. She didn't think her money would be enough to buy everything. But why did she have to go and lash out on her mom? They'd been getting along so well, all things considering. But maybe it was the holidays coming up, and Max had been out of the country for a semester abroad. Maybe she and her mom needed a break from each other.

Ana María must have thought the same thing, because she didn't come back to offer help. Stevie looked at the crying baby, and a horrible voice in her head wished that he didn't exist. She immediately regretted the thought. She hated herself. Where had that thought come from? What kind of person saw the most perfect human in the world, the only person who loved her unconditionally, and wish he didn't exist?

Stevie played soothing music. She paced with him in her arms until they shook. Finally, he fell asleep. She kissed his head, sniffing that intoxicating scent of milk and newborn sweat. Even though he looked just like Stevie, dark hair and eyes that

All Roads Lead to Rome • 81

kissed in the corners, when he was sound asleep, he looked like Liam.

She hardly ever thought of Tristan's father, but when she was scrolling on her phone, she'd seen a picture of him in a baseball stadium. For a little while, she allowed herself the luxury of fantasizing how different her and Tristan's life would be if Liam had chosen to share his life with them. Financially, things would be harder, because they would've needed an apartment. There was no way Ana María would've allowed them to live with her. But it didn't hurt to dream like this. It was better than the other kind of fantasy, where she was still a normal high school girl, and her biggest headache was that her prom dress wasn't as nice as the pictures had promised.

She didn't really wish Tristan didn't exist, but there was like a whirlwind in her chest. She felt nervous, and she didn't know why. Later, Stevie would wonder if the anxiety that she felt in her heart had been a warning. She'd felt the same thing the morning her dad had died. But she thought it was just her frayed nerves, the fear that Elise was late with the payment, and the sleep deprivation.

She woke up because the sun shone in her face. It was late November, and the sun would be buttery soft all day, but the glass of Stevie's window acted like a magnifier and burned her skin. At first, she was confused. She glanced at the clock, and when she saw it was nine, she struggled to understand what the time meant. For a fraction of a second, as she looked at the baby-blue sky beyond the window, she wondered if everything had been a dream, a really terrible one. If she never was pregnant. If she was late for school, and now she'd get a detention for being tardy. But then she saw his face in her mind, and again, her rock-hard breasts full of milk throbbed.

"Tristan," she said, rolling off the bed. "Tristan."

A gnawing feeling in her chest became a lead ball with chomping teeth. He was still asleep in his crib, and she smiled at herself. She'd been so silly. Getting nervous because her wish had been granted and he'd slept through the night.

"You learned how to roll over?" she said in a high-pitched voice, wondering if she should wake him up. He was sleeping on his tummy, but his face was to the side. She could see his chubby cheek, and his puckered lips. Her breasts throbbed desperately. If he didn't wake up to nurse soon, she'd die.

Like countless mothers in history, she gingerly placed a hand on his back. She waited one, two, three heartbeats.

He was eerily still.

"Baby," she said, "Tristan!"

She picked him up. What was the worst that could happen? That he'd wake up? She'd nurse him. She was wide awake after the first full night of sleep since she'd woken up from her coma. But Tristan was cold and stiff like a baby doll in his little sleeper.

At first, Stevie didn't know what to do. She was paralyzed. Her baby wasn't breathing. Finally, a loud voice broke through in her mind. He needs CPR. Call for help.

Only a few hours ago, she'd told her mom she didn't need any help. She didn't want it. And now she wailed, "Mami, help me! Tristan!"

Her baby was dead.

Tristan was gone.

Chapter 8

"Nothing is sadder than a baby coffin," someone said at the funeral.

The words kept echoing in Stevie's mind, like so many others.

If only she had woken up earlier.

If only she'd thought of taking him to the urgent care, just in case.

If only she'd paid attention to the nagging feeling she had in her heart.

If only she'd accepted her mom's offer to help.

If only. . . .

Then perhaps Tristan would still be alive.

Perhaps her heart wouldn't be shattered.

People wouldn't look at her like she was a murderer.

Even though she wasn't religious, her neighbor had offered to hold the funeral at the local church. Stevie sat on the hard pew and looked ahead, beyond the baby-blue casket. In this building, there wasn't a crucifix. She fixed her gaze on the old man playing the piano. Sometimes in the mornings and evenings,

84 • *Yamile Saied Méndez*

they'd cross paths when she was walking Tristan in the stroller and the man walked his Yorkie on a leash. They always complimented each other's babies as they went their separate ways.

Stevie's milk dripped, but she'd put pads in her bra to contain the moisture. Why hadn't she thought of that before? Her brother, Max, was speaking now. He'd come back from his study abroad to support her. Once again, coming to the rescue, putting his studies aside for her. Ana María held Stevie's hand and, every once in a while, she pressed it. It was almost as if the motherly instinct to see if her child was breathing, alive, had reawakened in her now that Tristan was gone.

Max was done speaking. After all, what kind of eulogy does a six-month-old baby get? He didn't even have time to live, and yet, with his last breath, he'd taken everything that held Stevie together.

Madi and Nadia and their families were there, including Nadia's sister and her baby girl, who was just a few days older than Tristan. Stevie couldn't even look at her. Every time the baby whimpered, it was like a knife sliced through her soul. She had no more tears to shed.

That terrible morning, once the ambulance and police had arrived, and the doctor had pronounced that Tristan was indeed lifeless, Stevie had to answer a myriad of questions. Everywhere, in the hospital, at the police station, back at home, people asked her the same questions, as if trying to catch her lying. She always replied the same; that she'd nursed the baby, and once he was asleep, she put him in his crib at the opposite side of the room. Yes, on his back. No, there weren't any pillows or even blankets that could've suffocated him.

The investigators declared that everything looked right in her room, and even the first responders said there hadn't been any signs of foul play or violence. Just an intrusive thought of *what if* the night before and then in the morning, a fantasy of what her life could've been like if Tristan didn't exist. All her life, her dad had told her that thoughts are powerful. That they create our world.

That thoughts lead to actions. She hadn't acted on her exhaustion. She'd only loved her baby. She adored him like she never imagined she could adore another human being. And yet, he was dead.

The official report said that it was sudden infant death syndrome. Abuela Yolanda had fainted when she heard Max explain it to her, because she just couldn't understand what the doctors meant. Stevie knew of SIDS and SUDI before, of course she did. She'd read about the boogie monsters of parents on the baby and pregnancy websites she scoured, trying to teach herself everything she could about being a good mother. She'd made sure there weren't any toys in the crib with him. Yes, he'd rolled over by himself, but he was a strong baby. How many times had she and her friends laughed that he could do baby pullups since the day he was born? He had enough neck strength to turn his face.

Now Tristan's death was another statistic.

At the hospital, the doctor, a man in his fifties, explained to her that no one knows why some babies die in their sleep. He said there could be a strange genetic disposition. Maybe Tristan had a problem that hadn't been flagged at birth. Stevie agreed to the autopsy, because she needed to know why this had happened to him. When she changed him for the last time with the favorite outfit of hers, she'd cried seeing the scar on his small chest.

The autopsy had been for nothing. The doctors found no clues. He just stopped breathing and died. Since Tristan had passed hours before Stevie found him, they couldn't even donate his little organs and honor his life by helping other babies that might have been waiting for a lifesaving procedure.

Tristan had been so healthy, and he'd loved her so much. Now she was an empty shell of a person, so she sat with vacant eyes as people told her he was in a better place. Stevie thought, *What better place could he be than snuggled next to her breast?*

She was also told that God needed another angel. *Why hers? Didn't he have enough babies who had already died?*

That everything happened for a reason. *What reason could it be?* She hated this one the worst.

86 • *Yamile Saied Méndez*

Why had God let her get pregnant and love this baby so much? What was the reason? To punish her? Why was she still breathing, and Tristan in that tiny casket being lowered to the ground?

Stevie had no answers. She went through the motions like a shadow, looking up every time she imagined his cries, but it was all in her mind. It was worse after the funeral when everyone went home and even Max returned to his apartment.

Her room was full of baby stuff. How could a little human who couldn't even crawl occupy so much space and make such messes? Her closet, once full of trendy clothes, cool-looking sneakers, and dressy heels, was now bursting with tiny outfits that still had the new price tags dangling from them and Tristan would never wear. Grief is strange. A person's heart can break, and yet, life continues.

Max had loved Tristan; he'd been the best uncle, but after the Thanksgiving holiday, he had to go back to school if he wanted to graduate on time. Ana María was destroyed, but she had her job at the flower shop, whose owner had provided the floral arrangements for Tristan's memorial service. Even Abuela Yolanda had her routine at church and the community center.

Tristan had touched so many lives, but none more than Stevie's. Her whole world gone, Stevie spent all day and night in bed. She imagined that if she stayed still, maybe she would suddenly die, too. There was no point in staying alive. But her stubborn heart kept beating, even though it was so broken. Each time it drummed, it jagged her inside.

Her family tried to be there for her. One night, her mom sat next to her and said, "I know what you feel. When your dad passed away—"

Stevie immediately tuned her out. She was almost catatonic, barely aware that her mom was crying, but now, those cries didn't move her like they had in the past. Her friends came over, but Stevie couldn't even pretend to smile. Sometime later, a doctor showed up at the house. Maybe Ana María had called him.

All Roads Lead to Rome • 87

Stevie didn't even know. He poked her arm with a needle. They were feeding her to keep her alive.

She let them do whatever they wanted, but that didn't change the fact that Tristan was dead. He had been smiling and snoring until he wasn't breathing anymore. How was that fair? If there was a God, why would HE do this to her?

Stevie hadn't wanted to be a mom, but she had loved Tristan more than she thought was possible. Was she really such a horrible person for God to take her baby like this? Had her mistake been that she had thought life was finally looking up? That after ruining her family, she had the possibility of rebuilding herself? How had she been so arrogant?

When Tristan was born, she had been unconscious. When he died, she had been asleep. All she wanted to do now was sleep forever.

"Stevie," a voice said, as someone held her hand. "You need to get up, or they're going to take you to the hospital, and I just can't lose you, too." Max was crying next to her.

Max—another casualty of all her terrible mistakes. "Please don't do this," he said. "Come back."

Stevie saw a little light in her mind, and she wanted to go toward its warmth, but she couldn't move. In the background, Nadia and Madi were talking to her mom. Their parents were also there. Abuela Yolanda was yelling at Ana María. Stevie thought that if she just refused to move and died once and for all, everyone's life would be infinitely better.

Yes, they'd cry and perhaps even miss her. Just knowing that made her feel better. She knew she was loved. However, down deep inside, Stevie believed she didn't deserve that love, like she hadn't been worthy of being adored by Tristan. If her mom told anyone she'd wanted to terminate the pregnancy, everyone would hate her. In her opinion, she deserved their hate. But truth be told, she already hated herself more than she could explain.

"Stevie," Max said. "I know you can hear me. I know you

88 • *Yamile Saied Méndez*

think you want to die. But I love you, sis. I'm here. Don't leave me. Don't prove them right. Don't let them win."

Max never cried. All his life, he'd been kind and sensitive—the perfect obedient son. Their parents' pride and joy. He was Stevie's biggest cheerleader. Even though she was three years younger than he, she'd always defended him and been there to shield him from the world. She didn't know why she'd been born with the fiery personality that made her burn everything around her. She was destructive, toxic, but she loved Max. There was no way she could see or hear him suffer.

She turned to look at him and said, "I'm sad."

Tears spilled from his eyes, but hers didn't even prickle. She was a desert; nothing lived inside her.

"I'm sad, too," Max said. "But you have to eat. You have to come back to us."

"What for?"

To his credit, Max didn't reply right away. "To make sure Tristan is never forgotten. To show everyone that he didn't ruin your life. That he gave you a reason to reach a potential no one else wanted to see. He was little, but he knew you're the most amazing human in the world."

"Because I fed him?" she asked.

Max smiled, satisfied. If she was being her acidic, usual self, she'd be okay. Maybe not now. Maybe not for months. But one day she'd show *them*, whoever they were, and the whole world that she wasn't done living yet.

They didn't hospitalize her, but the nurse came three times a day to make sure the IV fluids were working. Madi and Nadia sat with her, combed her hair, and softly filled her days with fluff. They told her about things that happened at school. The boys they liked. Nadia was still with that loser. Hopefully one day, she'd realize she was worth so much more. And Madi had trapped herself into thinking there was just *one* person who could love her and didn't see that she was pretty much everyone's dream girl.

All Roads Lead to Rome • 89

Slowly, Stevie regained her strength. One day, she was brave enough to open her closet and face the rack of still-unused clothes her baby never got to grow into. She took out her favorite outfits, his little toys, and placed them in a box. His blanket still smelled like him. Something cracked inside her, and finally the knot in her throat rose up to her eyes. Tears made her eyes burn, but stubbornly, she held them back. She was still hugging it when her mom walked into the room.

"Oh," Ana María said, a hand on her chest.

Stevie turned around, embarrassed at being seen at this moment of vulnerability. She felt worse than if her mom had walked in on her having sex with Liam. She felt feral. Why? Why did her mom take the liberty of walking in on her? Why couldn't she respect her privacy?

"What? What do you want?" she barked. Her voice was hoarse from the lack of use. She saw how hurt Ana María looked but didn't back down. "Knock before you come in."

Ana María had shrunk at first, but now the hatred from Stevie seemed to infuse her with strength. "A *please* and a *thank you* would be nice. I've been worried sick about you. I heard noises and came in to see if you were okay." If she'd stopped talking then, maybe things wouldn't have escalated. But like Stevie, Ana María didn't know how to stop her words before it was too late. "After all I've done to support you. I'm not the one who hurt you. I'm suffering, too. I loved Tristan, too."

"Don't say his name," Stevie yelled. "Don't even mention him!"

"Why? You want to pretend that he didn't exist?" Ana María said, inexplicably. "The pain won't go away just because you put his things away. I say this from experience. When your dad died—"

"Stop!" Stevie said, putting her hands over her ears. "You keep bringing up Papi, but this isn't the same! You can't even imagine what it's like to lose a child."

The words echoed and rebounded on the walls. On mother and daughter. From one's mouth to the other's heart.

90 • *Yamile Saied Méndez*

"I feel like I have lost you, even though I've done all I could to support you. Maybe he deserved a chance at a real family, and you denied him that."

Stevie's heart hardened. "At least he loved me. You won't ever get that from me." She knew the words were too much, but she wanted someone to hurt like she was hurting, and the only person in front of her was her mom.

Ana María didn't step back. She lifted her chin and said, "At least I kept you alive as a little child."

Stevie felt like she'd been stabbed. There was no air in her lungs. Her whole body was tingling. She'd had one job—keeping Tristan alive and happy—and she failed. All he'd ever done was love her, and she had failed him. Her mother had hurt her, but it was true: Stevie was still alive. She hadn't even been able to end her life, because she would hurt Max, and she couldn't do that.

"Thank you for keeping me alive," she said. "You don't have to worry about me anymore. I'm leaving, and you won't ever have to see or hear from me again."

Ana María crossed her arms. "Really? You're going to run away? Where? You have nowhere to go. No money. No education. You'll be back soon enough. And I'll be here when you're ready to apologize." Now that she'd had the last word, Ana María left Stevie's room.

Stevie packed a few things in a duffel bag. At the last minute, she put Tristan's little muslin blanket, the one with the elephants, in a pocket. She texted her friends and left the house where she'd grown up without looking back.

She stayed at Nadia's for a few days, not even a week, though. Nadia was busy at school all day and then had her job and her volunteer work. Stevie spent most days looking for a job and then working at a bakery. But Nadia's dad didn't approve of their friendship. Nadia's parents were nice, but once Stevie overheard the dad saying that he didn't want Nadia to end up like Stevie. It hurt, but she didn't blame them.

All Roads Lead to Rome • 91

Nadia was mortified when she found Stevie packing her things. "You don't have to go. My mom said you're welcome to stay indefinitely, since Isabella's room is empty."

In the sister's room was a crib for when Olivia stayed over. Stevie could hold her shame in check and ignore how embarrassing it was not to have a home, but she couldn't put herself through the hell it was seeing Olivia and hearing her whimper in her crib. It brought back memories that overwhelmed her like a tsunami. She didn't have the luxury of collapsing again.

Next, she moved to Madi's. Her mom spoiled her and fed her until she looked like her old self. Finally, her milk had dried up and her T-shirts were fitting again. She was treated like another daughter, but one night, Madi wanted to sneak out with a boyfriend and asked Stevie to cover for her.

"I can't do this to your mom," Stevie said.

Madi looked at her like she'd suddenly sprouted another head. "What? Since when do you care about what my mom thinks?" She didn't say anything else, but there was no need to.

Stevie wouldn't hold this against Madi for long, and she agreed to cover for her friend. But this was the sign she needed to find a place for herself. She'd finally gotten her first check from the bakery. It wasn't much at all, but enough to rent a room for a week. She had kept her car because it was a gift from her dad, and she wasn't going to give it to her mom. Fortunately for her, she was still on the family phone plan. That was the only thing that bonded her to her mom. She was determined to get her own number the first chance she got.

The room she rented was clean, and she shared the rest of the house with a woman who had three kids, ages ten to fourteen, two boys and a girl. The other renter was Mireya, a single woman from Mexico, who was working on getting her PhD and came to the US to cook for a chef during the summers.

"There's a lot of money in that industry," Mireya said to Stevie. "If you're interested, I can hook you up."

92 • *Yamile Saied Méndez*

At first Stevie was interested, but when she saw the salary range, she balked. Maybe it was enough to support herself—in Mexico, but not in Utah.

Although this possible job opportunity wasn't going to work out for her, it lit up an idea in her mind. She could relaunch her baby-food company. She could still use Tristan's Treats with her baby's silhouette in the logo. She'd only had Elise Llewellyn as a customer, but maybe, when she heard what had happened to Stevie, she'd be understanding and help her out.

Elise, after all, still owed her for two weeks' worth of food. Stevie wanted to forgive that debt, but she really needed the money. Elise, though, never returned her messages, and then, Stevie realized Elise had blocked her on social media.

Why? she wondered.

When she told this to Nadia, Nadia looked her up on her phone. She gasped, staring at the screen.

"What?" Stevie asked, imagining the worst. For a second, she thought something had happened to her client. Or, Heaven forbid, to the girls. What if they'd gotten sick because of Stevie? She couldn't survive that, but she had to know.

Nadia clenched her teeth. Her dark eyes flashed. "This is horrible. But you can sue her. She can't get away with this; what a bitch."

Stevie thought it must have been terrible, because Nadia never swore. When she saw what had made Nadia so angry at first, Stevie didn't feel anything. Her soul simply detached from her body. She saw the images as she scrolled through them as if they were from far away, like it wasn't her life's work and Tristan's memory that had been violated.

In Mrs. Llewellyn's profile, there was a link to another account: Twins' Treats. The logo was the silhouette of one of the twins, while the other's was superimposed. In the feed, there were photos and videos of Elise cooking and packaging the meals in jars with her girls. The feed also featured how her company had grown in just a few months.

All Roads Lead to Rome • 93

"She stole all my recipes," Stevie yelled. "She stole my company!" She was blind with fury.

Stevie couldn't even think straight as she drove down Provo Canyon. The last time she'd made the drive, Tristan had been with her, and he'd cried so much on the way there. But she'd been hopeful and happy that their lives were going to be better. She was going to get her GED and then go to college. That was the night he had died.

When she arrived at the house, there was a line of cars all along the street, and she had to park two blocks away. She rang the doorbell. It sounded like inside there was a party with chatter, laughter, and live music.

The same housekeeper opened the door. She studied Stevie's face, but she did not recognize her. "Are you one of the vendors? Everyone's going on back."

Stevie nodded and went around the house.

It was a glorious spring day. And there was Elise Llewellyn. She was finishing stacking jars upon jars of Twins' Treats on a shelf. There was a TV camera positioned in front of her, but it wasn't recording. The twins, now toddlers, were running around on a tennis court, chasing a good-looking blond man who must have been their father.

Stevie's voice vanished. She just stood in front of Elise, until the woman turned away. They stared at each other for what seemed like ages. Stevie wanted to say so many things, but she didn't know how to start.

"Oh, hi," Elise said. She actually had the nerve to smile. "I almost didn't recognize you."

"You stole my idea," Stevie said outright.

Starting with a full-on attack was the wrong way to go. It gave Elise an easy way out. They were at her house, with family, friends, and the press as support. To others, Stevie looked and sounded deranged as she raged at the woman. She didn't really remember what she said. She just had flashes of the twins crying, and an assistant taking them inside. The man she saw

94 • *Yamile Saied Méndez*

earlier was by Elise, a hand on her shoulder, facing Stevie, who felt so small and wrong that she wanted to disappear.

"I don't know what you're talking about, sweetheart," Elise said with an infuriating high-pitched voice. "Thanks for helping me out at the beginning, but I didn't steal anything from you. How could I when I have everything?"

Stevie held back a sob. If she hadn't cried when her baby had died, she wasn't going to cry now. Her mom's callousness, life's cruelty, Liam's betrayal had hurt more. But this act took her faith in humanity away.

"When you lose everything, you'll think of me and come crawling to apologize to me," she declared, channeling the little strength she had left. "You'll regret this. Maybe not now. Maybe not in a few years. But I swear you will. You had everything. And still you had to take what was mine? I curse you."

She turned around and walked away, because the husband said he was going to the police. They probably had security cameras, which is why Stevie held herself back and didn't smash the whole display to the ground. She wasn't driving through Provo Canyon. She couldn't face the memories. She went through Parley's Canyon toward Salt Lake, and when she got the first glimpse of the city's beauty, her car broke down and died.

An hour later, Max was there, rescuing her again. He smiled at her as he walked with a canister of fuel.

"Thank you," she said, and hugged him.

She was shaking, and he just held her. "Want to come to my apartment for the weekend?"

She looked at him, and he added, "My roommates are out until Tuesday. They went to a selling trip."

"Selling?"

"Yes, they call it a blitz," Max said hesitatingly. "Drew is selling knives, and Oscar is selling alarm systems. This is a short one, but come summer, they'll be out selling until August when school starts again."

All Roads Lead to Rome • 95

She only knew Oscar and Drew superficially and liked them okay. They both came from really well-off families, and she appreciated that they were hustling anyway. Now, more than anything, she was happy they were gone and she could finally crash at a safe place with her brother. She was grateful for the room she rented, but she craved the peace and quiet.

Max lived in an old townhouse in The Avenues neighborhood of Salt Lake. He had the smallest room and Oscar and Drew shared a loft that always smelled of weed, even though they swore they didn't smoke. As soon as she arrived at Max's, Stevie collapsed on his bed and slept like the dead.

Stevie woke up just as the sun was going down. Like a vampire, she couldn't sleep normal hours anymore. Madi had said it was PTSD, but Stevie couldn't afford therapy.

She was saving to rent a proper apartment. It would be so nice to share one with her brother. Their mom never came to visit, and Max complained he always had to clean the bathroom because his roommates never did. She could even take the small room, and she'd cook for him every night.

She threw the idea at him that night while they ate rice bowls from their favorite Korean barbecue food truck. "What do you think?"

Max looked sadly at her. "I'd love to, Munchkin, but I'm moving to England next month."

"What for?" she asked, dismayed.

He sighed. "I'm doing an internship at this financial company."

"Finance? Weren't you going to do literature?"

He smiled sadly again. "That was before Papá died."

Even if he said it casually, Stevie's heart still jolted at the reminder that their father was gone. She'd never get used to living in a world without him and Tristan.

Tristan.

Tristan.

"I have to do something practical now," Max elaborated

96 • *Yamile Saied Méndez*

further. "Maybe I'll write on the side. Maybe if I save enough money to make sure Mami and you are taken care of—"

"You don't have to worry about me," she said, the guilt gnawing at her again.

He gave her a look of concern.

"No, really, Max. I'm okay. I'll be okay, especially if I know you won't be around to bail me out like this," she said, smiling.

Still, he looked worried. "Are you sure? Stevie, you can't work at minimum wage all your life, or you'll never get to move out of that tiny room," he said. "Without an education. . . ."

He didn't have to finish the sentence. She already knew all of that. "I'm not going to be a burden to you," she shot back.

Why did she always lash out at the people who loved her? She wanted to stop doing that, but she didn't know how. "I promise that I'm going to get my high school diploma. Next time you see me, I'll take you to a fancy dinner, I promise."

He smiled so sadly that it broke Stevie's heart. She didn't tell him what had happened with her baby-food company. She didn't want to abuse his kindness. Hadn't her job always been to protect him? And he'd saved her twice already. She wouldn't forget, but she wouldn't call Max for help ever again.

"When are you leaving?" she asked.

"In three weeks."

"Send me postcards, okay?"

"Okay."

While she stayed at her brother's townhouse, Stevie cooked and left food in his freezer to last him until he departed for London. When she looked at her bank account, she'd been surprised to see a lot more money than she remembered. It was from an email account she didn't recognize, but the sender had been in Park City. She imagined it was Elise Llewellyn, trying to buy her forgiveness. She'd never forgive or forget. On the other hand, she could really use this money.

While her brother went to school, she read his roommates' sales books, and the pamphlets from the marketing companies

All Roads Lead to Rome • 97

they worked for. When they came back, boasting about all the money they'd made in just a few days, Stevie was curious. She drilled them with questions. When they both reassured her that there were also girls who did summer sales, she was convinced. She didn't want to sell knives. The alarm systems paid more per account, so she signed under Oscar.

By the time Max left for England, she had been to two training seasons. It was incredible how the marketing companies tried to lure sales reps. They promised many things that seemed too good to be true, but she had nothing to lose. If the plan worked out, she could sell during the summers, and with all the money she earned, she'd be able to support herself and go to school.

And that's what she did.

The first sales trip, she stayed at the rental house with all the guys. At least she had a small room to hide from the bad-smelling men, who were out all day selling. She didn't join their drinking games at the end of the day. Some of the guys were married with young families, but most were kids right out of high school, and a few had just gotten back from their missions for their church.

Like Austin. He was twenty years old, and he had the same hunger that Stevie had. He wanted to prove to the world that he was more than everyone gave him credit for. In a short span of time, he was the top sales rep, and he had no problem helping Stevie with her pitch.

All she owned was in the closet of the rental, stuffed in a small duffel bag. Hidden at the very bottom was Tristan's blanket. Stevie was starved for love, for human contact. The night she broke the company's record for installations, she kissed Austin. That a woman had broken the record made her feat even more historic.

Austin's eyes widened as the whole room clapped for her. The recognition and validation were the best reward, even more so than the promise of the check heading for her account over the weekend. Austin had a pull on her she couldn't avoid. He was honest and immovable in his convictions. She secretly fell in love with him—hard.

Their relationship was a secret that everyone in their summer office knew about, but no one dared to mention it. Their make-out sessions became steamier and steamier, but this time, Stevie was determined to play it smarter. She went to a Planned Parenthood and got an IUD, just in case. She was never going to make the same mistake again.

She told Austin about the birth control, thinking that he'd be relieved, hoping she could tell him about Tristan. Instead, as soon as she started talking, he pulled away from her, mortified. "What? I'm not going to do it before marriage, Stevie. I thought you knew that."

She looked at him, confused.

"There's other things we can do, though. But I'm getting married at my church," Austin said. "The person I marry will hopefully be also saving herself for marriage. It's the right way."

"So, if I'm not a virgin, you won't even think of me as a long-term relationship?"

"It depends . . . but that's not what I wanted from life, babe."

"I'm not your babe," she snapped back.

Austin exhaled, frustrated. He wasn't that much older than her, but he was a lot bigger and taller. He was intimidating. "You make it so hard."

"What do I make hard?"

"Loving you, Stevie. You keep pushing me away, and I just want to find a partner who has the same mindset. You're the hardest working person I know, but you have no interest in forming a family in the future. You have all these plans that don't include anyone but you. You might also be the most selfish person I know, which is saying something, as we work with all these guys."

"Selfish?" she asked. "If I don't take care of myself, then who will?"

All Roads Lead to Rome • 99

"I want to do that, and you don't let me," he said.

They'd parked their car in a forest in California. All around them, the windows of the other cars were steamed.

"I'm not a virgin, for your information," she said. "So, take me back before I tempt you and ruin your dreams of a saintly wife."

His face was pure disgust. "I deserve someone who's decent. I can't do this. Sorry," he said, and then drove back to the house.

No one in the office understood why the perfect couple had broken up, and why the next day, Stevie transferred to another team.

Stevie didn't care if Austin ever got his fairy-tale ending. But in the last two years of her life, she'd learned that her mom had been right. Even if she'd tried to make good decisions, she was already ruined forever. No decent guy would love her for who she was. It was a good thing she hadn't told him about Tristan. She didn't even tell Brady, when he came along, a couple of years later. Virginity long lost, she saved the memory of her baby.

The only pure and sacred thing she had.

Stevie turned into a working machine. During the summer, she was the first one at the doors and the last one to leave. Her second season, she and Brady managed an office together. They had a brief fling, and even though he promised her he didn't care what religion she was or wasn't or whether she was a virgin or not, Stevie vowed not to let her fantasies run wild like they had with Liam or Austin. She'd made the mistake of giving out her heart twice. There wouldn't be a third time.

At first, only three other women were on her team, all over twenty. With Stevie's training and leadership, they became so successful that the area managers had her travel from office to office to train other women sales reps.

Of course, the guys complained about it. Stevie wasn't only the top female rep, but also the top salesperson overall. Her numbers shattered all records. She didn't care about the rumors

100 • *Yamile Saied Méndez*

that preceded and followed her like a shadow. They were true. Yes, she used "all" her feminine charms to get more sales. She used everything she had to achieve her goals. Cleverness, cunningness, determination. Pure spite and grit. Her strength, mental and physical. She gave it all. That summer, her team had won the company-wide competition for top installations.

To be honest, all the things people made up about her couldn't compare to the truth. She was a terrible person. She'd been a terrible mother. She couldn't protect her baby. Every time she mentioned this to Nadia and Madi, on late-night calls when the loneliness was suffocating, her friends tirelessly repeated that what happened to Tristan hadn't been her fault.

"If that had happened to my sister and her baby," Nadia said, trying not to cry, "would you have said that it was her fault?"

Stevie was appalled. "Of course not! SIDS is a real thing, but there's a higher prevalence to babies of teen moms," she said in a monotone voice. "Isabella wasn't a teenager when she had Oli."

"Stop torturing yourself by going online, Steve!" Nadia exclaimed. It took a lot for Nadia to lose her cool.

Stevie chuckled. "I did go online, and I researched more about that fact, and it's true. Every part of it."

"It doesn't make it your fault, Stevie, please. You need to stop blaming yourself. It won't bring him back," Nadia stressed.

The silence that followed was a like a long-distance slap. Nadia's words shook her. Nothing would bring Tristan back. "I have to go," she said in a strained whisper. "Love you, Nadia. Thanks for talking to me."

"Of course," Nadia said. "Anything for my Stevie."

Stevie achieved everything she'd set out to do. There was more money in her bank account than the inheritance her dad had left her.

Without telling Max, she made a huge deposit in his school

account. "It's like a miracle," Max said when he called to tell her the news. He was now living in San Francisco. A thinker and writer trying to be a finance guy. It was a tragedy. "Mami said that maybe it's residual from the life insurance. Are you sure you didn't get anything?"

She smiled at his happiness. "No. I didn't."

Stevie could practically see his smile fall, and she couldn't have that. "But I'm happy for you, Max!" she said in her cheerleader voice. "Maybe there is some justice in this universe after all."

"Maybe there is," he replied, giddy again.

He'd met a girl.

"I . . . I really don't know how she fell in love with me. I'm at work more than at home."

"She loves you because you're a teddy bear, Max," she said. "She better treat you well, or I'll come beat her up."

He'd laughed, but there was worry underneath. "Ummm, no, please. Maybe I won't bring her home for Christmas, after all."

"It will break Mami's heart, and she can take disappointment from me but not you. I don't care if she blames me, but . . . no. You have to be home for the holidays."

There was a pause, and for a second, Stevie thought the call had dropped.

"Have you talked to her?" Max asked. For the last year, he'd tried to be the bridge between his mother and his sister. Stevie wasn't going to put herself in a vulnerable situation with her mom again, but they started texting again, and occasionally talking on the phone, although it was always about superficial topics and Max, the only thing they had in common now.

"Not really," she said, "but don't worry. I promise I'll be on my best behavior."

"Okay, because with Abuela Yolanda in Peru, I need at least an ally at home."

"What do you mean?"

"I think I'm going to propose."

102 • *Yamile Saied Méndez*

Stevie's eyes misted for a second. She blinked, and the emotion was under control. "Congrats, Maxi!" she said. "You're the best guy in the world. And don't worry, I'll take care of Mami."

She hung up before her voice broke and Max could ask her what she meant, exactly.

That Christmas, she and her mom were indeed on their best behavior. They were polite and gracious to each other. When Max commented that their coldness was worse than standing in the blizzard outside, Stevie tried to amp her charm to at least pretend their family was normal, for his sake.

The charade was a success, because when Max popped the question, Erin accepted immediately. In the best Utah style, they were married in the spring, before Stevie left for her next sales season. Stevie's hard work with her mom paid off. The next Christmas, Erin and Max were spending it with her own family, so Stevie and her mom were off the hook.

At first, she felt guilty that her mom was all on her own. Abuela Yolanda was still in Peru, so Stevie almost called her mom to say she was coming home. Right before she did, she found out two things that rattled her world: Brady was getting married in Rome to a French girl. And Stevie's mom was dating someone.

Now that Max had his own family and Abuela was on the other side of the world, Stevie had no more ties to her mom. Ana María was taken care of. It hurt that her dad could be replaced so easily, so fast. No one could replace a child, though, especially one she kept hidden in the darkest corners of her heart.

She flew to Rome, thinking that with Brady married, her time of summer sales was over. She didn't know what she'd do after. Maybe it was time to put her plan in motion—finally.

Chapter 9

After Rome

Stevie's best sleep was always on airplanes or borrowed beds. Although her mind was a whirlwind of thoughts and her heart a pond of murky water, on her flight from Rome to New York, she slept like the dead.

If only the dead could dream.

During both flights, her dreams were full of Cristian's accented voice. The taste of that one kiss awoke something in her she thought she'd never feel again. The warmth of his hand in hers when they had crossed the street or walked on the ancient cobblestones by the Colosseum.

Sometimes, she met a person so charming that she let herself fantasize about a future together. She allowed her imagination to run wild and create happy fairy-tale scenarios, like she was a character in a video game. Then, she snapped her fingers and went back to reality.

However, with Cristian, it was different. That night at the hotel, tired from walking all over the city and sharing their dreams for the future, Stevie had dreamed about him the whole

104 • *Yamile Saied Méndez*

time. Him and Tristan, but not the baby version. In her dream, Tristan had been ten years old, the age he'd be now, and he ran into Cristian's arms. The look of love in Cristian's eyes had made her cry and cry.

She woke up, and the pillow had been wet with tears. She washed her face and stalled in her hotel room as she decided what to do next. Stevie knew she could ask Brady for Cristian's number, but her friend was on his way to his honeymoon, and she wasn't going to intrude. She had left her phone charging overnight, and this morning, although there were plenty of messages from Max and Erin, Nadia and Madi, and—shockingly— even her mom, there was no sign of Cristian. It was as if he hadn't existed. As if the previous night, including the coin wish, had been nothing but a distant dream.

When she saw the blue gloves and remembered the look on his face when she put them on, she thought that perhaps this was a sign that she'd been forgiven for her previous sins. One doesn't meet a person like Cristian every day. Over the years, she had known so many guys and been tempted to break her promise of never getting involved with someone she met through a friend, but never had that urge been as strong as now.

Granted, she had only met him for a few hours, but his face was imprinted in her mind forever. The scent of his skin all around her. His family still lived in Nevada, but she didn't have an anchor anywhere. Maybe . . . maybe she'd let herself hope. Stevie dressed herself simply and didn't even put any makeup on. If he'd been deceived by the makeup and the hairdo, this was a chance to set him and his expectations straight.

She ran across the street. It was snowing—in Rome! It felt like a sign from the universe, like she would get to live something out of a romance novel. Maybe this was a page turning in her life. When she arrived at the reception area of the hotel and gave his name, the receptionist shook her head and said, "So sorry, madam. Mr. Alvarez checked out an hour ago."

All Roads Lead to Rome • 105

Stevie stood rooted in place, trying to make sense of what the girl said, even though she'd spoken in flawless English. She was too proud to beg her for a phone number or an email. After all, this wasn't a movie, and privacy laws were a real thing. She went back to the hotel and packed her stuff. She almost left the blue gloves behind, but at the last minute, she stuffed them in her jacket's pocket.

She snapped a picture in front of the mirror, posted it in her stories, and left for the airport.

If hell existed, it would be a customs line.

She tried to tune out the droning sounds a boy not older than one tired of crying made. His mom rocked the stroller while she looked at her phone. Stevie and an older Asian woman exchanged a look, and then she heard a mean voice in her head say, *Who are you to judge? She could be looking at information about her family, or her business. After all, she was able to keep her baby alive, and you. . . .* She bit her lip to refocus her thoughts on her physical pain instead of the emotional one.

Accidentally, she made eye contact with the kid, and he froze mid-cry and then smiled at her. Why did this always happen to her? Kids loved her, and she wanted nothing to do with them. Still, she wasn't the kind of person not to return a smile, especially coming from a child. One thing led to another, and the next thing she knew, she was playing peek-a-boo with the boy, who played back, adorably hiding his eyes behind a pudgy hand. He was so cute. He, too, had a dimple in his left cheek, just like Tristan.

The customs officer called the mother and son duo to a booth. The mother quickly headed there. Losing sight of Stevie, the kid started crying again, and the mother shot her a look of such disdain, she was momentarily speechless. "Ungrateful bitch," she muttered, and for the next following minutes debated if she deserved this treatment or if she would get points in Heaven for a good action that went unnoticed.

106 • *Yamile Saied Méndez*

"What was your reason for going to Italy?" the officer asked. He was a young, handsome Black man.

Stevie was too tired for this. "I went to a wedding," she replied, instead of playing hard and saying it was none of his business.

"Fun. Fun," he said, and then added, "Smile for the picture." She stared at the camera without moving a muscle.

"Welcome home, Ms. Choi," the officer said, with a genuine smile that made her feel bad for being in a rotten mood.

"Thanks," she replied, and walked away.

Maybe the kindness she had shown to the baby gave her points after all, because her luggage wasn't flagged for another random check, and she was able to move it from one carousel to the next. When she headed to the closest Sky Club, she glanced up and saw the back of a man's head that made her heart jump into her mouth. He had the same blond curls around the ears as Cristian and matched his height. What were the odds that they'd meet up at the airport in New York?

Trying not to be too obvious, she tightened her steps to catch up to him. She didn't know what she'd say, but if this were a movie, this would make a cute scene, the start of something special. But when she almost reached him, she saw a little blonde girl holding the man's hand. Feeling her gaze on him, he turned around and looked at her for a second.

He wasn't Cristian.

The man didn't look like him, after all. His eyes went past her to someone behind her; a tall blonde woman who looked like his twin smiled at him and the girl. She joined them, and they continued walking to wherever it was they were going, holding hands. Something inside Stevie screamed that this was what she wanted, and more than anything, she wanted to drown that voice. She knew how. With a good dose of working on numbers until her flight was called up.

Stevie boarded with the first-class passengers, and when she saw she was sitting next to a guy, she put her headphones on

All Roads Lead to Rome • 107

to shield herself against any kind of attempt to talk. All she wanted to do was sleep and hope to dream with Cristian. She wasn't about to waste the delicious comfort of the white noise of the airplane, but she felt too wired up. She turned on her phone and scrolled through her social media accounts. And there she saw it, a post of Brady and Céline arriving in Thailand, already looking tanned—madly in love, happy, completed.

She clicked on the *like* button and wrote, "Have fun, kids!"

This should quench any remaining rumors once and for all. Before she logged out, she saw she had a new notification, and thinking Brady had replied, she smiled.

What a goose. . . .

She opened the app again, but it wasn't Brady. It was Cristian. He'd liked her comment and sent her a DM. He'd reached out first! Her heart started galloping. Just then, the captain announced that due to a mechanical error, there wouldn't be Wi-Fi service during the flight and apologized profusely at the chorus of complaints that rippled through the cabin. She bit her lip, and her hands trembled as she tried to decide if she should read the message now or hours later, after she landed in Salt Lake. Knowing herself all too well, there was no way she'd survive the flight not knowing what he'd said.

What if he had written that they should forget about the stupid engagement? Or the kiss? What if he confessed he was indeed the player Brady had warned her about and that he had a real-life fiancée? She almost took the ring off and left it inside the pocket in the seat in front of her. Anything to avoid feeling embarrassed in advance. She wasn't a coward. If it was going to hurt, she wanted it to do so for real.

She opened the message and was relieved to see it was more than a mere *Hey* like the countless other messages she got from weirdos online.

Ciao, ragazza americana.

108 • *Yamile Saied Méndez*

Her insides melted, hearing his voice in her head. The airplane was lifting. She'd soon lose connection, and he was typing another message that arrived in chunks, which felt like precious drops of water for her parched soul.

Last night, or was it the night before? It felt like a fever dream, like those fairy tales my Nonna used to tell me when I was little. Like the women in her island that weaved lace with thread from shells that are found only at the bottom of the ocean. . . . Sorry for rambling. I'm not drunk. I'm just very tired and still dazed, trying to make sense of what happened, and honestly? Kicking myself in the ass for not acting like I should have.

Stevie swallowed and closed her eyes for a second. This is where he'd say he never wanted to hear from her again.

I checked out of the hotel and went to the airport, but I felt like I was being torn in pieces. I went back to your hotel, but the lady in the reception wouldn't give me your room number. I didn't know what else to do. I texted Brady but he never replied. He must have been enjoying his honeymoon. Anyway. I didn't know how to contact you and left a note with the receptionist. I hope you got it. But then I saw your comment in his picture and thought it was a message from the universe to take a breath before ruining everything.

What happened was pretty magical. The walk. The talk. The ring. The kiss.

I know you said you don't want anything serious now, that you want to be free to explore life and really, really live. But I'm serious when I say that I'd love to be your friend. Your best friend. I don't know. I just wanted to reach out first because if you're okay with it, I'd love to check in once in a while, and more often than not.

Forgive me again for this rambling note. I was in New York

All Roads Lead to Rome • 109

waiting for my flight to Las Vegas and I kept seeing you everywhere. Here's my phone number.

From your Plan B fiancé,

Cristian

Her signal died as the plane gained altitude, and she wished she had a parachute to jump out. She was giddy, looking at the clouds, hugging the hand that had the ring, his ring, against her chest.

Stevie wanted to reply a resounding *yes*, she'd be his best friend, but maybe it was a good thing the connection was lost so she had the chance to really think through the words before typing them. She'd always been impulsive, and now she had four hours to craft her reply, which she sent as soon as the airplane touched down in Salt Lake.

"Good flight?" the man next to her asked.

"The best," she said.

She was floating as she headed to get her bag, even though outside everything was covered in snow, her least favorite landscape. Winter had never been her favorite, but now she had memories of Rome to keep her warm.

Stevie was going to head to her apartment, but Max had also texted her saying that even though Ana María was with the boyfriend's family, their mom had sounded a little sad when they talked on New Year's Day. Stevie had nothing else to do, and she owed Max a favor, or many. She told herself that she was heading home to stand in for the Chois among her mom's new chosen family.

She thanked her past self for having the foresight to park her SUV at the more expensive spots at the airport, and headed to Orem, still soaring every time she thought about Cristian, and the way he had written about their night together, where two souls had met and not burned in the light.

Stevie tried to prepare herself, but when she arrived at her childhood home, the wave of nostalgia hit her like it did every

110 • *Yamile Saied Méndez*

time she drove into her neighborhood. In front of her house was a line of cars, and although it was only past noon, the Christmas lights were all lit up. Her mom had decorated with things Stevie remembered from her childhood, like the giant skeleton her dad liked to dress up as Santa Claus. But there were new things, too, like a life-size nativity scene.

She hadn't seen her mom in more than a year. She was jet-lagged after a transcontinental flight, and her heart started pounding with nerves. She held on to the gift bag with the present for her mom. Cristian's message had left her tender-hearted, feeling like her soul was a delicate thing. If a stranger could see so many good things about her, surely her mom would, too.

Stevie tried to open the door, but it was locked. She entered the code in the keypad. She'd gotten her mom a full security system the first year she started working. Ana María never had to pay a cent, but she always complained about one thing or another. Not that she had to update Stevie on everything, but it hurt that she couldn't get into her house because her mom had changed the code on the system Stevie had installed.

She rang the bell, and although there were sounds of laughter, no one came to the door. She looked back at her car, thinking maybe she should just go home. But she had driven an hour from the airport, and if she went back to her apartment, Stevie knew she wouldn't want to make the trek south again for at least a week.

Instead, she could go to Madi's or Nadia's, whose parents were in the neighborhood, but she didn't just want to drop in at their houses without notice. She'd done it too many times before, and she was always welcome, but now she just wanted to be home, and this house had been the last place that had been a home for her. Tristan had lived here.

Braving the snow piled around the house like it was a moat, she went around to the back door through the walkout basement. She opened to a sight she'd never seen at her house because their family had been so small. The family room was

All Roads Lead to Rome • 111

filled to the brim with people of all ages. A woman who looked in her twenties had a baby strapped to her chest in a baby sling. The baby looked only a few days old. He had a full head of dark hair, like Tristan.

Stevie felt as if she'd walked into the wrong place. She almost turned around, but right then, her mom was heading downstairs, and they locked eyes.

Ana María's eyes lit up brightly for just a second. It had been like the flare of a shooting star that dies before you have the chance to make a wish.

"Hi, Mami," Stevie said, waving. Her voice had been soft, but she might as well have screamed, seeing how everyone went quiet around her, even the kids. And was that a dog sleeping on the couch? Ana María had never let Max and Stevie have a dog, even when they were teenagers.

"Stephanie," Ana María said in a breathy voice. "What a surprise! Was that you ringing the doorbell upstairs? I must have missed you by a second!"

Stevie was rooted in place, aware that snow was blowing in. Her mom hated when they tracked dirt or snow inside. But now everyone in the room was wearing shoes. She almost took hers off, but she didn't want to risk looking even shorter than everyone around her.

"Sorry," she said, her cheeks burning with embarrassment but mostly regret. She shouldn't have come like this. Yes, her mom had sounded sad when she'd been talking to Max, because of course she missed *him*. But Stevie dropping off like this was a bomb.

"Come in, Stephanie," said a man, gently leading her in with a hand over her shoulder. Her first reaction was to flinch at the touch.

She felt the irrational urge of being a bitch with everyone and treating this man the way her mom had treated Liam, the one boyfriend she'd ever brought to the house. Besides, who was this man who welcomed her into *her* father's house? Everyone

112 • *Yamile Saied Méndez*

was looking at her, so she sent him a smile, before turning back to her mom. "Sorry," she said again. "I should've called, but I wanted to surprise you."

"And you did!" Ana María said cheerfully, but the sound grated in Stevie's ears. Then she looked around the room and said, "Familia! This is my daughter, Stephanie."

"Hi, Stephanie!" everyone chorused.

Needles prickling her skin, she said, "Please call me Stevie."

She went around saying hi to everyone in the room, guided by her mom. She didn't hear one single name, except for Tiffany.

"She's Frank's daughter. She just had a baby, Tysin." Ana María beamed at Tiffany.

"Hi," Stevie said, and even though she'd tried her best, she knew she sounded colder than an iceberg.

The girl leaned in for a hug, and the scent of the baby's head made Stevie dizzy with longing. "We were in math together in junior year, before. . . . Well, I knew you back in high school. Now we'll be sisters."

"Sisters," she repeated, but her mind was stuck in all that Tiffany had said.

Stevie felt such a shame. She felt as though she should be in jail for not keeping her baby safe.

Tysin stirred in the carrier, and the same look of adoration shone on Ana María's and Tiffany's faces. Envy made Stevie's blood boil. Her baby would be ten years old. He should've been the prince of this house, running all over the place, laughing, getting in trouble.

Tiffany took the baby out of the carrier. He was all curled up like he was still in his mom's belly. Stevie realized she was staring when Tiffany looked up and said, "Do you want to hold him?"

"No." Stevie took a step back, and then seeing the hurt look on Tiffany's and Ana María's faces, said, "I mean, I'd love to, but I've been at airports for the last two days, and before that,

All Roads Lead to Rome • 113

with lots of different people at my friend's wedding in Rome. I don't want to risk passing on a germ."

Tiffany's smile returned, but her eyes were misty.

"Right," she said. She looked around for someone, and then found a young guy who must have been her husband. "Excuse me," she said, smiling tightly at Stevie, handing over the baby to the guy, and making a show of washing her hands in the kitchen sink.

Ana María never allowed anyone to wash their hands in the kitchen sink. The bathroom was right there. But now she never said anything. In fact, she followed Tiffany around the room like she was a precious being that needed constant supervision.

Frank, her mom's boyfriend, cleared his throat. "It's nice to meet you, Stevie. Your mom has told me so much about you."

Stevie glanced at her mom, but Ana María only had eyes for Frank. She'd never seen her mom look at her dad like that. Maybe she had when they were younger? Maybe before Stevie became so problematic and drove them apart?

She knew she was supposed to say something, but her mom had never talked to her about Frank, and she couldn't lie. She wouldn't. "Nice to meet you," she said.

Then she turned to her mom and said, "Sorry for barging in on you like this. I just barely landed. I have a headache. I'll head to my room and take a little nap?"

Ana María's face reddened as she made a gesture with her hands. "Ay, Stephanie."

Stevie felt like she was a young teen being told off yet again. "What, Mami?"

"I had no idea you were coming. Frank's family knew I'd be spending the holidays all by myself, and they kindly agreed to come here to share the whole week with me."

She was agitated, and Stevie didn't know what she'd done to provoke this reaction. Stevie wanted to head to her room before she said something wrong and ruined this moment for

114 • *Yamile Saied Méndez*

her mom. But it seemed that no matter what she did, she ruined everything anyway.

"Tiffany is staying in your room," Ana María finally said in Spanish.

Still, the words had been obvious because, rushing to Ana María's side, Tiffany said, "I can move elsewhere."

"No," Ana María replied. "The baby's things are already set up there." She turned to Stevie, who was, for once, speechless.

Stevie wasn't welcome here. She had no business in this house. It hadn't been her home in a long time. Without another person to bridge the differences between Stevie and Ana María (her own dad, Max, Abuela, or Tristan), they had nothing in common. They just knew how to hurt each other.

And Stevie hadn't intended to fall into the same old patterns.

"Happy New Year, Mami. Nice to meet you, Frank. You have a nice family. They look perfect. I'll head to my apartment. Mom, call me if you want to catch up, okay?"

She turned around and headed upstairs. Like hell she was going to wade through the snowdrifts. For all the acting like the perfect boyfriend, the guy Frank could've at least cleared the sidewalks and paths outside. There was a perfectly good snowblower in the garage that she made sure was kept in tip-top shape, so Ana María never had to worry about anything.

By the time she made it to the first floor, Stevie was out of breath, bordering on hyperventilating.

"Wait," Ana María called. When Stevie stopped and looked at her, she added in a whisper, "Don't embarrass me in front of him, please."

Stevie scoffed. "That's why I'm leaving, Mamá. I'm clearly not wanted here. I don't fit."

"What do you mean? I haven't seen you in a whole year. I never hear from you. You didn't show up for Thanksgiving or Christmas. What was I supposed to do? Was I supposed to be all alone waiting for you? How is that fair?"

Stevie was tired. She had nothing else to say to her mom.

She just wanted to be in her apartment. She should've stayed in Rome. She should've booked a flight to Las Vegas and met up with Cristian. She should've flown to the moon. Anywhere but here.

"It's not fair. You're right. I'm sorry," she said, and opened the door.

"Don't leave. You can sleep in my room, hija."

Had Ana María said that a minute before, things would have turned out a lot differently. But Stevie couldn't stay here a minute longer. She had made up her mind.

She kissed her mom on the cheek, gave her the gift bag with the gloves, and left.

Her car was freezing already. She told herself that's why she was shaking as she drove north to her lonely apartment.

The view from her bed was magnificent. The whole Salt Lake Valley was sprawled and glittered like jewels on dark velvet. At twenty-seven, she could afford anything she wanted. But not what she wanted and needed the most—family.

After her nap, she laughed at how dramatic she'd been. She texted Nadia and Madi, and they agreed to meet up for drinks later. Nadia had started working as a lawyer at a new firm. This would be her last free night for months. Madi was planning her new yoga workshops and needed advice on the best essential oils to use. Stevie would recommend Cristian's family's brand, of course. She'd already curated the best stories she would tell her friends. But she wouldn't tell them about Cristian—not yet. She'd keep him secret and sacred, like Tristan.

She never looked at pictures of Tristan. It was too difficult. In her nightstand drawer, she kept that little muslin blanket with the elephant print. She allowed herself two minutes of hugging it, imagining the force of the love he'd had for her. When the time was up, she put it away.

Still, she had a couple of hours before she met her friends, and she didn't know what to do.

116 • *Yamile Saied Méndez*

Stevie, always on the move, had a hard time sitting still. She thought of texting her mom to smooth things over, but she didn't have the bandwidth for that today. Her mom hadn't texted or reached out, anyway. Max was too busy with his wife. She wasn't going to ruin the holidays for him, even if their mom got to him first with her version of what had happened. She wanted to text Cristian, but she didn't want to come across as needy and problematic.

For the next little while, she went over her plan for a catering business that she'd started fine-tuning a couple of years ago. After earning her GED, she'd taken culinary arts classes, but she needed to learn how to operate a business. Wanting to be prepared so she didn't ruin her dream before it started, she'd signed up to audit a restaurant administrator class, but she hadn't heard back from the admissions office. The semester started the next day.

Stevie tried to shake her mind off the past and the present and started planning the summer for the team. She wasn't sure if she and Brady would be working together, but in any case, she needed a spot for her team and their families. She was deep into studying the maps of several small towns in Alabama when her phone chimed with an incoming text message. It was a picture of Cristian, eyes bright, hair all messy.

Good night, Stevie, he wrote. *It's chaos with the family here. Hit me up if you decide to come to Las Vegas for a weekend. I'll be the perfect tour guide.*

At the same moment, she received an email from the community college where she had signed up to audit the class to administer restaurants, and a new spot had opened up. She was so tempted to head south on I-15 all the way to Vegas and Cristian, but instead, she replied to the email and said she accepted the offer.

Some people have goals other than partying forever, she wrote to him. *If you want an accountability partner, I'm your girl. But don't tempt me!*

All Roads Lead to Rome • 117

She sent him a selfie, although she'd broken out on her forehead and chin. She was fanatical with her skin routine, but her lotions and serums could only do so much against late nights, long flights, and junk food. She saw that he was typing for several minutes. She went to take a shower, and when she came back to the phone, she saw he'd texted, *You're perfect.*

He couldn't see her, but she shook her head. "If only you really knew me, Cristian. If only you knew who I really am."

She was a fraud, far from being perfect. The sooner he learned that, the better off they'd both be.

Chapter 10

Cancún Querido was so loud and warm that if she closed her eyes, Stevie could swear they were in Mexico and not in cold, dark Utah. The view out the window belonged in a Hallmark Christmas movie set, but she was already tired of the snow. At least she was in good company.

"Cheers for our student!" Madi exclaimed, raising her glass for a toast. She was the designated driver, so she was only drinking a Shirley Temple with three cherries on top.

Nadia and Stevie were drinking a Moscow mule and a prosecco, respectively. "Cheers!" they both chimed.

They all took a sip from their drinks, and Nadia side-hugged Stevie. They were at their reserved booth at their favorite restaurant, sitting side by side. "I'm so glad to have you back and anchored here for a while!"

"What do you mean *anchored*?" Madi asked.

Nadia briefly shook her head, exasperated. "That's because she's taking this class until April—we'll have her here all winter!"

Madi's eyes were wide as realization set in. "After your busi-

All Roads Lead to Rome • 119

ness class, you can come to my soundbath! You can just relax and sleep, I promise. But I'll get to see you! Ah! I love when things line up."

Stevie hated the phrase *everything happened for a reason*, but she had to admit, sometimes things did happen for a reason. Maybe her past self was protecting her from her own impulsivity. Having to go to class would keep her busy and excited for the future, and most of all, safe from driving to Las Vegas and getting into trouble with Cristian.

She hadn't told her friends about him yet, but she had to say something, so she added, "Yep. Sometimes everything lines up. Besides, with all the changes happening in the company, I can't afford not to be in the thick of everything."

"What changes?" Nadia asked, giddy as Alfredo, the server, refilled their tortilla chips for the best guacamole in the world.

Stevie didn't want to talk about work, but it had been such a long time since she'd seen the girls that she owed them a detailed update.

"There's rumors the company's going public, so things are shifting in leadership."

"What does that mean for you? Will you get a promotion?" Madi asked.

Stevie shrugged. "I don't think I want a promotion. I don't love this job. I just love that it allowed me to make a lot of money in a short period of time, and I learned many lessons. I don't want to switch from the doors to an office and deal with all that drama."

"But Brady might," Madi said.

"Brady will," Stevie replied. "Especially now that he's married. I don't see Céline traveling from town to town and living in those horrible motels for weeks at a time. I don't imagine she'll stay behind."

"Austin lives in Florida, though," Madi said, narrowing her eyes as if she were trying to figure something out.

"He's from there, Madi," Stevie said. "He has his support system. Just like I have mine here."

120 • *Yamile Saied Méndez*

She clutched her friends' hands. More than her support system, they were her lifeline. Without them, she'd be lost.

"Do you want to hear something that happened at the wedding?" she asked, rubbing her hands as if she had a delicious morsel in front of her.

Madi and Nadia leaned closer.

"You haven't even shared a single tidbit about the wedding," Madi said, offended. "How dare you!"

"Seriously, Stephanie." Nadia did such a perfect impersonation of Ana María that Madi and Stevie shivered. "You owe us! Tell us everything!"

So, she did. She went over every detail of the wedding ceremony, and the reception. She left out the part where Céline had snubbed her by sending her to the most distant table at the venue and others that would only upset her friends. She only told them the shiny parts, like catching the bouquet.

"You caught the bouquet!" Madi screamed, her sugar high reaching its peak.

"I sure did!"

"Now we must find someone you can marry!" Nadia said.

The food arrived just when Stevie was going to tell them about Cristian. But Nadia was sharp, and she noticed the new ring on her finger.

"What's that ring?" she asked.

"That's so pretty, Stevie! It has diamonds!" Madi said, grabbing her hand and inspecting the ring.

After that night at the fountain, Stevie hadn't really looked at her ring, not really. But now that Madi had mentioned it, she realized it glittered not only because of the gold, but also a thin line of diamonds all around it. She'd given Cristian a fake ring that she paid ten dollars for on Amazon.

"This . . . this is from my Plan B fiancé," she declared.

"Your Plan B what?" Madi said.

Nadia was the one who answered. "Her fiancé." She turned

All Roads Lead to Rome • 121

to look at Stevie and crossed her arms. For Nadia to ignore the smoking sweet pork enchilada in front of her, it meant the news had rattled her.

Stevie shrugged and rolled her eyes. "I met this guy at the wedding. Cristian? Remember Brady—"

"Hates him?" Nadia said.

Stevie had been really good at keeping her friends at a safe distance from the guys from work. No one from that crowd deserved her soul sisters. But there were occasions they'd crossed paths, and she hadn't been able to keep them away. Like the one time Stevie got an award, and her friends had surprised her in the audience, walking into an auditorium full of salespeople holding blue and gold balloons and a crown. Because she was a queen, of course. That time, Brady had forced an introduction, and among the few words they had exchanged, he'd managed to let them know he hated a guy named Cristian.

Nadia, who had the memory of an elephant, remembered every word that had left his lips.

"That's because he feels threatened by other men who are more accomplished and handsome than he is," Madi said. "Show me a picture of this Cristian."

Stevie wasn't going to, but she couldn't help showing him off to her best friends, who had her back no matter what.

Nadia did a double take.

Madi audibly gulped.

Stevie looked at the screen to make sure she hadn't accidentally shown them a random picture of Maluma, her celebrity crush. But no. It was the shot he'd sent her right before she left to meet the girls.

"Wow," Madi said, fanning herself. "I'm not into blonds, but—"

Nadia interrupted her. "But he looks just like a young—"

"Matthew McConaughey," the three said in unison, and laughed.

122 • *Yamile Saied Méndez*

"When's the wedding?" Madi asked, propping her chin on her hand, her eyes dreamy, as if she could picture the whole thing already.

Stevie shook her head. "Not until we're seventy."

Madi exclaimed, "What?"

So, she told them about dinner and the walk, the fountain and the coins. Their wishes.

"But why seventy, Stephanie?" Nadia said, like this was a personal affront. "Normal people say like . . . thirty, something more practical. Seventy! What were you thinking? His equipment won't even work!"

Madi shuddered again. "Do you know how many guys are the hottest and then they hit forty and turn into the Grim Reaper?"

Stevie shrugged. "It's not a romantic engagement. It's just so that if we haven't found our significant other . . . how does your mom call it, Nadia?"

"¿Media naranja?"

"Yes, half orange. If we don't find our person by the time we're seventy, we'll get married to make sure we always have good company, good food—"

"And good sex?" Madi always asked the important questions.

"Maybe," Stevie said. "The main thing is that I wanted to throw my coins into the fountain, but when I learned the tradition says that if you do, you'll fall in love, get married, and return to Rome, then I chickened out."

"You don't want to fall in love or return to Rome?" Nadia asked. She didn't have to look into Stevie's eyes to see into her soul. They knew each other's greatest dreams and hopes.

"I do. And I want to go back to Rome. And maybe I'll want to get married someday. But not yet. Not yet."

Her friends knew her, but they didn't catch the *Gladiator* reference.

"I don't know, Stevie," Nadia said, attacking her enchilada, although by now it was cold. "A guy who's willing to wait until you're seventy?"

"And gives you a true diamond ring," added Madi.

"Is a guy that fell in love at first sight, whether you want to see it or not." Nadia nodded as if this were the final statement before a judge.

Stevie rolled her eyes, but inside, there were fireworks. "You two are impossible. What can he have seen to fall in love? And do I want a guy who loses his head after meeting me one time? Wait until he knows the real me."

"I'm excited to see that," said Madi, and then she looked around, as if she expected to see Cristian walking into the restaurant to join them at dinner.

"Don't let your hopes rise," Stevie said, grabbing one of her tacos al pastor. "He lives in Las Vegas, and then he says he'll go back to Argentina, you know how I feel about long-distance."

"Ooh," Nadia said in sing-songy voice. The Moscow mule had definitely gone to her head on an empty stomach. "Las Vegas is practically the end of the galaxy! No two souls were ever divided by a greater distance." She placed the back of her hand on her forehead and pretended to laugh.

The girls. What would Stevie ever do without them?

Chapter 11

"I keep saying I'm allergic to winter, and no one believes me," Stevie said with the last thread of voice she had.

Nadia gave her a side-eye and quickly turned her attention back to the road. She was driving to the ER for the second time this month, and on consecutive weekends, too. The first time had been strep throat, which soon morphed into something else that had Stevie feeling like she was knocking on death's door, the one door she hoped was a no answer for a long, long time.

"You might be a plant, you know? You looked radiant in your pictures in Rome, but even the night you arrived, you were already coming down with something. You kind of withered away fast after that."

"You mean I went downhill fast? Thanks, Nadia. Just what my confidence needed."

Nadia laughed, and then swerved to avoid hitting a Cyber-truck that was weaving through rush hour traffic on I-15. "Mothereffers, thinking they're in a *Fast and the Furious* movie,

All Roads Lead to Rome • 125

ruining everyone's day, who does he think he is?" she muttered in one breath, and then fanned herself.

What a friend she is, Stevie thought. To do this for her when she was so busy with work and the weekends were the only free time she ever had. Nadia didn't particularly hate winter, but she had an aversion to driving in the snow.

"It was winter in Rome, too," Stevie said. She should stop talking, because every time she tried, it was like a giant serrated spatula was scooping her pharynx.

"But it was ROME!" Nadia said, slapping her thigh for emphasis. "And you're here while you could be anywhere else."

"I just can't let you and Madi get in more trouble without me. I'm your Jiminy Cricket," Stevie said, and started coughing again.

"Drink this, because Madi will be offended you never even tried it." Nadia passed her a bottle of water that had who knew what in it, a concoction of lemon, honey, and spices Madi had conjured up, but which had kept her germ-free for months.

Stevie took a sip, and shockingly, it was so soothing to her throat that she drank almost the whole thing.

"If only Madi had a brew for not stumbling on the same stone twice, she'd become a millionaire," Nadia said sternly.

It was, of course, directed at herself.

She and her idiot fiancé, Brandon, had broken up again. The reason this time was that she'd dared to ask if they should start planning their wedding for this coming September, like he'd said last year. He totally freaked out and left. It had broken Nadia's heart. A month had gone by, and now that the holidays were over, he'd started texting that he missed her. Typical Brandon. The worst was that Nadia was seriously thinking about taking him back.

"More than a brew, she'd have to create shoes that not only prevented you from stumbling on the same rock twice, but also made you kick Brandon's ass all the way to Pluto, you know?"

126 • *Yamile Saied Méndez*

Stevie's voice was totally gone by the time she reached the end of her sentence, but Nadia still laughed.

They arrived at the ER, and when Stevie didn't have the strength to walk from the curb to the entrance, Nadia insisted they needed a wheelchair. Stevie went along because she had no voice or strength to complain.

In the examination room, the friends were making a joke about it, until the doctor said Stevie needed to be admitted. "She has pneumonia, and she's badly dehydrated" was his verdict, like this was a tribunal and Stevie's adulting was being judged.

To prove her innocence, she raised the hand that was still holding the water bottle.

"That's what I was afraid of," Nadia said, clutching her hands under her chin. "That's why I drove her here before it got worse. Bacterial or viral?"

The doctor, a youngish guy who looked faintly like Jacob from the *Twilight* movies, shrugged. "It might have started as a virus, but it morphed into a bacterial infection."

"No honey and turmeric are going to heal that," said Nadia.

The doctor chuckled. "No, they're not."

Stevie sobered up. No. She couldn't get sick, because she couldn't imagine calling her mom, or worse, Max, with the news. No. Her brother would rush to rescue her, and he had a family of his own. Ana María would also come see her, but the whole thing would turn into how Stevie was always doing extreme things to grab her attention, which wasn't true. It's not like she had gotten sick on purpose. Hell, if she had that superpower to get sick on demand, she wouldn't get sick on a weekend when she could drive to Vegas and renew her friendship with Cristian, who, with time and distance, became more and more attractive in her mind.

"Can you just like give me an injection or something? I want to go home." she said, but her voice was like the croak of a dying animal.

All Roads Lead to Rome • 127

"That shot hurts like. . . ." He winced, either thinking of past pain or regretting how close he'd come to swearing. "It hurts more than you think. Just stay for one night, and we'll give you the medicine through the IV. We'll watch you until your fever goes down. I know this isn't anyone's favorite hotel and the food has a bad reputation, but the flourless chocolate cake is the best in state."

Nadia furiously typed on her phone. Probably to Madi, rallying forces.

Every time the young doctor looked at Nadia, he blushed. He seemed really shy. Poor guy. Shy and having to see people all day long. But he had to be smart to be a doctor, right? And smart enough to notice Nadia, who was just wearing sweats, but her hair was a true thing of beauty. Even without makeup, her skin was glowing. She had a natural beauty and needed a serious distraction from Brandon. Stevie decided to sacrifice herself for her friend.

Like the doctor said, it was just one night. Stevie hated hospitals, but at least Nadia had been aware enough not to drive her to the one where Tristan was born, and where they took him afterward . . . and she went home with empty arms. How heavy was the emptiness of those babyless arms!

"Okay," she said, nodding, "just one night. I have to go to my class on Monday."

That should be plenty of time for Nadia and the doctor to fall in love.

It took two nights and several doses of antibiotics for the fever to break. The doctor fell in love, not with Nadia, but with Stevie, or at least the girls thought so. She wouldn't know since she'd been sleeping every time he stopped by to check in on her. He didn't have to. He was just the ER physician, and Madi was sure the day before had been his day off.

Stevie's voice now sounded like she was an eighty-year-old who had been a chain smoker all her life, but it was audible, at least. "But how could he have a crush on me?" she asked as

128 • *Yamile Saied Méndez*

Madi filled in Nadia on what had happened earlier that day when Dr. Edward Taylor—for real—had stopped by with flowers to cheer her up.

"I've seen myself in the mirror," she said with a groan.

Her eyes were swollen and bloodshot. She looked paler than a paper towel. Her skin was all drying out. If her mom were to see her in this state, she'd start making the flower arrangements for the funeral.

"Even Cristian said I look hideous when I told him about the doctor! I look like . . . like . . . like Frodo after Shelob stings him in the cave!"

"Shelob?" asked Madi.

"Frodo?" said Nadia.

"When the giant spider almost kills Frodo in the second *Lord of the Rings* movie? The book? Remember we read it in high school?"

"The Precious guy?"

"Are you guys illiterate?"

Nadia and Madi just laughed, which brought Stevie out of her moodiness, a little. She was just upset that by sacrificing for her friend, she'd only put herself in an awkward situation, and these two were making fun of her. Also, Cristian had agreed that she looked hideous! Ugh!

"I don't understand," Stevie said. "What is it? Do ER doctors really work so much they don't care who they hook up with?"

Madi rolled her eyes. "Listen. There's nothing wrong with wanting to hook up with a good-looking, smart, successful person."

Stevie kicked the blankets off as if she couldn't stand them. Now that her fever had come down, she felt hot, burning. It could also be the way her blood pressure had gone up when she saw Cristian's text. "I . . . he's cute, but I don't like him that way."

Under any other circumstances, she'd have gone feral about a Jacob doppelgänger.

All Roads Lead to Rome • 129

"I was talking about him wanting to hook up with you, the good-looking, smart, and successful woman," Madi said.

"You say that because you love me." Stevie sighed. "How can he know me? We only exchanged twenty words at most."

"We say that because we love you and it's the truth," Nadia replied.

"See?" Madi said. "Smart. You even know how to count."

Stevie threw her a pillow that Madi wasn't quick enough to dodge and hit her straight in the face.

A nurse came in just in time to avoid a pillow fight. "Ready to go home, young lady?" She was proper and efficient, and at the sound of her voice, Stevie sat up in bed, at attention.

"Readier than ever," she said with raring enthusiasm.

"Well, then," the nurse said. "You can go home, but you must promise to follow the discharge protocol; otherwise, Dr. Taylor will be so sad his favorite patient isn't improving."

She gave Stevie a side-eye and Nadia exclaimed, "We knew it! You noticed that he's flechado, too? See, Stevie?"

Stevie had no idea what flechado meant, but it must have had something to do with flecha, arrow. Among the three amigas, Nadia was the most bilingual and fluent in Spanglish, since her family spoke exclusively in Spanish at home. Stevie was only fluent in swear words, but she got the gist of what her friend was saying. She covered her face with her hands to hide her embarrassment.

"Tell me," Madi said, walking toward the nurse and taking her gloved hands. "Does he fall in love with everyone? Is he trustworthy? What can you share?"

The nurse laughed, throwing her head back. "I don't think he's ever been smitten by a patient before. He's a good kid. You should give him a chance."

Stevie rolled her eyes again, even though the back of her eyeballs still hurt because of the high fever. "If that's the price to walk out of this place, then I guess I have no other choice."

Stevie would've agreed to anything, just so she wouldn't

130 • *Yamile Saied Méndez*

have to stay in the hospital another night. She'd started having nightmares again. Besides, the longer she stayed here, the more chances that her mom would find out, and then there would be all kinds of drama for not having told her.

The nurse sent her away with a prescription longer than a CVS receipt and all kinds of recommendations that included lots of rest, breathing treatments, and good nutrition.

Madi had to go back to the yoga studio, so Nadia offered to take Stevie home. She lowered the visor to see herself in the mirror. Had Cristian been serious that she looked terrible, or had it been a joke?

"You always look like the goddess that you are, and you know it," Nadia said, navigating the freeway like a Formula One driver now that the snow had thawed out. Or it might have been her urgency to get to a gas station because the car was running on fumes.

"I think he's just desperate because Valentine's Day is a month away, and he must not have a date, poor devil. Imagine fishing for one in the ER!"

The friends laughed, and only stopped when Stevie started coughing like a lung was going to come out.

Nadia offered to go in and get the medicine, and Stevie stayed in the car. "I might just clone your card," Nadia said, joking as she waved Stevie's credit card. It was a fancy one that had no limit.

Stevie rolled her eyes. "Treat yourself to some chocolate, Nadia, but don't go too crazy. That money was earned with the sweat of my brow and the drips between my boobs in the hot Laredo summer."

They always joked like that. Nadia earned well, but she was starting out at her job, and she had to help her family. Madi was cruising on new-age vibes and the mercy of the universe. The only one of the trio who had any real money was Stevie. Not that she could retire anytime soon, but her summer job and the

All Roads Lead to Rome • 131

amazing residuals she got from it made it so her bank account had a comfortable cushion.

Nadia headed to the pharmacy, and Stevie stayed behind with her thoughts again. She couldn't deal with them, so she opened her phone like every time she needed to self-soothe. She only posted from a very well-curated collection of pictures in case Liam or Austin or any of the other losers who had broken her heart were keeping track of her. For a split second, she imagined what would happen if she posted a picture of her looking sad and sick. Would guys pop in trying to come to her rescue? Would her mom call her first for once? No matter how bad things got for her, Stevie would never show weakness like this.

She searched through her camera roll and saw a shot of Rome that looked like it was taken out of a fairy tale, like Cristian had said. Cristian had been holding her hand as she recorded the path ahead of them as they walked away from the Colosseum, and then he took the camera and filmed her.

Yes. She'd looked radiant in Rome; with a guy she didn't really know. She'd been free in the fact that he didn't know anything about her. That there would be no strings attached. That the way he looked at her was because of the now. She'd been happy, and the city shone behind her, and only Cristian's hand with the cheap ring from Amazon. No one else but her—and yes, him, but only if he saw it—would know what the ring meant. People would be curious. And maybe telling guys she was taken would shield her from all the idiots in the world.

Chapter 12

Stevie went ahead and posted the picture. After doing so, Nadia drove her home, and she went to sleep. Hours later, when the sun was just a glow over the horizon, she wasn't sure if it was the daytime or the night. She checked on her phone, which marked five, but it still didn't say much to her.

Finally, she realized it was the afternoon. She had a couple of new messages. Nadia, asking if she felt better. Stevie closed her eyes again to assess how she was feeling. She did feel better. She didn't have a fever, and she'd slept most of the day, which she might regret later, but they were doctor's orders, after all.

The other was from Edward.

"Hey, Madi gave me your number. I hope it's okay. This is out of character for me, but I was wondering if you wanted to go out for coffee once you feel better? I don't think you remembered me from high school, and every time I stopped by the room to catch up, you were sleeping. We were in different groups, and I'm a year older than you, but my sister played in

All Roads Lead to Rome • 133

your softball team. Remember Bella? Anyway, let me know if you're interested. Just as friends."

Stevie didn't remember ever meeting Edward, but she didn't have to strain her memory much to know who Bella Taylor was. As soon as he'd mentioned his sister, the face flashed in her mind. Dark hair, vivacious eyes, a killer arm. Bella had been the most talented player in her team.

After Stevie, of course.

Bella had gone on to become an all-American and even played in college and the Olympics. Stevie tried to imagine what her life would've been like had she not dated Liam and gotten pregnant. It was impossible not to be filled with regret.

She wasn't in the right mental state to reply back to Edward. She couldn't even think about anything until she ate. She was starving. She craved something hot and salty. Something delicious. Something from Cancún Querido, which unfortunately, didn't deliver.

Nadia had left her a few staples like bread and olives, but nothing sounded appetizing at the moment. She looked at her phone, hoping there was a way to order what she craved, when another notification popped up.

Cristian. Her heart jumped straight into her mouth. *I saw your post. Does this mean my fiancée is still alive?*

It was all a game, a gimmick. Still, she giggled. Alone in her apartment, she didn't have to hide or pretend that a message from him made her giddy. It was so good he lived hours away. Who knew what would happen if he lived any closer. She'd call him. He'd come over. They'd hook up and then she'd be completely in love and then brokenhearted when he broke up with her, because how many times had he told her he didn't want anything serious just yet? And neither did she, for crying aloud.

I'm alive, she wrote back.

Do you miss me? Is that why you posted that picture from Rome?

134 • *Yamile Saied Méndez*

You wish, she replied. She almost left it at that but knew he wouldn't believe her.

That was a strategic post, she typed. *It should keep me safe for Valentine's Day.*

There was a pause, and then he replied, *Are you trying to shield yourself from every guy until you turn seventy so you can finally marry me?*

She laughed again, but then worried that he might have a point. He was so annoying. She'd have to do something about dating, or she was going to end up with him and then would have to hear him boast about how he'd been her only true love to the end of their lives.

Didn't looking like death put the doctor off? he texted.

You don't have to keep saying that I looked hideous, okay? I get it. And for your information, the doctor knew me from high school, so he'd seen me, not at my peak, but close enough.

Picture or it didn't happen, he texted back.

Stevie searched through her gallery, but a picture from high school wasn't a part of her curated collection. She looked into her mom's Facebook account, and true enough, there was a picture from when they'd won state in sophomore year. She'd been so little and full of herself. That day, everything had seemed at her fingers' reach, and then she'd thrown it all away.

Her heart clutched for her younger self and everything that was coming her way. She sent it before she got tempted to go through all the other pictures her mom had on her Facebook. She'd stopped posting about Stevie right after that.

Well, I can comment because we're contemporaries, but let me tell you little Stevie was way cuter than the one whose picture you sent this morning.

What about you, Alvarez? she shot back. *I'm sure you weren't even that cute in high school to make you have such an ego at the threshold of your thirties.*

She could see the three dots dancing on the screen for a few minutes, and then the picture came in.

All Roads Lead to Rome • 135

"Damn!" she said aloud.

Cristian in high school had been stunning. If she'd met him at that age, she surely would've made the same mistakes she had with Liam. While sad to admit, it was the plain truth. A part of her told her young Stevie and this older, more jaded version weren't that different, after all.

Nice, was all she texted back. Anything else, and he'd have incriminating evidence that she had a bad crush on him, and she couldn't allow that.

She saw he was texting again, and she braced herself. But his message said, *Beyond all the teasing, how are you feeling? I was worried when I saw your picture. Appalled, but also worried.*

He was annoying, but beautiful nonetheless, and he knew how to lighten up a situation. *I'm alive,* she texted. *I have pneumonia. The antibiotics helped and I feel like a human again. A very hungry human, but since I can't cook or even drive, I'll just have cereal and maybe ice cream?*

Ice cream? he replied right away. *What's your favorite kind?*

Rum raisin, she said, adding a few laughing emojis, anticipating the most common reaction.

Interesting. I always think rum raisin is like a sambayón, he said. *Rosario is the cradle of the Argentine flag and fútbol, but most importantly, we're known for having the best ice cream in the world, and that's saying something, as I lived in Italy for so long. We have something called crema rusa, Russian cream, that's very similar to your rum raisin and incredibly delicious. It must be the liquor in it.*

Her mouth watered just thinking of ice cream. *That sounds incredible. Next time we're in Rome we'll have to go gelato tasting,* she said.

Or you can join me in Argentina, he countered.

She laughed to hide the uncomfortable tickle in her stomach.

I'm leaving next week, he texted. *Armando and Ross are happier than a dog with two tails.*

136 • *Yamile Saied Méndez*

That's so sweet, she typed. *Well, my stomach is trying to eat itself. Let me go scrounge for something in my kitchen.*

Buon appetito! And if you're going to ignore my invite to come to Argentina, maybe we can meet another time. Get well soon, unvalentine.

She wasn't going to get into those muddled waters. The promise of summertime in Argentina with him was a temptation she wasn't going to resist for long. It was best to take it out of her mind and not even acknowledge it being a possibility. She had her classes. He had his unfinished business to solve.

And maybe, maybe, a date with Dr. Taylor wouldn't be that bad. Her mom would be impressed she was talking to a doctor. It wasn't the same as becoming one, but it was better than talking to a retired athlete who was still trying to find himself. Besides, they had time. All the way until they were seventy.

Thanks, unvalentine, she replied, and then added, *Don't break too many hearts. I'm very jealous and territorial.*

Noted, he said.

Stevie looked into her fridge and the pantry, but there was nothing good to eat. It had started to snow again. She felt so much better than even just a couple of hours ago, but after considering it for a while, she decided she couldn't drive in her condition.

She was about to make do with a bowl of cereal when someone knocked on the door. A part of her imagined it was her mom. She was equal parts delighted and horrified. But maybe Nadia had told Ana María how sick Stevie was, and how lonely she'd felt. Even though Stevie had lived at her apartment for two years, Ana María had never visited her. Stevie thought that her mom would think it was beautiful.

She opened her door. Her hopes crashed to her feet. It wasn't her mom after all. It was a delivery guy, but he was leaving.

The guy heard the door opening, though, and turned around with a huge smile. "I'm glad you're home. I have something for you."

All Roads Lead to Rome • 137

"For me? Who sent it?"

"Someone who surely loves you a lot."

It had to be her friends. Who else could it have been?

The boy, who was really just a teenager, hoisted a big wicker basket higher on his arm and then passed it to her. It was heavier than it looked. "We don't usually do deliveries," he said, "especially not during an incoming blizzard, but the person who called promised me a tip I couldn't say no to." He smiled ruefully. "Oh! I almost forgot. He said to tell you 'Happy unvalentine and enjoy.'"

Stevie's heart jolted. Could it be? But how? In a daze, she went inside and looked into the wicker basket. There were several trays of food and a small paper bag. A scent rose as she rummaged in the basket to study its contents: lavender and lemon mixed with the spicy sweetness of her favorite restaurant in the whole world: Cancún Querido.

The paper bag contained an assortment of teas and essential oils from a brand she recognized very well, since it had been a household name in the valley for years: Luna Living Oils. Lavender, chamomile, and a lemony flu-buster combo. Her eyes prickled with sudden tears of gratitude. She lined up the bottles and the box of tea and grabbed the first tray of food. It was her favorite grilled chicken quesadillas. The other one contained the fixin's for burritos and tacos to last her a week, and one more had soup. She put the food next to the oils and the tea and snapped a picture.

She texted Cristian. *Was this you?*

She added the picture, and while she waited for an answer, she grabbed a plate and real utensils to eat. She hated to eat with disposables. When she returned to her phone, there was a reply.

You're sick and this is the least I can do for my virtual fiancée.

Stevie laughed. She'd never been a fiancée before, not even a fake one. She'd never even been anyone's official girlfriend.

She texted: *Thanks, but . . . How did you get my address? It's kind of creepy!*

138 • *Yamile Saied Méndez*

He replied right away with a cringing emoji. *I asked Brady. I know it's bad etiquette for me to ask, but since soon I'll be a continent away, he saw no issue. I hope you forgive me. I promise I'll never ever show up at your doorstep before receiving an invitation from you.*

Stevie had been promised the moon and more by guys of all backgrounds and ages. She had only believed Liam, and things had ended in the worst possible way. He'd killed her faith in the human race. But for some reason, she trusted Cristian.

Okay. But how did you know Cancún Querido is my favorite restaurant?

You mentioned it to me in Rome, remember? At María's restaurant?

She was speechless. Not only had he been listening, but he remembered.

Thanks. That's very kind of you.

You're welcome. That's what friends are for.

Later, her belly full of her favorite food, snuggled in bed watching *Gladiator* for the umpteenth time, she fell asleep with a smile on her face. Her mug of chamomile tea was on her nightstand, and the scent of lavender that she'd rubbed on her feet, as the booklet indicated, enveloped her.

For Stevie, food was the ultimate expression of love, and even if Cristian was a virtual fiancé, a Plan B she wouldn't ever have to deploy—her seventies were an eternity away—she relished the feeling and fell asleep.

Chapter 13

Pneumonia vanquished, Stevie had pressing matters to attend to.

Valentine's Day was days away, and although she thought the holiday was a commercial trap, she wanted to show Cristian that she had better prospects than waiting until she was seventy to celebrate it, even if it was with her friends.

If only her friends hadn't ditched her at the last second.

Against all their recommendations, Nadia had gone back to Brandon. This was his last chance, she promised her friends. Stevie had rolled her eyes, but kept her mouth shut.

Madi was dating a guy named Javier Rice. His initials matched the dreams about soulmates she'd had as a child, but Stevie doubted he was the one for her friend. Again, she kept her opinion to herself, because she knew from experience that the heart wants what it wants, no matter what reason says.

Meanwhile, Cristian was in Argentina. He'd posted a picture with a large group of friends, the majority of whom were women. Beautiful women. He'd sworn he wanted nothing seri-

140 • *Yamile Saied Méndez*

ous with anyone, but Stevie didn't want to get left behind, aka, be by herself.

On a whim—and yes, a fit of jealousy that she had no right to feel—Stevie accepted Edward's invitation to meet at a quaint coffee shop in Salt Lake. He'd arrived on time, looking way younger in street clothes than he had in a doctor's scrubs. Maybe he just looked more rested, because there was no trace of the shy guy she remembered.

"Hey," he said, and gave her a brief hug. She was hyper-conscious of the scent of his cologne. There, but not overwhelming. A point in his favor. "It's great to see you feel better."

"Thanks," she said, a little self-conscious when she thought back on how she'd looked that day in the ER. "It's great to see you . . . outside the hospital."

He chuckled. "It's great not to be there, to be honest."

Stevie was immediately curious. "What do you mean?"

Before he got the chance to answer, the waitress came by to take their order. He had a London fog, and she had an almond latte. It seemed like a non-issue, but in their super conservative Utah community, by ordering a caffeinated drink, they might as well have waved a flag that said, I'M NOT MORMON.

They both nodded at each other in acknowledgment. There was a brief pause, and then Stevie cleared her throat.

"Oh, right," he said. "A doctor who doesn't like the hospital. Why? I actually do like it, just not the long weekend shifts."

"Do you work every weekend?"

"Most," he said, and sighed. "I know. Not a great way to meet people, hence my excitement to see you that day. Not that I was happy that you were so sick, but . . . yeah. . . ." The way he blushed was so adorable.

"I work all summer long, the weekend of the year in a way," she said, taking a sip of her latte. "I understand."

"What do you do?"

Stevie thought back on the day she'd met Cristian, and the

All Roads Lead to Rome • 141

way he had made fun of Americans asking what the other person did for work as a way to form an idea of who they were.

"I'm a door-to-door sales manager," she said. "I manage a team of about twenty people, mostly guys. We go to an area, knock all summer. Come home in August."

"No weekends off?"

"Just Sundays . . . sometimes."

Edward swallowed. "That sounds intense. Is that what you plan on doing long-term?"

She shrugged. Not that he'd had a tone of prejudice, but he was a doctor. Certainly, he had an idea of what kind of people would choose sales, and she imagined it wasn't the best. In other circumstances, she'd quickly say that of course door knocking wasn't her long-term goal. She'd said that for years. But she felt defensive and protective. Who was he to judge? He had no idea what sacrifice the guys made. Some had college degrees and could only do their dream jobs—like teaching or writing music—because of the freedom selling gave them.

But she didn't know Edward enough to bare her heart to him like she had with Cristian.

"Yep. And you? Plan on being in the ER for the long-term?" She knew she sounded confrontational, and she didn't know why. But she wasn't going to pull back.

Edward blushed a darker shade. His brown hair had red undertones. "Maybe. I'd like to go into OB-GYN, to be honest."

Alarms went in her mind. "Why would you like to do that?"

Maybe her tone was too cutting for him, because Edward's eyes shot to hers. He bit his lip as if he were trying to decide if he could share something with her. Stevie held her breath. She wanted to know what drove a guy to want to look at women's hoo-has all day. Was it the money? Was it something worse? Would he tell her if so?

Edward ruffled his hair and said, "Actually . . . I helped de-

142 • *Yamile Saied Méndez*

liver my youngest brother. Nico." His eyes flittered to his hands. He was wringing them. "He was okay. He's okay," he said and chuckled, glancing at Stevie. "But my mom almost didn't make it. Nico was her eighth kid in fifteen years. She was a pro at it, but her placenta wouldn't detach." He was pale now. "There was so much blood! Luckily, the ambulance arrived, and she had surgery, and now she's okay."

Stevie placed a hand on his. "That's terrible. I'm sorry. How old were you?"

"Eighteen," he replied. "That happened during my senior year."

They exchanged a charged look.

"That's around the time I had my baby," she said.

He nodded. "I remember."

The silence that followed was too deep with memories.

Edward sighed. "The conversation took a sharp, dark turn, didn't it?" He laughed, but there was sadness in his voice. Stevie's heart twinged for him. He seemed like a nice guy.

"I think your plan's pretty amazing," she said. "I'm cheering for you."

He seemed surprised by the warmth in her voice. "Thanks. Now let's talk about more pleasant things—what do you like to do for fun when you're not raking in money from sales?"

She smiled. "How do you know?"

He shrugged. "Come on, we're in the Utah valley. I have buddies in sales who all rave about this girl that outsells them all. They're all terrified and starstruck by you."

"And you're not?"

"Terrified and starstruck? Of course!"

Their laughter finally broke the ice between them.

Still, Stevie felt no . . . attraction to him at all. She liked him, though. If she kept seeing him, she could be accused of stringing him along or friend-zoning him. But how was she going to get to know anyone if she didn't agree to go on a second date?

Maybe she shouldn't have, but he invited her to a Valentine's

All Roads Lead to Rome • 143

dinner, and she agreed. She wasn't desperate to marry anyone anytime soon, but she didn't want to be lonely anymore.

A second date turned into a third, and finally, the fourth time, they went out on Valentine's Day, and Edward kissed her. After the flowers and chocolate and the great dinner, she knew it was coming. She wanted him to do it. But she didn't know what the kiss would lead to, so she was nervous. She still didn't feel anything for him.

The whole time they were kissing, Stevie's mind flew to the last time she'd been kissed.

She had enthusiastically returned the favor.

Rome.

A tall, blond boy.

A real diamond ring—her first and only one so far.

A silly promise that that had been made, one she wanted to fast-forward almost forty years into the future.

Stevie decided she should text Cristian and ask him if he'd meant to give her this expensive ring, or if he wanted it back. Maybe he had more urgent things to do in Argentina, where he seemed to be having a blast.

Edward pulled back and smiled at her. Stevie smiled back, but she looked down in case he saw the truth in her, that there were no fireworks exploding inside of her, that she'd kissed him but had been thinking of another.

There was nothing wrong with him. It was all her. The one normal, decent guy she'd dated in forever, and she felt nothing. Edward was a gentleman, and when she didn't invite him to her apartment, he didn't act like he was offended or hurt.

"See you in a few days, Stevie," he said when she got out of his car. "Have fun in Texas."

She rolled her eyes and chuckled. "Thanks. Have fun in the ER."

Edward's smile was blinding. Its brightness was seared in her eyes as he drove away.

* * *

144 • *Yamile Saied Méndez*

Spring was rolling around, but Stevie was in full summer mode. To make up for her days being sick, she went back to work, visiting sales offices all over the Southwest. Brady joined her in Texas. As she had expected, their relationship had a coldness that made things extra awkward.

"I think you're mad at me," he said, his eyes on the back of the room where Céline was waiting.

They had just trained a group of about two hundred prospective salespeople in El Paso, Texas. Brady had been so awkward the whole time, not even looking in her direction, that Stevie had to work extra hard to turn on the spark for those who came to see if this was a possible career for them. For her, the job of pitching started here, in the lobby of a cheap hotel as she tried to motivate people to give this job a chance. Those who believed her, who believed in themselves, went on to do great, but those were only a small percentage. Brady had acted like a diva the whole time. He was so full of himself that she'd be surprised if a tenth of a percent of the attendees came back for the season.

"I'm not mad at you, Brady," she said. "I . . . don't understand what you're doing, to be honest." She bit her lip. She'd started spending so much time with Edward that she was talking like him now.

"If you're mad at me because I gave Cristian your address, just say so."

She inhaled to tell him that his giving Cristian her address was the last on the list of things she was upset at him for.

"I didn't care about that."

Céline was watching them, sending electric vibes with her eyes. Stevie's head started hurting, which pissed her off, because she had to do homework for her restaurant management class, and if the headache turned into a migraine, she would never get to it.

"I hope he doesn't do anything stupid," Brady continued, clueless as always. "I think he has a crush on you." He snorted as if this was the funniest, most bizarre thing he'd ever heard of.

All Roads Lead to Rome • 145

"Too bad for him," she said, shrugging.

Brady pulled back to look at her like he didn't believe her. "What? You mean you don't like him back?"

"I'm dating someone," she shot back, a wave of relief and gratitude going over her that this wasn't a lie.

Brady thought she was lying. "What? Who? When?"

She sighed. "So many questions. He's a doctor, for your information."

Brady's face darkened. "Really? Hmm."

"What's that supposed to mean?" she asked, crossing her arms.

"Everything okay?" asked Céline, walking in their direction. She stared at Stevie like she wanted to drag her for misbehaving.

"Everything okay, mon amour," Brady said in the worst French accent Stevie had ever heard.

Céline put a protective arm around his waist. She looked at Stevie, demanding a reply.

"I was just telling him I'm dating a doctor."

Céline, too, did a double take, but unlike Brady, she didn't ask any follow-up questions. She just said, "Is that so?"

They walked away without even saying goodbye. Brady looked over his shoulder and mouthed, "I'm sorry," at Stevie.

She wasn't sure if he meant that he was sorry for his or Céline's behavior, which hadn't really bothered Stevie before, but now it was getting old. Céline had married the guy, who, by the way, Stevie had never been interested in. What else did she want? Who was she to imply Stevie couldn't be dating a doctor?

Brady hadn't mentioned anything about accepting a position with corporate. If he didn't do so soon, Stevie would bring up the topic herself to make his decision easier. She had no intention of putting up with a jealous wife all summer or ever.

Maybe it was time Stevie managed an all-girls team for the summer. Not that there wouldn't be romantic entanglement if it was an office of just girls, but it would eliminate the feeling of being looked at with suspicion by the wives and girlfriends

146 • *Yamile Saied Méndez*

when all she wanted was for the guys to produce the best, so she could one day break free of this soul-sucking job and finally live her dream of being a cook.

On her way to her rental apartment, she got a notification. Her mom was calling her. Ana María *never* called her. The last time had been when Stevie's dad had died. Her parents had been hiking Mount Timpanogos. They'd been doing that at least once a week that summer. Stevie knew that on that day, they had been arguing. She suspected it had been because of her, because the night before, Stevie had come home way past her curfew. Her mom had been waiting for her in a chair in the kitchen, alone in the dark. How dramatic. They'd argued in loud whispers so as not to wake her dad. But her mom must have told him anyway. And who knew what she had said, because he died of a heart attack that night.

Both mother and daughter suspected they were the reason Federico had died. Neither would ever bring up the topic. They had avoided talking on the phone ever since. Maybe something had happened to Abuela Yolanda or Max. What if her mom needed her, and she was alone in her house? Not that Stevie could teleport back to Utah, but she'd take a page out of Cristian's playbook and figure something out.

Right before the call went to voicemail, she answered. "Hello?"

"Oh, hello," Ana María said in a breathy voice. "I thought you were going to let this go to voicemail."

Why did she always do this? Why did she put up a wall between them every single interaction they had? Why was Stevie always in a bad mood whenever she and her mom talked? Stevie didn't know what she was supposed to say to this.

"Are you there?" Ana María asked.

Stevie took a deep, calming breath. Her blood had already reached a boiling point, and they'd only exchanged a couple of words. "I'm here, Mami. Everything okay?"

All Roads Lead to Rome • 147

Ana María scoffed. "Of course, Stephanie. Why wouldn't it be?"

This time Stevie couldn't hold her words back. "Hmmm. I don't know. Maybe because we haven't seen each other or talked since Christmas? It's March, Mom."

Now it was Ana María who paused. Was she trying to compose herself? Was she trying to find the right words to cause the most exquisite kind of pain? What was she trying to do?

Then Stevie heard a sniffle, and a man's voice in the background say, "Don't cry, my love. Just hang up. You don't have to put up with this abuse."

Stevie almost hung up, but she was paralyzed. Her mom never cried. She hadn't cried when Stevie's dad died. When Tristan died. Not even when Max had graduated with all the honors a person could receive and thanked her during his valedictorian speech that had gone viral.

"What is it? Are you okay?"

Ana María sniffled and finally said, "Yes. I am okay . . . I just wanted to tell you that Frank and I are engaged."

Stevie had to pull over. She was shaking so hard, and her vision went all black. She wasn't ready for this. She was both sad that her dad had been replaced by someone who was nothing like him, and relieved that her mom wasn't alone anymore. But she couldn't feel happy. She wasn't going to lie.

"Congratulations," she said.

"You could sound like you're happy for me, you know?" Ana María answered back.

Stevie bit her tongue until she tasted blood. "Congratulations," she repeated, in a cheery voice that sounded like it belonged to another person. "When's the big day?"

"It's in the middle of August. I know you're most likely not going to be there since it's the peak sales season for you, but the date works for the rest of the family."

Stevie felt like she was becoming smaller and smaller by the

148 • *Yamile Saied Méndez*

minute. "Maybe I can make it," she said, stubbornly. "Thanks for the heads-up."

Maybe there had been other dates that could've worked, but no one had asked her, had they? Well, she just knew her mom didn't want her there to ruin her day, but she'd show up just the same, even if it was peak season, just to spite everyone.

"Okay, I won't get my hopes up. I know you're married to your job," Ana María said.

Stevie saw her chance and shot back. "I actually have a boyfriend. He's a doctor."

She could practically see Ana María's jaw drop. She heard someone scoff. It must have been Frank.

"He works at the ER in the new hospital in Salt Lake. Remember Bella Taylor?"

"From the softball team?" her mom asked, a little breathless.

"Yep. Her brother," Stevie said.

"I wonder how long that will last," Frank whispered, but the sound carried all the same. "How is that going to work?"

There was a sound like her mom had covered her phone and was telling him off. Ana María should've pressed the mute button if she didn't want Stevie to hear this argument. Stevie didn't feel proud of the satisfaction that rose inside her that things weren't as perfect in paradise as her mom made it seem.

"Are you there?" she asked.

Ana María cleared her throat and said, "Yes, congratulations, Stevie. You're welcome to invite him to the wedding, of course. Everyone will be thrilled to meet him. I'm sure." There was another long pause, and then her mom added, "Well, I wanted to let you know. Bye."

Later, Stevie didn't even remember if she'd said bye back or if she'd just stayed silent. The news had devastated her.

Chapter 14

Brady didn't get the position with corporate. All summer long, Stevie tried to keep the peace with her long-distance boyfriend, her unsupportive family, and Brady's jealous wife. Every spare second she had, she followed her mom's social media account to catch at least a glimpse of the preparations for the wedding. In every post, without fail, Frank's daughter, the one with the baby, proudly stood in the place that by all means should've been hers. At least Max was front and center everywhere, of course, he and his wife Erin.

Stevie liked and commented on everything, while inside, jealousy ate her up. She wondered if she should've introduced Edward to the family so he could at least represent her for some things, but back in April, their relationship was too new, and now, in August, it wasn't that much more stable. He was close to his family, and he couldn't understand why Stevie didn't drop everything and run to her mom's side, or his, for that matter.

"Why don't *you* drop everything to come visit me, Edward?" she asked on their weekly video call. "That's what most part-

150 • *Yamile Saied Méndez*

ners and wives actually do. Those who can't stay here long-term come visit every once in a while."

"You work all week," he said, sighing. "It will be a waste of my days off."

"Working during the week is the normal time to work. Besides, we could hang out at night," Stevie retorted.

Although their first kiss had been underwhelming, the few nights they'd shared together hadn't been bad—not at all. Wasn't the promise of more enough for him?

"It's not the same, Stephanie. Those other partners are wives and girlfriends. They're supposed to support their boyfriends or husbands who are working hard for their family."

She was glad they were miles away and she couldn't climb through the screen to have this conversation face-to-face. He'd never hinted that their mismatched schedules or her job were an obstacle, until now.

"I'm working hard, too," she said. "And if we're going to get nitpicky about money, I'll remind you that I make more than you do."

Edward clenched his teeth and took a deep breath. "Really? Are we going to measure in money? I save lives, Stevie. And you? You sell security systems."

He might as well have spat in her face. Edward had no idea what her job entailed. In one of the groups she managed, she had people ages eighteen to forty-plus. Some were right out of high school, and others had professional careers. They saw her as their leader, and even though she was single, they came to her for advice on everything; from financial decisions to couple and parenting problems. They loved and respected her. They were there for her when she needed them. Edward wouldn't even know what to do if one of his teammates was kidnapped and driven to Mexico in a case of wrong identity, as she had to sort through with one of her guys only a couple of weeks ago.

She was too tired and busy to even try to explain it to him,

All Roads Lead to Rome • 151

though. Still, he must have realized he'd crossed a line and said things that would leave permanent scars.

"Stevie, I'm sorry. I didn't mean it like that."

"Whatever," she said, "I have to go. Bye."

She closed her laptop before he could explain exactly how he'd meant it.

Stevie was heading to the gym when she got a text from Cristian.

Hola, Estefanía, I'll be in Utah next week. Wanna meet up? I know it's your mom's wedding. Do you need moral support? Unless you're ready to introduce the boyfriend to the family? I promise I'll just be there as a friend and won't even mention you're already engaged to me.

She couldn't help smiling. Cristian seemed to have a radar that knew exactly when she was feeling the lowest of the low. Without fail, every time she talked to him, she immediately felt a thousand times better.

Stevie looked at her calendar and studied it as if she could make extra days appear out of thin air. Her mom's wedding was on Saturday, which was the semifinal of the cup, the annual companywide tournament. Her team was the favorite to win it all. But if she left Friday night on the red eye, she could make the ceremony and surprise her mom. If the team hustled hard, the missed sales from her wouldn't hinder them too much.

What kind of person wouldn't attend her own mom's wedding? On a whim, she booked the flight. She texted Max, Madi, Nadia, and Cristian. The message for him was a little more detailed.

Stevie: *Hello, Cristiano, How come you'll be in Utah? How was Argentina? I'll pop in for my mom's wedding and head back to El Paso. But I'd love to see you. Want to be my plus one for the wedding?*

Cristian: *And the boyfriend?*

Stevie: *Boyfriend? I don't know him.*

152 • *Yamile Saied Méndez*

She wasn't even joking. She didn't really know Edward. Just because he was a doctor and he'd been nice at the beginning didn't mean he was a decent guy or good enough to be her person. Everyone had bad days, but what he'd said about her job must have been simmering for who knew how long?

Cristian texted back: *Tell me the place and time and I'll be there* 😉

Brady wasn't thrilled at the news that she'd be missing such a crucial Saturday, but he had no right to complain. How many times had she covered for him when he was late at trainings because—in his words—Céline wouldn't let him get out of bed?

His moody silences didn't affect her. Stevie imagined the surprise and joy on her mom's face when she saw her. It would eclipse the surprise and joy on Brady's face when he'd seen her in Rome. With this vision and the promise of seeing Cristian as incentives, Stevie worked harder than ever so the day she'd be gone wouldn't hurt her team's chances of winning the cup. Besides the glory of becoming the best team, each person would receive a substantial bonus and a trip to Tahiti, all expenses paid.

When the day of the trip arrived, a hurricane somewhere in Florida grounded airplanes and ruined plans all over the nation. Most importantly, ruined Stevie's plans. Like always, the fates were against her. Defeated, disappointed in herself, she went back to her apartment. But instead of sitting and wallowing in self-pity, she went out to try and rescue a couple of sales.

On the day her mom got married and started a new chapter in her life, Stevie broke her sales record. Since there was nothing she could do to change the image her mom's new family had of her, she tried to overcompensate with her friends. She sent presents to Madi and Nadia: cowgirl boots and sombreros. She even sent a package to Cristian to apologize for not making it to the wedding when he'd been ready to escort her. He would've looked so handsome in his rented tux. What a waste of good looks!

All Roads Lead to Rome • 153

The next week, he was heading to Lake Powell with his grandma and a group of friends. From there, he was leaving straight to Vegas and then back to Argentina. Stevie would miss him by a couple of weeks. One night, during their endless text threads, he mentioned that Ross loved Texas barbecue. Stevie sent her a box of every barbecue sauce she could find, and Ross invited her to join them in Powell the following year.

Her team won the cup, and Stevie invested her bonus in a high-interest-earning account and gave her spot to the trip in Tahiti to one of the guys, Fernando, so his wife could travel with him. Before she knew it, the holidays came around. In spite of her mom's words that she was welcome to visit, Stevie didn't feel like she could show her face. She didn't have the strength to show up at her mom's and ruin their perfect holidays. And she couldn't intrude in Madi's and Nadia's families anymore. She didn't like feeling like an orphan, but that's what she was.

Through social media, she found out that Frank's daughter, Tiffany, was pregnant again. Ana María was in Heaven, judging by the many pictures she posted online. Stevie tried to overcompensate by posting pictures of her skiing and ice climbing with her friends. She knew her mom saw her posts, but never commented, never even gifted her a thumbs-up. It was like she didn't exist anymore.

On a whim, she texted Edward, just to see how he was doing. It took him three days to reply.

Hi, Stevie, sorry for ghosting you. That last conversation wasn't my best moment. I'm sorry. I'm seeing someone else at the moment. I wish you the best in everything. I really do.

Stevie knew she deserved this reply. She had ghosted him, too, and although they hadn't officially broken up, she hadn't planned on attending the wedding with him. She'd actually intended to go with Cristian, hoping that his good looks impressed her mother's family more than Edward's degree.

She had opened a breach with everyone that now felt unsalvageable. Sometimes she felt like she didn't belong in the world

154 • *Yamile Saied Méndez*

anymore. These intrusive thoughts scared her so much, she was ashamed of them. She didn't dare tell anyone, not Madi and Nadia. Certainly not Brady, who was on an anniversary trip in Paris. Not even Cristian.

Right on cue, when she was spiraling fast, sometime in December, Cristian texted:

Hi, Stevie, I'm heading to Egypt with a group of friends. One of the girls had appendicitis and she won't recover in time to make it. Her spot's open. Wanna come?

She immediately texted: *I'm in.*

She booked the flight to Cairo right then, without even asking who else was going or what they were doing. All she cared was that she'd be gone over Christmas and New Year's. She'd be back in time for the draw, when the teams chose their areas and started recruiting for the summer.

It wasn't until she landed in Cairo, trying to make sense of the cacophony of voices and announcements on the intercom, that she wondered if she had lost her mind. She'd never imagined that so many people would spend their vacations in Egypt, but a lady from Mexico, who was waiting for her luggage next to Stevie, told her that because of the heat, winter was the high season. Stevie had been sweating bullets, and she couldn't imagine how hot this place would be in the summertime.

Now that she was surrounded by people, she felt alive again. Her brain was alert, trying to make sense of a new place. A place she'd only ever seen in history books and fun movies. Ever since Cristian had texted her the invitation and she'd accepted it, she'd been reading up on this country. She was fascinated by the history and the weight of time. This was one of the cradles of civilization.

Stevie had never cared about history, but the hunger to learn all she could about this place gnawed at her insides. She was worried her group hadn't made it when she heard a familiar voice next to her.

"It's good to see you, Stevie."

She whirled around, and there he was. He looked more hand-some than she remembered. There was a softness to his face. The light in his eyes when he looked at her was so genuine that it grounded her to the world of the living—for now.

He went in to kiss her cheek, but she hugged him.

"I keep forgetting you're so American!" he said, hugging her tightly.

It was the first time she'd hugged another person in months, and the hunger to be connected to another human had over-whelmed her.

Chapter 15

A part of Stevie had hoped that in person, Cristian's charm would grow dim. She hoped that the tickles she felt in her stomach when they texted until the wee hours of the night or seeing that he'd sent her a fun meme would die as soon as she realized that her loneliness and overactive imagination had built up a persona of him that didn't exist in real life.

True, he looked sleepy and disheveled after the long flight from Argentina. Heaven knew, she did, too. But the way his blue eyes shone like stars seeing her wasn't her imagination playing tricks on her. The way he kept an arm around her waist wasn't just her wishful thinking, either.

"I'm so glad you made it," he said, tightening his hold. "I half feared that you wouldn't show up."

"Why not?" she asked, playfully slapping his shoulder.

He shrugged. "Because we only really met in person once and, I don't know, most people wouldn't just join a group of strangers."

"I'm not most people," she said, grinning.

All Roads Lead to Rome • 157

"I know," he replied, and the rumble of his voice grounded her. Then he turned around and waved over a group of mismatched people who somehow looked like they were all in the same group. "I'm excited for you to meet my friends. They're all amazing. You're going to love them."

When the group of two girls and three guys joined them, Stevie tried to squish down the jealousy she felt at seeing the girls. They were beautiful, like real-life brunette Barbie dolls. Silky long hair, legs for days, and the kind of confidence that glows like an aura.

Because she was intimidated by them, she took a step forward, put out her hand for them to shake, and said in English—although she didn't know if they spoke it—"I'm Stevie Choi. Nice to meet you."

The first girl's eyes lit up. "What? Finally!" She hugged Stevie before she could brace herself. "I'm Connie! I've heard so many great things about you!"

Stevie shot Cristian a look and said, "What kind of things?"

"The best," he said.

The other girl—her eyes were hazel, and she had a septum piercing—said, "I'm Aldana." Then she looked at Cristian and said, "So she's real. I thought you were talking about an imaginary girl the whole time."

Cristian narrowed his eyes and pouted at Aldana. "Of course she's real."

The guys introduced themselves to Stevie with the same kind of disbelief on their faces as had painted the girls'. The tall one was Franco. The one who looked just like him but shorter was Santiago. They were obviously related. Both had hair so dark it was black, but Santiago had pale blue eyes, and Franco's were dark brown. Santiago also had tattoos covering both arms. The other one was Lucho. He had long, reddish hair, and a serious demeanor that intimidated Stevie as much as the girls' confidence. Lucho eyed her curiously, but other than hello, didn't say another word to her.

158 • *Yamile Saied Méndez*

"Is this the whole group?" Stevie asked, her face aching from smiling so long.

"Yes," said Lucho, for once showing any emotion. He looked truly disappointed. "Too bad Vero couldn't make it."

Stevie remembered that she was filling the spot of one of their friends who'd been too sick to travel and remembered her manners. "I'm sorry about your friend, Veronica? I hope she's doing better."

"Oh, she's recovering well," Lucho replied.

"At least it happened at home and not when we were traveling."

"Or on the balloon."

"Or the cruise!"

The girls spoke right above the other, and Stevie wasn't sure who said what, but her mind got snagged at *balloon* and *cruise*, and she felt alarms go up in her mind. She should've asked Cristian what the itinerary was. But there would be time for that later.

"Everyone got their suitcases?" Cristian asked.

When everyone nodded, including Stevie, he said, "Time to go through customs, then. Let me find our guide, Ahmed."

From what Stevie had read, Ahmed was the most popular man's name in Egypt, but with uncanny skill, Cristian found their guide without a problem. With his help, they went through customs and headed to their hotel.

So many times during the ride, Stevie wanted to tell them to stop the car so she could catch the first flight home. But then she saw the city and fell in love with it. She couldn't open her eyes wide enough to take everything in. She was fascinated. Traffic was busier than she'd ever seen it in the US or in the European cities she'd been to just to catch the perfect photo for social media before she headed back to the hotel. Under every bridge was a small city of people selling and buying wares, men carrying enormous baskets of flat bread on top of their heads, and dogs.

All Roads Lead to Rome • 159

Dogs of every size and color everywhere, weaving in and out of people and cars.

She realized that everyone around her was quiet, and when she looked inside the van, she saw that everyone was asleep while Cristian and the guide, who was also their chauffeur, chatted animatedly in Arabic.

Cristian must have felt her eyes on him, because his words stopped in mid-sentence, or so she thought. He turned around, and seeing the look of admiration in her eyes, beamed at her. "Do you need a drink?"

She blinked rapidly and said, "No. But wait, do you speak Arabic?"

Cristian blushed like he was embarrassed, and he started stammering in Spanglish when the chauffeur said in a booming voice, "Yes! He speaks in Arabic. Now, he has a strong American accent, but he's decent."

"American accent?" asked Cristian and Stevie in unison. He sounded affronted. She sounded amused.

Ahmed waved a hand at Cristian and said, "Don't be offended. You have a tiny American accent. But you're doing well. You'll get better. Don't get shy."

Stevie scooched to the edge of her seat. She could have placed her chin on Cristian's shoulder, and she almost did, but at the last second, she placed her hand on his shoulder anyway. He was sweaty under his shirt. "So, Mr. Talented," she said, "how many languages do you speak?"

His blush went up his neck all the way to his ears, as if knowing more than one language was something to be ashamed of. It was adorable. They locked eyes in the mirror, and he counted with his fingers. "Let's see. Spanish, Italian, English, Arabic, Portuguese, and some French and German?"

Ahmed said something in French, and Cristian chuckled and said something back. Stevie had no idea what they were saying. She only knew that if he'd sounded sexy in Italian, she

160 • *Yamile Saied Méndez*

had no definition for him in French. Good thing they arrived at their hotel. It was right in downtown Cairo, and the street was bustling with life. Everyone in the cab woke up, and they too looked surprised at how fancy the hotel was.

"I don't think it's the gift with languages that opens doors for you, but that face. You're a freaking genius," Lucho said, ruffling Cristian's hair, as he got off the van.

"Coming from an actual physicist, that says a lot," Connie said to Stevie.

A physicist. Surely, Lucho fit the stereotypical image Stevie had of scientists, but she also had an inkling that besides IQs, he and she coincided in a lot of things—mainly, their opinion of Cristian. He had no clue of the power his smile had on people. He had charisma, what the Spanish called duende. She'd had a glimpse if it in Rome, of course, but now it was blazing for the world to see.

Cristian and his friends moved and acted with the same ease she felt with Nadia and Madi. When it had been just the two of them, she suspected they both put on an act for each other that wouldn't hold around friends. And she was right. Seeing Cristian with these people who had known him for years showcased things about him that she had never suspected.

Suddenly, Stevie wanted not only to impress him, but them, too. She wanted them to like her. At the same time, she didn't know how to fit in with their group. While the guys took care of the luggage and the girls distributed water and hand sanitizer, Cristian navigated the check-in process. Since he apparently had reserved everything with credit card points, they were getting amazing discounts.

Stevie had been nervous about the accommodations, but not because she was picky. Plenty of times, she'd slept in the back of a van full of stinky guys, or on the floor of the cheapest motels she could find for her team. One time, she'd gotten into bed, and had started itching uncontrollably. After Brady confirmed the bedbug infestation, she'd abandoned her luggage in that town.

All Roads Lead to Rome • 161

No. She wasn't picky, but she'd been nervous about sharing a room with these people she didn't know.

She didn't know their backstory yet, but they all behaved among each other as if they'd known each other forever. There were a couple of times when they talked, and it seemed they had long-standing inner jokes between them. Once again, she felt like an outsider, like she always did. Like an impostor. These were people her age, but she felt much older than them—more jaded.

When Cristian called them to distribute their room keys, her fears vanished.

"Aldana and Connie, here are your keys." He looked at Stevie and explained, "They're sharing, of course. But you, Estefanía, get your own."

"Awesome," she said, taking her key from his hand. "Because I snore like a bear." She did a little curtsy, and they all exploded in laughter. Even Lucho cracked a smile.

"Well, then," Cristian said, "it all worked out after all! Here. These keys are for Santiago and Franco, who get the extra-large pharaoh-sized bed."

The way he said it made everyone laugh. Everyone but Stevie, who had to rearrange the mental connections she'd made about the group.

"You mean . . . you're together?" She asked this as nonchalantly as she could, but it was hard not to laugh when everyone around her was cracking up.

"They're cousins, which I know makes it sound even worse," Cristian said for her benefit. "Don't mind us. We're still ten in our minds."

"Okay," she said, still confused as to what their relationship was. Not that she cared, but she wanted to be sensitive of everyone and not assume.

"And this last one is for Lucho."

Everyone was on the same floor.

"Do you guys want to freshen up and meet up to go eat some-

162 • *Yamile Saied Méndez*

thing?" asked Cristian. "Tonight is a little more spontaneous, because I wasn't sure how long the check-in process would take. I wasn't counting on arriving at the hotel for a couple more hours."

Stevie was relieved to get a little time on her own to regroup. She was hungry, but still hadn't figured out the dynamics of the group and didn't want to muddle any waters by being in the wrong place at the wrong time.

"Let's meet here in an hour," Cristian said.

Stevie nodded. His eyes always turned crystalline and shiny when he looked at her.

Her room was luxurious. There was a welcome basket addressed to her, and a warm feeling of welcome that came over her surprised her. Cristian had thought about every detail.

She showered, put on a loose white dress, and at the last second, she remembered to grab a scarf. She wasn't sure how strict this country was with modesty rules, but she knew from experience that nights in the desert were always chilly. She didn't think it would be that much different in Cairo than in southern Utah.

When she and Cristian walked out of their rooms at the same time, she was surprised. They seemed to be synchronized.

"You look nice," he said, keeping his eyes on her face but making an overall motion with his hand.

She, on the other hand, took the chance to look him over. He was wearing a pair of jeans and a black T-shirt without any logos. In Rome, under layers of clothes, she hadn't appreciated how sinewy his arms were. On his right hand shone the cheap ring she'd given him, and a sense of reassurance grounded her.

"I figured I'd wear black during the night, since the sun is supposed to be pretty unforgiving in the daytime," Cristian clarified.

"You look very nice, too," she said, a little too late. She took a deep breath to steady herself, but it was a mistake, because he smelled even nicer, and the scent of his cologne was intoxicating.

All Roads Lead to Rome • 163

"Thanks," Cristian said while looking at his watch, perhaps to try to distract himself from the fact he was blushing again.

Stevie realized she liked doing that, making him blush. "Are the others downstairs already?" she asked.

He winced and shrugged. "As far as I know, Connie passed out as soon as she came out of the shower while she waited for Aldana to be ready. Aldana and Santiago are actually together, so I doubt they'll be joining us. They haven't seen each other for months, so . . . you know how it is?"

Her cheeks felt like they had caught on fire. She'd wanted to tease Cristian and tell him, no, she didn't know how it was, but she'd be lying, and they both knew it. They, too, hadn't seen each other in months, and although this was technically the second time they were together in person, this time she knew more about him.

Cristian seemed to be going through his personal internal fight, and once he swallowed, he continued, "Lucho is catching up on work he should've finished before the trip, and Franco said he'll get room service." He looked at her for a second. "It seems it's just the two of us, unless you changed your mind and want to get room service, too. I mean, you in your room, and me in mine." The more he spoke, the more flustered he looked, and the stronger his accent in English became.

She cocked her hip to the side and crossed her arms, tapping the tip of her foot on the carpet.

"Woman, you know what I mean. Don't look at me that way!"

Stevie laughed, and Cristian looked ecstatic, like he loved doing that, making her laugh.

"Why are you nervous?" she asked, standing next to him and gently elbowing him.

He shrugged. "I was afraid you'd think I had set everything up to get you all alone."

All of a sudden, the air between and around them felt charged, although his voice had sounded like a whisper.

164 • *Yamile Saied Méndez*

"Listen, you don't have to make up any tricks to get me alone. Your friends look amazing, but, I'll tell you a little secret." She said this last phrase in a fake whisper.

Cristian leaned closer to her, and she whispered for real this time, "Your friends terrify me."

He laughed and clapped his hands. "Really? They're all so, so, scared of you!"

"Me? Why? I'm just a wisp of a thing!"

"Your fame precedes you. Besides, what do they say about small bottles?"

She nodded slowly. She knew this saying, because her dad quoted it all the time. "The best perfumes come in small bottles." She made a dramatic pause and added, "But also the most potent and lethal poisons. Or is it venoms? I never remember the difference between the two."

"There's a difference? In Spanish, they're both veneno." His laughter echoed in the hallway. "Is the saying really true, though? Someone should test it!"

"Someone should. But not us. Now I'm hungry, Alvarez! I'm sure room service is delicious, but if I stay in the room, I'll get tired soon. If I go to sleep now, I'll wake up at three in the morning, and tomorrow I'll be a zombie for the pyramids." Then she added, "The pyramids are tomorrow, right?"

"Right," he replied, and then did a double take to look at her. "Wait . . . you actually went over the itinerary that I spent months crafting?"

She pursed her lips and shrugged. "Since I only heard of this trip three days ago, I don't know how much the months of planning were for me."

He pouted. "I promise they were. Even though you weren't part of the group until now, I was hoping the whole time that you were."

"Really?"

"Really."

She looked toward the elevator that had arrived at their floor.

All Roads Lead to Rome • 165

"So, let's go get food. Shall we? You can fill me in about everyone while we eat. I can't think when I'm jet-lagged and hungry."

He laughed and offered her his arm. "Your wish is my command, Empress Estefanía the First. Let's get going."

Arm in arm, they walked into the elevator. It jolted up, but then it smoothly went down, and Stevie breathed in relief. Getting stuck in an elevator in Egypt was the last thing she needed. Especially when she was so aware of Cristian's every breath next to her and how his hands kept fidgeting, like he was nervous, too.

Chapter 16

Before leaving, Ahmed had assured them that the hotel area was safe to walk around late in the night. The concierge confirmed his words. However, as they browsed along a night bazaar, Stevie felt unsettled. Maybe it was because she felt a such a strong magnetic pull to Cristian, even though the whole way to Cairo, she'd told herself not to do anything to ruin this friendship.

If she hadn't dived into a relationship with Edward when she felt nothing for him, not even a crumb of attraction, maybe they might have been able to remain friends. Now it would've been awkward to even be in the same room with him. They had, after all, slept together.

Stevie couldn't even imagine the misery and awkwardness she'd feel if she made the same mistake with Cristian—for whom she felt a host of things. No matter what, she didn't want to lose him like she'd lost Brady or Edward.

He seemed to sense that her mind wasn't on the Cairo late-night bazaar. "We can still head back to the hotel. There's a

All Roads Lead to Rome • 167

rooftop restaurant, and we can see the city from up there," he offered.

She shrugged and smiled. "No, I want to go to this place. Don't worry. My mind is all over the place, but I like walking."

If she heard how her voice wavered, then Cristian must have, too. They walked side by side in the bustling street, and he looked like he was trying extra hard not to even brush her side. When they were about to cross the street, following the initiative of the locals who weren't waiting for the green light, Cristian had been about to place his hand on the small of Stevie's back. She'd broken into goose bumps when she shivered, anticipating his touch. But he'd stopped himself just before he touched her.

In Rome, they held hands every time they crossed the street. Now her stomach twisted in knots of disappointment, but it was for the best. Once on the other side of the sidewalk, they passed a group of men sitting outside a pipe shop. No one glared or gawked at Stevie like in other places. In Italy, for example, she'd been catcalled nonstop. Sometimes in Mexico, she'd felt eyes glued on her, even if she wasn't dressed provocatively. But here, she didn't feel the stabbing laser-like glances from men trying to undress her or at least guess what she looked like under the fabric of her dress. She wondered if here, people didn't find her attractive, because everyone stared at Cristian.

How could they not? Blond and tall, he looked like a Roman god straight out of a mythology book or down from Mt. Olympus to walk with mortals. Finally, unable to resist anymore, she clung to his arm, which he bent into a perfect crook for her to place her hands, as if they'd practiced this all their lives. She felt the blond thin hairs on his arm bristle, and she pulled herself closer to him. He glanced down at her with a questioning look in his eyes.

She looked away but said, "I'm okay. I just didn't want to get separated when we walked through that group."

He chuckled. "I know. I was worried about the same thing. My question was more along the lines of, are you okay if we hold arms or something? I've been dying to hold your hand

168 • *Yamile Saied Méndez*

since we walked out of the hotel for fear of losing you, but I didn't want to break the rules."

Her heart warmed. "You're okay gently holding my hand to cross the streets or if you're afraid of losing me. Just careful where you grab me at, because you're way taller than me."

They laughed and continued walking.

"Here we are," she said when they arrived at the restaurant the concierge had suggested.

"Wow. I'm glad someone has a better sense of direction than me, or at this point, we'd be more lost than I don't know what."

She beamed at him and curtsied. "I don't have a lot of virtues, but my sense of direction is legendary. I never get lost."

"You mean you've never been here before?"

"No, I told you it's my first time in Egypt!"

"Then how?"

She shrugged. "I just paid attention to what the concierge said, glanced at the map, and that's it."

The way he looked at her—the admiration. She'd never been looked at that way before. It made her tingle from head to toe. She'd have to uphold her rules more strictly if she wasn't going to get them in trouble and ruin their new friendship.

"With my sense of direction and your language skills, we make a great team," she said, and he smiled at her.

The hostess walked them to a table under a canopy of green leaves. The air smelled of orange blossoms, a subtle sweetness. She looked around and realized they were seated in a mini orchard of citrus trees, right in the heart of Cairo.

"This looks like it belongs in a fairy tale," she said.

"Or an Indiana Jones movie," he replied. "I love this."

"What? Being out in the night with a virtual fiancée?"

"Yes, but also, walking off the plan. Discovering new things that aren't featured in a tour guide or even a Yelp review."

She pointed at a Yelp and Tripadvisor sign right next to her, asking guests to please leave reviews.

All Roads Lead to Rome • 169

He laughed, throwing his head back. "Well, I guess I like the appearance of being original. Stevie, don't break my illusions!"

She shrugged. "What can I say? Madi says I'm too much of a Capricorn moon not to see reality and lose myself in fantasy."

"Madi sounds interesting," he said, narrowing his eyes at her. "I feel like I know Nadia and Madi for all you talk about them. But you don't have pictures with them in your social media."

She didn't know what to say to that. She'd never intended to keep her best friends away from her public persona. But in the milliseconds that passed between Cristian's words and her reply, she knew the answer.

"They're sacred to me. I post things that will help me recruit people for work. I don't like to share important people with strangers."

"I'm honored you tell me about them, then," he said.

The waitress brought their order, an assortment of appetizers, bread, and fruit. Stevie was so hungry, she had to pace herself.

"What about you?" she said. "You post everything, but I've never seen your friends who are here, either. Tell me. What's the tea? I'm the outsider, and I'd like to know how things stand in case I risk messing up the group."

He shrugged. "I've been friends with all of them for years. Connie and Aldana were my neighbors when we were growing up."

"Ever dated either one?"

He bit his lip. "Both. But at different points of our childhoods."

"Both?" She playfully slapped his arm. "What a player!"

"Well, the last time I dated either one was before I turned thirteen."

"Who was your first kiss with?"

"Neither."

"What? Were there more neighbors that had some Cristian?"

170 • *Yamile Saied Méndez*

He laughed, and she loved the sound. "It was Vero, when I was fourteen."

There was a heavy pause, and Stevie's mind started tying knots with the clues she'd had so far.

"Is she . . . your girlfriend?"

He steepled his hands and leaned in toward her on the table, impressed with her bravery, she hoped. "No. Not now. We dated until I met Micaela, and then . . . Micaela was her best friend." He inhaled sharply and said, "I'll be honest. When I went back to Rosario from Rome, we tried to . . . you know? See if it worked between us."

"It didn't?"

He shook his head. "Vero's like a big sister to me now."

Stevie swallowed the knot in her throat. In spite of his words, Vero's presence loomed large between them.

He continued, "Vero's dating Lucho now, if you must know. That's how I know him. Franco and Santiago played fútbol with me in our local barrio club, ADIUR."

"ADIUR? It sounds French," she said.

He laughed. "A little. It stands for Asociación de Deporte Infantil Unión Rosario."

"Oh," she said. "I told you I'm horrible with languages." But she didn't want to change the subject. "Tell me: Isn't it awkward that you and Lucho are on the trip together?"

He shrugged again. "That's for them to decide. I don't meddle in her relationship, you know?"

"Is it weird to see them together?"

Stevie already knew she couldn't face Edward at least for a few decades, and often wondered how she'd react if she somehow met up with Liam, especially if he had a child by now. Judging by the way her blood started boiling, she imagined she wasn't ready to experience that in real life.

Cristian was different, though, and it was obvious in his answer. "I'm relieved she has someone, actually. I used to have so much anxiety thinking that Mica would want us to be together,

All Roads Lead to Rome • 171

you know? In a way, Vero waited for me for years. How selfish of me if I didn't give her a chance, right? But I didn't feel anything. I couldn't fake it either. That would have been more unfair even."

She nodded, her lips pressed.

"She's with someone who has the same goals and dreams."

"Lucho has dreams? I've only met him for an hour or so, and he acted like a robot," she said, and laughed.

Cristian laughed, too, but wagged his finger at her. "You more than anyone should know that appearances are deceiving. They're made one for the other. They're both all alone in this world, believe it or not. Vero lived with an aunt, who recently passed away. Lucho has a similar backstory. He lived with his grandparents, and against all odds, got a scholarship to the CONICET—" He guessed she had no idea what this was and added, "The prestigious Argentine government agency?"

She shrugged. "I don't know what that is."

"It's the National Scientific and Technical Research Council. Anyway, super hard to get into. He got a scholarship from them to research things that sound made up. He's a genius. And I'm happy they found each other."

"Can I see a picture of her?"

He took his phone from his pocket and showed her a picture of Lucho with a girl. She was tall and slender, but other than that, Stevie was shocked to see herself in some of her features. The same eyes, the long straight black hair.

"You have a type," she said, and he burst out laughing.

"I knew you'd think that when you saw her! But in my defense, I can say I just like pretty girls. Women, I mean. Do you have a type?"

"Other than Maluma? Nope," she replied, giving him the phone back. "The kind of man I idealize is just that. An ideal. No one like him exists in the world."

"Maybe you're looking in the wrong place. Maybe girls?"

From any other kind of person, like some of the sales guys, she would have taken offense at the comment. But Cristian seemed earnest. Where had he come from? And why weren't more guys like him?

"I've thought about that many times. Hell, I wished it was true more times than I can say. I love being around other women. They're all beautiful and generally smell great. But I've been cursed with an attraction to men."

"It can be a phase, you know? If you met the right person. . . ."

He was being sarcastic. How many times did people say that to her gay friends?

"I wish it was a phase. No. I like men. Although most men are the worst."

He pouted. "I'm sorry."

He didn't say *not all men* or any other such thing, and Stevie knew he wasn't just saying that to get into her pants. He'd had plenty of chances before, and he hadn't taken her up on those invitations. And he didn't push the subject at all.

Their meal arrived, and they paused their conversation to savor every bite. Later, satisfyingly full but not bursting, they smiled at each other.

"I loved everything," he said, patting his flat stomach. "The concierge was right. This is the best welcome to Egypt."

They politely turned down a shisha, the Egyptian fruit-flavored water pipe, but were excited to accept coffee. Neither one seemed ready to go back to the hotel.

Stevie continued her interrogation. "How did you decide to come to Egypt with this group? Of all the places in the world."

He sipped on his coffee and said, "My dream is to set up experiences for people. That's how I met Brady, you know? In Lake Powell? We had a connection through Céline's family, but I hadn't met him until then. Céline wanted to see the wild horses that roam in the mesas of Glen Canyon. My nonna had wanted to see them, too, so this one summer, I hired a helicopter company. Nonna Ross was gushing about it at the restaurant, and Brady overheard me. He asked me to plan the outing for him and Céline."

All Roads Lead to Rome • 173

"That's how he proposed," she said. "That's amazing. You set up trips for people? What are you, kind of like a travel agent?"

"No, I'm more like a bucket-list coordinator. But the best is that I know how to play the system. How to help people afford their dreams of certain experiences. You must have noticed that we're only paying a fraction of what this kind of trip usually costs."

She scoffed. "Incredible. Thanks for inviting me."

"My pleasure," he said, and she knew he meant it.

They had a packed agenda the following day, and although their meal had been light, the effects of having a full stomach, combined with the jet lag and the excitement and stress of being in such a new place, finally took a toll on Stevie. She yawned a couple of times, and he asked for the check.

She took her credit card out of her purse, but he stopped her with a firm voice. "I got it."

"What? You're using points or something?"

"Or something," he said, and then, as if he thought better of that, he added, "This is my treat for you."

She accepted it graciously. "Don't make a habit of it. I'm a modern woman, after all, and I don't want my feminist card to be revoked."

"Oh," he said, nodding. "I know you probably make more money in one summer than me in my whole footballer career, but let me treat you this time."

"Okay," she said, loving the way he seemed not threatened by knowing she made more money than him.

They went back to the hotel arm in arm, catching up over the last year, although she was sure to leave out super personal and private details, as she was sure he did, too. Even though he was sweet and charming, there had to be some shadows underneath his angelic smile. Every time he flashed that smile at her, she reminded herself that Lucifer was the morning star whose guile deceived people with his beauty.

Chapter 17

They arrived at the hotel to a surprise. A group of firefighters were leaving the lobby.

"Let me go see what's going on," Cristian said.

There was no way Stevie was going to stay put, so she trailed behind him. She overheard the receptionist tell him there had been a flood on the tenth floor.

"That's our floor," she said.

Cristian nodded and winced. "I know. I hope our friends are okay." He glanced at his pocket and said, "No messages."

"Let me check if your rooms were affected," the man said. "What's your room number?"

He clicked on his keyboard. The look of worry in his eyes belied the smile. "Your rooms weren't damaged, thank goodness. But we had to cut the water service in that hallway because of the suite at the end, which is where the problem originated. I'll have to move you elsewhere."

Stevie and Cristian exchanged a look. He looked so worried

All Roads Lead to Rome • 175

that she pressed his hand to let him know everything would be all right.

The man clicked on his computer, and then relief crossed his face. "Yes. This is great. We have a suite on the fifteenth floor available at the moment. Much better than your current rooms, although those are nice, too."

Cristian sighed. "That's great, right?"

Stevie was one step ahead of him. "Wait. You said one suite. We were in separate rooms."

The man scratched his head. "Oh, my apologies. In that case, I'm terribly sorry. We're completely full. We have just that one room."

It was one in the morning. Stevie was almost falling asleep on her feet. She wanted to find a quiet place to collapse for a few blissful hours. "Can we discuss in private for a sec? Excuse us," she told the man; grabbing Cristian by the shirt, she pulled him away.

"Listen, let's just share the room tonight. Tomorrow I can bunk up with the girls, anyway. Or maybe they may have fixed the problem by then."

"But you told them you snore like a bear."

"It was a joke!"

He shook his head. "Listen, I can share with Franco, since Santiago is most likely spending the night with Aldana. I hope he wakes up and opens the door for me."

"Don't be silly," she said. "It's a suite, which means there will be more than one bed. And even if there wasn't, I really can sleep anywhere." Which was true, in a way. It didn't mean that she got any rest, just that she could block out the world and pass out.

When he didn't reply, she said, "If you're still worried about boundaries or ruining anything, I swear I'll be on my best behavior. I'll keep my hands to myself."

He shook his head. "No. It's not that I'm worried about ruining, Estefi."

176 • *Yamile Saied Méndez*

Estefi. Liam used to call her that. No one else ever had. The sound of this endearment on Cristian's lips disarmed her. It was true that the love of a person can't be replaced with that of another. But it's also true that a new love, a new friendship, can strengthen your heart, rewrite the map of your life.

"What are you worried about then?" she asked.

He bit his lip and sighed. "I talk in my sleep," he said.

He'd sounded so serious that she laughed. "I won't tell. I swear." She raised her hand like a Boy Scout.

"I wouldn't expect anything different from you." There was no mocking in his voice.

They went up to the concierge to tell them their decision. "Nice!" he said, clapping his hands. "Follow me." He left the front desk to help Stevie and Cristian move their things to the new suite, a penthouse on top of the building. The Nile River glittered under the full moon, and there was a glow around the city. The view was magnificent. And the room was incredible. An ample bed sat behind a set of arched doors. Stevie peeked inside a smaller room to the side, and sighed with relief. At least they weren't going to be stuck with the dilemma of sharing a bed.

Stevie was heading to the smaller room when Cristian intercepted her.

"I promise no one will revoke your feminist card, but I can't let you sleep in the small room," he said.

The concierge gave them a side glance as if saying they didn't need to pretend in front of him. Stevie tipped him generously, and he kissed her hand. "Sleep well, madam, and sorry for the inconvenience."

"No inconvenience at all," she said, but when she turned around and saw Cristian, standing there, arms crossed as if waiting for instructions, her heart started racing. She hoped at least a few hours of sleep would clear her mind, because she didn't know how she was going to last the whole week without messing this friendship up.

All Roads Lead to Rome • 177

"It's only for one night, right?" she asked, scratching her head.

"One night," Cristian confirmed.

"Okay, then, I'll take your offer and the big bed. Only because, look at it, it's majestic. You can shower first."

"Wait," he said. "We can shower at the same time."

"What?" she said in a choking voice.

He had a straight face as he said, "There are two bathrooms, aren't there?"

"But that one's just a powder room with a toilet and a sink. And yes, a bidet," she said. "Unless there's a partition between the tub and the shower in the other bathroom?"

They both turned to look at the bath suite, and no. It wasn't going to work. Glass surrounded the shower stall, and a big, footed tub sat in the middle of the room. At least the toilet area had a door.

"Thanks for the invite, but no, thanks. You go first," she said. "I wanted to take a long bath, anyway."

Now he was the one blushing as he headed into the bathroom. *Good. That will teach him not to joke like that.*

Stevie's victory was short-lived. For all she pretended the teasing hadn't burrowed under her skin, once she heard the water going in the bathroom, she had a hard time keeping the image of Cristian in the shower, droplets of water sliding down his golden skin, out of her head. And she was so thirsty. . . .

She wasn't a prude, but even she got scandalized at the things her mind was conjuring up. Hoping to get some reprieve from her subconscious fighting to rise to the surface, she covered her eyes with a face mask, put cancelling headphones on, and tried to plan for the next day. They had a full agenda, after all. Cristian had sent her detailed notes on what to pack, and she had been happy to see that she owned most of the things on the list, due to her years mountain climbing and hiking in the desert.

She wasn't sure when she fell asleep, but what must have been a few hours later, she heard a voice nearby. She must have taken

178 • *Yamile Saied Méndez*

off the gigantic headphones in her sleep. Her hair had tangled around the headband. Carefully, she freed herself and checked on the clock on the nightstand. Six a.m. flashed in red.

Stevie sighed with frustration but also a touch of relief. She'd fallen asleep before she'd set up an alarm for seven. They were meeting as a group at eight, and she figured she'd get ready before Cristian woke up. As soon as she remembered he was sleeping just a thin door away from her, her skin prickled. It had been silly and dangerous to flirt like that the night before. She'd have to be more careful from now.

"Estefi," he said clearly from the next room.

"Yes?" she asked, and listened for his answer.

Cristian was talking, but his words sounded slurred and mumbled. He didn't say her name again, and she figured he was talking in his sleep. That hadn't been a lie or an excuse. He'd said her name, Estefi. She put a pillow over her head to mumble the groan of frustration at how much she loved to hear this nickname pronounced by his lips. There was no way she was going to sleep now. So she got up and dressed for the day.

Cairo in December wasn't scorching like it would be in the summertime, but it was still going to be hot. She dressed in long hiking pants, hiking sneakers, and a sports bra, over which she wore a gauzy long-sleeved shirt. She braided her hair and wrapped a gauze scarf on her wrist. She had remembered to bring a bucket hat and hooked it to a clip on the waist of her pants. A small backpack completed her attire.

Cristian hadn't talked in his sleep again. Maybe like her, he got his best sleep when it was time to wake up. She peeked through the curtain and gasped at the view from the window. She walked out to the balcony just as the morning call for prayer was ringing from mosques all over the city, their sound joined in a symphony that resonated deep inside her.

After Tristan, Stevie had stopped believing in God. She hadn't been very religious before, not even as a small child. She wasn't

All Roads Lead to Rome • 179

interested in spirituality enough to label herself as an atheist, but she just didn't even think about the existence of a greater power. With Tristan, it's not that she started believing in God, but she couldn't deny there was something divine in him, the purity of his eyes, the fierce force of his love for her, and hers for him.

Sometimes, when she checked on him before falling asleep, she'd do the sign of the cross on his forehead, like Madi's abuela used to do with them when they were little. Obviously, when Stevie did it, the protection hadn't worked.

After Tristan, this faint belief in goodness disappeared. If there was a god, then, what kind of heartless deity would allow an innocent baby to pay for her sins? Furthermore, was loving Liam a sin? Was speaking up for herself against her mom also a sin? What had been so wrong about her that God had punished her by taking what she loved the most? If that God existed, Stevie didn't want to worship him, even though her mom had told her she had to make an effort to be a good human if she wanted to see Tristan again. What kind of sadistic God would use an innocent baby to punish her?

At seventeen, she'd too been a child. Twelve years had passed, but she couldn't help tearing up when she thought of the heartbreak of that girl whose baby had just died. God and religion weren't for her, but she was moved by other people's faith. And hearing the call to pray, she lowered her head and just offered her gratitude to whatever force was out in the universe—to Tristan.

She went back in and finally gathered the courage to peek into the room where Cristian was sleeping. She stifled a chuckle when she saw him sprawled over the tiny bed, his curly hair sticking in all directions, his slack jaw leaving his mouth open. He was bare-chested, and his feet stuck out from under the covers because the bed was too small and short for him.

"Psst, Cristian," she called from the door.

180 • *Yamile Saied Méndez*

Cristian took a deep breath, and under his lids, his eyes moved like his body was slowly waking up, but his mind needed a little extra time.

"Cristian, I'm heading down for breakfast. I think it's time to go," she said, this time a little louder.

In that moment, his alarm went off, and he sat up so abruptly, he startled her.

"Ah!" she screamed.

"Oh, wow, sorry for scaring you," he said.

He blinked and looked around him, as if he were trying to make out his surroundings and understand where he was. "It wasn't a dream, then?"

"What are you talking about?" she asked, still laughing at how he'd scared her.

In the blink of an eye, she imagined a whole life waking up next to him, traveling all over the world. What would it be like to wake up next to Cristian? What if instead of waiting until they were seventy, they became exclusive travel partners now?

But Tristan was buried in Utah. And Max and Erin were having a baby. She had to be around in case her mom ever wanted to mend the rift between them. Stevie knew that even if she ever had another child, which she absolutely wouldn't, her love for Tristan would never vanish. Her mom had never showed her love in the way she had craved all her life, but Stevie knew she was loved. Even if she kept posting about Frank's daughters and kids, Stevie knew that deep down, her mom had to love her, right?

No. She couldn't leave Utah for all she wanted to run away from it, and Cristian didn't have a place to call home. There was no future for them together. Stevie would have to be happy with a long-distance friendship and hope that they'd see each other on outlandish trips every once in a while until they grew old and decrepit.

Cristian sighed, and now fully awake, he looked sheepish as

All Roads Lead to Rome • 181

he raised the sheet to cover himself. "Sorry I miscalculated time again. Another one of my flaws."

"Do you want me to wait for you?" she asked.

He shook his head. "No. Go down and eat with the others. I'll be there in a few."

She had been nervous about seeing the others if they found out that she and Cristian were sharing a room. But this way was perfect.

"Okay," she said. "I'll see you soon." She looked over her shoulder just as he was getting out of bed. He was chiseled by the gods themselves, and feeling her brief gaze on him, he covered his privates with the sheet.

The attraction was mutual, then. She smiled all the way to the lobby.

Chapter 18

Everyone was refreshed and excited for the new day. Stevie got some coffee and a cheese Danish and sat down next to the others, very much feeling like the new girl at school. It wasn't that she didn't enjoy other people's company, but the problem was she didn't know where she fell into this group yet. Clearly, she wasn't the leader. Nor was she the leader's girlfriend. Really, Stevie could have been anything she wanted to be, and yet she felt like the tagalong.

If Madi were here, she'd say it was only her ego speaking, the mean part of her psyche that had her mom's voice. But Stevie knew it was only her consciousness. They had all been speaking Spanish, and when she joined them, they switched to English. She appreciated the gesture, but she wasn't going to subject them to it. She knew how hard it was to joke around in a language not your own, how stilted and artificial the words felt and sounded.

"No, don't worry," she said, trying her best for her tongue to speak Spanish like it sounded in her head. "Even if I'm quiet, I understand what you all say. Don't switch to English for me."

All Roads Lead to Rome • 183

They all looked at her in delight.

"How did you learn to speak so well? Your accent is perfect," Aldana asked, instantly becoming Stevie's favorite.

In that moment, Cristian joined them. He had showered again. Droplets of water darkened the shoulders of his white linen shirt. The image of him in the shower flashed again. She blushed at the impudence of her thoughts and noticed Aldana and Connie hadn't missed a beat. They exchanged a charged look that said more than words. Stevie wished she could correct their wrong assumptions.

She shrugged and said, "My best friends are from Argentina and Puerto Rico. And my parents are from Peru."

Funny how in other circumstances, she'd said she was Peruvian, but now with actual Latin Americans, she'd hesitated to call herself a Latina. Maybe because she saw the confusion in the others' faces when a US-born Latine person talked about belonging.

"Before that, my grandparents were from Korea, via Japan. It's complicated," she explained, even though they hadn't asked about her family tree. She felt so awkward, she shrugged.

"You were born in the United States, though," Connie said, not unkindly. It sounded like she just was genuinely curious. "You feel American, Peruvian, Korean, or Japanese?"

It was hard to answer that question. She'd been to Peru several times when she was young, but she'd never been to Korea or Japan. She didn't know how to convey the subtlety of nationality in a language that was her mother tongue but not the one she navigated the world in.

"My language at home was Spanish. My parents made a little Peru, and I was like one person there and another out in the world. I guess, I feel more American," she said, looking at Cristian, expecting him to tease her, but he didn't. In fact, his eyes were soft when he looked at her.

Once again, not missing a beat, Aldana saw Cristian and said, "Kind of like this specimen here. He was born in the US,

184 • *Yamile Saied Méndez*

to Argentine parents. His Italian grandmother lives in Las Vegas. He lived in Italy for the last decade, but he feels like an Argentine, or so he says."

"Argentines are born wherever they want," Lucho said, quoting the famous meme.

"Thanks for being the only one coming to my defense," Cristian said.

The others laughed, but Stevie just watched him, hoping he'd go deeper into this topic. She was always fascinated with how others navigated the muddled waters of those born in between cultures and languages.

He didn't disappoint her. "Argentina's the country where I grew up, and where my heart planted roots. I have the privilege of moving around the world with a passport that has automatic entrance pretty much everywhere. Maybe if I wasn't well off, or if I'd grown up under other circumstances, I'd have a different idea. I don't know. My nonna loves the US because she could achieve her dreams there. She made this life possible for my mom and me."

"That's what my nonno says about Argentina," Aldana said. "He doesn't remember Italy, even though he lived there until he was ten."

"Maybe we belong where our heart is," said Lucho, surprising everyone. "Maybe the heart really is the most important organ, and not only because it pumps our blood and keeps us alive, but because without our loved ones, we die."

"Ah! Listen to Lucho! A scientist and a poet!" Santiago exclaimed, and they all teased Lucho until he blushed to the tips of his ears.

"Aren't all scientists poets in essence? And all poets who have to measure the force and metric of their words, scientists?" Franco added.

"Franco's a philosopher now, ¡qué lo parió!" said Cristian, and they all laughed again.

All Roads Lead to Rome • 185

In that moment, Ahmed, their guide, arrived to take them to their first stop, the national museum.

"Ready?" he asked.

"Ready," everyone replied, and followed Ahmed.

Stevie would've been last in line, but Cristian slowed his step to walk by her side. It probably was a coincidence, but it made her feel included.

The way the sun hit even in December was something Stevie hadn't been prepared for. It was similar to standing on the red rocks of Lake Powell in July, the dry hot air like an oven. They had a short ride in the van and then arrived at the museum. Usually, she didn't like museums, but she was fascinated by what she saw. The mummies, the sculptures, the way carved words remained thousands of years later after their meaning was lost. Maybe the world had forgotten why Nefertiti's head had been purposely shaped like a cone —had she been an alien, like some conspiracies say?

No matter the reason, she was famed to have been the most beautiful woman of that era. Stevie wondered if she'd been born that way and, instead of changing herself to fit the standard of beauty of the times, she'd changed everyone's ideas of beauty so that everyone wanted to be like her. She envied that kind of confidence, and that legacy. If Stevie were to die now, what would people say about her?

That she'd been a good friend, the kind you know would help you bury a body if the need popped up.

A dependable, hard-working leader.

A bad student.

A rebellious daughter.

A little sister who hadn't found her way.

A maverick type of girl who says yes to any adventures at the last minute and makes a pact to marry you, even though you've only met a couple of hours ago.

Someone who never got the chance to speak would say she'd

186 • *Yamile Saied Méndez*

been the best mother a kid could dream of, even though she'd been a kid herself.

In a few years, those labels would disappear, too. What would remain? Did it matter? Who was Stevie when she was by herself? If she went ahead and opened her catering company, even if someone copied her recipes, she'd be present in some way, even if her name was forgotten.

Stevie brushed her fingers through the relief of hieroglyphics and promised herself that she'd leave a legacy that would endure, even if monuments crumbled, the empire fell, and the sound of her name was lost to memory.

When it was time to come out, Stevie felt like she'd had a spiritual experience—in a museum. Who would've thought? Not her history teacher, that's for sure.

"The pyramids are next!" Ahmed told the group.

Stevie was relieved she wasn't the only one pretty much bouncing with excitement. It wasn't necessarily surprising, but Lucho actually squealed, "The pyramids!"

Cristian turned around and locked eyes with Stevie, who had to look out the window not to start laughing, and risk offending one of his friends. The more time she spent with them, the more she saw through the shields they, too, put up for the world. Lucho, serious and aloof, was still a kid at heart. It was obvious why he'd still come on this trip even though his girlfriend was sick. This also spoke highly of Veronica, that she didn't get offended that he'd still travel without her. It was a once-in-a-lifetime opportunity, but Stevie wasn't sure she'd have had the moral fortitude Veronica seemed to possess.

No wonder Cristian once had a crush on her. But she didn't want to wallow inside her mind and turned back to the excited conversation in the van.

Everyone in the group respected the rule that once you claim a seat, that seat is yours forever. She happily sat in the middle seat in the second row so she could scooch forward to eavesdrop in the conversation between Ahmed—who looked like a

All Roads Lead to Rome • 187

younger, taller Al Pacino—and Cristian, even if she didn't understand what they were talking about. She loved the cadence of their rapid Arabic and was happily surprised to notice that Cristian's English accent was less noticeable.

One moment they were zipping on the highway along multi-family buildings that reminded her of the government housing apartments where Nadia had lived in Argentina (Stevie had seen pictures), and the next, there was a slice of desert with the pyramids sitting on top.

"Is that them?" Connie asked, pointing out the window, her voice and face hardly containing her excitement.

They all turned in her direction, and Stevie's breath caught in her throat.

Chapter 19

The pyramids were just like Stevie had imagined, but the surroundings were not. "I never believed they were in the middle of the city," she said. "I always thought they were out in the desert, like hours into the desert!" She was glad when the others shared her surprise. She didn't feel like an idiot as she would in a similar situation with other kinds of people.

"In a couple of years, the entrance will be brand-new," Ahmed said, pointing at construction along the highway. "There will be a new museum of history. But for now, we still go this way."

The van trudged along a ribbon of pavement in the middle of the sand. It was still early, a little past noon, but already groups of tourists lined up outside a building.

"That's the visitors' center," Ahmed said. "They have great food there. We'll go into the big pyramid. Then you all will ride horses, and then have lunch. Does that sound right?" he asked Cristian.

Cristian nodded. "You're the boss!" he said in English.

Stevie's heart was pounding with nerves. She couldn't wait

All Roads Lead to Rome • 189

to see how her pictures turned out. How her mom would be poring over the images, trying to guess who was who, and how she'd be so curious to know how Stevie had met these stylish people. Of course, in time, Stevie would tell her all the details. Nothing would make her happier. Maybe one day, her mom would want to go on a trip with her.

As soon as they got out of the van, Stevie's body startling prickling with sweat. She took a sip of water and followed her group.

"Miss Choi, you'll need the scarf," Ahmed called from behind her, handing her a scarf she'd purposely left in the car.

"But I'm so hot," she said, waving his concern away.

Ahmed wouldn't be deterred. "No, you don't understand. The scarf will protect your face and your arms from the sand. Believe me. Also, it will keep you cooler."

She bowed her head and took the thin scarf from his hands. "Thank you," she said.

She turned to join her group and realized that Cristian was watching her. He had a strange expression on his face, and she felt self-conscious, although she didn't know why.

"Let's go!" he said, and led the group as if he'd been here before.

A multitude of people selling scarves and decorations swarmed around them, but Ahmed barked a couple of things, and they all dispersed. A woman was sitting on the ground, at the shade of the pyramid. She had a thin brown dog on one side, and a little kid on the other. Her face was tanned dark, and her eyes were a stunning bright green. Stevie and the woman made eye contact, and they smiled at each other.

She continued walking, trying to tie her scarf like Aldana and Connie had around their heads, but the wind kept ripping it from her hands. She felt someone tap on her shoulder. When she turned, she was surprised to see the woman. They were about the same height, and probably the same age, although lines fanned from the woman's eyes. She was missing a couple

190 • *Yamile Saied Méndez*

of teeth in the back of her mouth, but her smile was dazzling. Stevie was alarmed at first, but then she smiled.

"Let me help you, amiga," the woman said in perfect Spanish.

Stevie was shocked. "How do you know I speak Spanish? How did you learn?"

The woman was deftly arranging the scarf around her head and tucking the ends under Stevie's chin.

"I learned in school, and you look like you're from a Spanish-speaking place."

Stevie couldn't believe it. Then the woman chuckled and pointed at the rest of her group with her chin. "They were all speaking Spanish went they walked past me, and you're with them. So, I assumed. But you're more comfortable in English, right?"

Stevie nodded, more surprised by the minute.

"How do you know all that?"

The woman glanced at the pyramid looming behind Stevie and said, "It's the divination power I get from the pyramids." She laughed again. Stevie laughed, too. She liked this woman a lot. In other circumstances, they could be friends. They had a similar sense of humor.

"Your accent, darling," she asked. "Colombiana?"

"Peruana," Stevie replied.

The woman snapped her fingers. "But from the States, right?"

Stevie nodded.

"There," the woman said. "You look so pretty."

Stevie took some money from her pocket, and a sadness passed the woman's eyes. "No need. This is my gift to you."

Stevie placed a hand on her heart. She was moved by the gesture. "Thank you." Then she glanced at the boy and the dog sleeping on a rug a few feet away. "Is that your son?"

The way the woman's eyes lit up made Stevie light up, too. When she had Tristan, and people asked her if she was the baby-sitter, she had once said yes, because she'd been embarrassed to

All Roads Lead to Rome • 191

say she was his mom. Not because of him; because he was perfect. Stevie lied because she had cared if a stranger thought she was a bad person. Her eyes welled up with tears. Through them, she saw the woman had necklaces hanging from her arms.

"Do you sell these?" she asked, sniffing.

The woman nodded, still with pride. "Yes, for good luck."

Without really looking at the charms hanging from the strings, Stevie grabbed two and gave the woman some money. She only had dollar bills.

The woman's eyes widened. "This is too generous, madam."

She tried to give the money back, but Stevie shook her head.

"A blessing, then," the woman said.

Her eyes were so expressive. In them, Stevie read an assurance that she could trust this person. She nodded.

The woman grabbed Stevie's hands and glanced at her palms very quickly. Stevie wondered what she had seen, because when she looked up, there was compassion in the stranger's face. She said words in a language Stevie didn't know but sounded like Arabic. She felt the softness of the words soothe her burned-up heart, and a knot of tears grew in her throat.

"Stevie!" Cristian called her.

The woman finished her blessing and, cupping Stevie's face with her hand, she said, "Go back to your beloved. He's been waiting for you."

Stevie looked over her shoulder. Cristian was frantically waving her over. "He's not my beloved," she said softly, but even as she said it, she knew it wasn't true.

"Well, he loves you. Can you not see? It's glowing from his face and his whole body," the woman assured her.

Stevie's body trilled with her words. But that mean voice in her head told her that no matter what Cristian felt for her, she didn't deserve his love, or much less, his admiration. He didn't really know who she was.

"Believe me," the woman said. "There's a light inside you. Let it shine."

192 • *Yamile Saied Méndez*

Stevie clasped the woman's hands in hers and kissed her. This was her gift.

She turned to join Cristian and the rest, who were already lining up to go into the pyramid.

"Everything okay?" he asked, glancing behind Stevie.

"Yes," she replied. "She gave me a blessing."

Cristian was about to say something when Ahmed came up to them. He held tickets in his hands. "You go in here, climb to the inner chamber, spend a little time inside, and take pictures. Then you come down the same way. Ready?"

"Yes!" they all said in unison.

They headed in, except for Ahmed.

"You're not coming with us?" Franco asked.

Ahmed shook his head. "I've already been in too many times. My ticker isn't what it used to be." He patted his chest, meaning his heart. "I'll wait here for you."

Stevie saw a look of worry pass on her new friends' faces. How hard could the climb be? She'd gone up the Arc de Triomphe in Paris, and yes, arrived short of breath, but the view had been worth it. Like it was her custom, she was last in line, although Cristian kept trying to have her go in front of him.

"Stop doing that," she said, sneaking past him on her way to the entrance, a mouth on the side of the pyramid.

"What?"

"That thing when you try to be all gentlemanly with me," she said.

He shrugged. "It's not only with you, Stevie. I want to make sure everyone's with the group. I let you stay for a moment, and you stayed talking to that woman forever. If we hadn't been waiting for the line to go in, we could've left you behind."

"I can take care of myself."

"I know that," he said, already panting. He'd covered his face with a light scarf, too; only his bright blue eyes were visible, but she saw in the glow of his skin that he, too, was sweaty.

They didn't talk for a while. There was too much noise of

All Roads Lead to Rome • 193

voices in every language to have a conversation. Besides, the little path along the pyramid was narrow, and where it widened, they had to weave around people selling scarves or necklaces, and even sleeping dogs. Stevie's heart clenched for them.

She was impressed at the size of the pyramid. She'd always imagined the sides would be smooth, but in fact, they were the opposite, roughhewn stones, tightly packed together. They went into the entrance and then saw why there was another line. The way into the big chamber was a steep ramp that zigzagged all the way to the top. Rope handles were helpful, as well as the rungs on the ramp, and in parts, the ceiling was low, and Cristian, Lucho, Alana, and Franco had to hunch over.

The group was in good spirits. They joked along in Spanish, and although she didn't understand everything they said, she got the gist that they were teasing Santiago for his small size.

"At least I fit, not like you guys," he said, good-naturedly.

Stevie didn't know why she looked over her shoulder. Maybe to see if Cristian was laughing, too. But when she did, she saw that Cristian had stopped several feet away from her. In the distance, she saw a worker was holding the line. Maybe there was an occupancy limit in the grand chamber. A woman had a baby in a stroller, and the man next to her was carrying a toddler in a backpack. Stevie couldn't hear what they were saying, but she figured the attendant was explaining that the carrier wouldn't fit.

The couple exchanged a worried look. If they wanted to go in, they'd have to split up. Stevie felt bad for them and had the impulse to go help them. But then, she figured no one in their right minds would leave their children with a stranger.

Cristian hadn't stopped to look at the couple. He leaned against the wall, holding his head. Stevie thought that he'd hit it and went down to see if he was all right.

"What happened?" she asked, gently brushing his hand that grasped at the rope handle like it was a lifeline.

He didn't say anything for a second. His breathing was loud

194 • *Yamile Saied Méndez*

and deep, and she moved the scarf from his mouth. "You're going to hyperventilate," she said.

She could feel his pulse racing on her fingertips. "Do you have anxiety?" she asked again, in that soft voice that she wasn't sure was hers.

He shook his head and then shrugged. "Claustrophobia, which really, is a form of anxiety, right?"

She placed her hand on his shoulder. Since she was a couple of rungs above him, she towered over him. "I'll walk down with you," she said. "You don't have to do this."

His eyes were desperate. "All my life," he said between gasps, "I wanted to see the inside of the pyramids. I'm here. I can't turn away now when I'm so close."

She laughed, but not in a teasing way. "You've seen the inside. You're inside right now."

He shook his head, and she knew then that trying to convince him to go back was futile. It would only hurt him. She understood the need not to quit just because things got difficult.

Her mind scrambled to find a solution. The she remembered the necklace in her pocket. "Here," she said. "I'm going to give you a talisman against fear. The woman outside the pyramid gave it to me, along with a blessing."

While she talked, she unwrapped the scarf from his head and his neck. His blond curly hair was plastered to his scalp. His face looked gaunt, but he was still beautiful. She clasped the necklace around his neck. It was the cheapest kind, a piece of twine with a metal clasp. The important thing was the charm. It was one half of the Isis eye against evil. She'd seen it all over the place, in all shapes and forms and colors. She saw that the other necklace held the other half. *What a coincidence,* she thought. That of all the necklaces that she could've grabbed from the woman's giant tote, she'd taken a perfect match.

"Here," she said, clasping its twin around her own neck. "Now the strength that I have will transfer to you."

All Roads Lead to Rome • 195

"You keep giving me jewelry, woman. Do you want to sleep with me or something?" he asked, in a joking tone, but Stevie's cheeks felt aflame, and not because it was hot inside.

"Stop with those dirty thoughts," she said, playfully slapping his arm. "I'm trying to make you feel better."

"And I do," he said, straightening up, or trying to because he was way taller than the ceiling.

"In that case," she said, gently clutching his arm and leading him in front of her, "let's get going. We're holding up the line. It's because of people like you, Americans, that the wait is unbelievable!"

That made him laugh. "Hmmm. American. You hit all the boxes."

Slowly, they trudged up. The rest of their group was inside the chamber already, judging by their loud cheers that echoed all the way down.

"I think they're having the time of their lives," Stevie said. "You're the best experience planner."

She turned around just in time to see the color return to his pale face. He smiled in gratitude. Before they went in, he stooped closer to her and kissed her head, before walking ahead to join their group.

They finally made it to the top. Stevie didn't know what she had expected to find, but inside the grand chamber was nothing but a sarcophagus. And an energizing, electric atmosphere. Maybe it was the music that the group had gone in ahead of them was playing—tambourines, maracas, and other bells. Maybe it was the soft light that filtered through a window high on the wall, or the aftereffect of that kiss on her head that robbed her of all conscious thought.

Whatever the reason, Stevie allowed herself the chance to join the dancing around them, although she was hot. For once, she truly didn't care what anyone thought about her. She was inside the great pyramid, with a group of people who yesterday

196 • *Yamile Saied Méndez*

had been strangers and today felt like friends. And a stranger that in the last few months had become the closest friend she'd ever had.

Once or twice, she caught Cristian laughing, clutching the necklace she'd clasped around his neck. He'd hold onto it and smile, and that made Stevie smile, too.

Later, when they exited from the pyramid for the next group to go in, Stevie and Cristian saw that the couple with their babies was heading toward the exit. They were so blond and tall, Stevie thought they might be Scandinavian. Cristian made eye contact with the man, who said, "It sounded like a party up there."

"You're not going up?" Cristian asked.

The man shrugged, and the woman shook her head. She was older than Stevie had thought when she first saw her. "The babies won't go to sleep. We thought that if they did, we could take turns, but my son cries when either one of us tries to head up."

Cristian glanced at Stevie. The experience granter, he couldn't help himself, could he? "You don't know us, but we can watch your babies for a bit, if you want."

The couple exchanged a look that Stevie couldn't read, but they were obviously considering the proposal. Were they crazy? She stared at Cristian until he winced at her, as if her looks hit him.

"We can give you our passports," Cristian said. "We'll watch the babies in the stroller, and the guard here can supervise us."

The couple shrugged at each other. Stevie loved that they could apparently talk with their thoughts, because neither one had said a word.

She elbowed Cristian, and he said, "Sorry. I should've asked you first. But in my opinion, they'd feel safer if there's a woman instead of just a man."

It was all crazy, anyway.

All Roads Lead to Rome • 197

The couple nodded and spoke their language with Cristian. Stevie was too shocked to say anything to stop them. They started climbing the ramp, not even running like she would've if it was her kids staying with strangers.

"Are you out of your mind?" she finally asked him.

"It's a totally normal thing to do, Stevie, watch out for other people's kids. My nonna always used to say there's no such thing as other people's kids, and that's how I ended up with those guys as pretty much my siblings." He pointed to the exit, and she imagined he meant their group.

Just when she thought they had something in common, he did something totally out of the blue that made her realize she didn't know him at all. She'd only known him for one night and two days. She didn't know him at all.

"How can they do this?" she asked, a little affronted at the universe. "How do they know we're not evil and will take their kids or do something terrible to them?"

"What can we do? This is a public place, people all around us have their phones in case something happens, and they'll only be gone for a few minutes. But they'll leave with a renewed sense of humanity and the experience of their lives."

She was hyperventilating now. The little boy in the stroller saw her worried face and started pouting.

"Now, calm down before you make them cry," he said, rocking the stroller. "It's not that deep. You smile at the girl. She's smiling at you."

"I'm not going to smile at no one," she said, wondering how in the world she'd ended up being stranded inside the pyramid with a guy who knew no strangers and apparently could speak every language known to humans.

In spite of what she'd declared, though, when she saw the grin on the baby's face, her defenses crumbled. "Oh" was all she said, as her insides melted from the cuteness overload. All her body tingled with tenderness. If she ever had a baby, she'd never leave her with strangers. She'd never even trusted her mom with

198 • *Yamile Saied Méndez*

Tristan, which was a constant source of endless fights and reproaches. In fact, the worst thing that could have happened had occurred while he'd been under Stevie's care. Her eyes prickled, but she smiled at the girl anyway.

"Try rocking her for a bit," he said, showing her how to do it with the other stroller.

To make matters worse, he started singing a lullaby.

"I can't believe this," she said, questioning how a boy could be so perfect and yet, so wrong for her. He liked children, that much was obvious. For all he said he wasn't ready to settle down now, it was obvious that he'd be the kind who would have a quiver full of kids (to label it as the scary group of people who popped babies nonstop). She never wanted that. She could never be trusted with a baby. She knew that.

If it hadn't been because the couple had her wallet with her passport, she would've left right away to get a cold drink before their turn to ride horses.

"What language were you speaking with them?" she asked, eager to do anything so the time would pass quicker.

"Oh, we spoke Dutch, but they're from Sweden."

She looked at him like he was speaking gibberish now.

He smiled, and she looked away before she smiled, too. She just couldn't win with him. "Keep rocking the baby," he said. "She's falling asleep."

"Are you fucking kidding me?" she murmured, and this time even the guard tried to hide that he was amused by her predicament.

"You're a baby whisperer, Stevie," he said. "You have a magic touch."

The ghost of the smile that had been blooming on her face dropped. He had no way to know how this affected her. She had the opposite of the magic touch. In fact, she had the literal touch of death. Everything she loved died. The plants in her apartment. The classroom fish in kindergarten. The neighborhood cat that begged her to let him into the house. After months of

All Roads Lead to Rome • 199

resisting, she had fed him and loved him, and then one day, he didn't come back for his meal. She saw him dead on the side of the road.

Her dad. Tristan.

And he said this?

She couldn't explain without revealing this to the one person she really wanted to impress. So she didn't say anything. Finally, thankfully, the Swedish couple returned, all smiley and victorious that they, too, had been able to see the great chamber.

The woman's face was practically glowing as she beelined to Stevie like she was on a mission to report something. Maybe she was just really grateful that her babies were still safe and sound. But . . . she didn't even look to see if her babies were okay. She stared at Stevie in the eyes, who was so much shorter, she had to look up so as to not lose eye contact, and said, "I was meditating. I knew I only had a few minutes, but when you meditate and enter the astral world, time moves differently. I saw you in the future." She glanced at Cristian and beamed at them. "You two are going to be so happy. You shone like the midday sun."

Stevie wondered if there had been an exchange of forbidden substances inside the chamber that she hadn't known about and shrugged.

The couple realized their babies were asleep, and they gushed at Cristian and Stevie in a combination of English, Spanish, and Dutch, apparently overwhelmed. They tried to pay them, but Cristian's face stayed stern, and they accepted the favor. Chattering nonstop, the couple left looking back at them and waving every once in a while.

"Well, now that we've done our good deed of the day, ready for horses?" Cristian asked, clapping once and wiggling his eyebrows like a dork.

Stevie rolled her eyes. "Finally."

Chapter 20

There was only time for a sandwich, which Stevie regretted, because the menu looked delicious. One of her favorite things was trying new cuisines, and from what she'd seen in Egypt, their food was a combination of Mediterranean and Moroccan. But she didn't want to miss out on horseback riding, so she ate her food on the go and watered it down with her beverage of choice, Coke Zero. It hit differently here in the desert.

They didn't have to go far for their rides. The stables were near the pyramids in front of a two-story house painted aquamarine, although the paint was peeling like the bark of aspen trees in American Fork Canyon. Stevie shook her head at herself. All her life, she had said she'd run away as far from Utah as she could, and here she was, missing it and finding connections to it in everything.

Ahmed and the horsekeeper matched everyone with a horse. Up on the saddle, Lucho looked pale, but he held on to the reins for dear life. The girls squealed, and only stopped acting scared when their horses started pawing at the air with their front hooves. Santiago and Franco, too, looked scared, and although Cristian had a hard time getting on the horse, once he was in the saddle, he looked like he belonged there.

The horsekeeper looked at Stevie with not much trust, and she rolled her eyes. If only he knew that she'd taken horse-riding lessons all her childhood! She hopped in the saddle and, in the blink of an eye, had her horse doing circles one way and the other. There hadn't been time for her to get to know her horse, but he seemed to know what she was doing. He was a black stallion, like in the movie she loved to watch with her dad when she was little. His name was Jack.

Apparently, all the stallions here were named Jack and all the mares were Veronica, which started a round of joking and teasing, because Lucho's mount was indeed a mare, named Veronica, of course, like his girlfriend.

Stevie felt like she wanted to absorb her surroundings. They rode in the middle of a neighborhood where there were children everywhere, chasing after their horses. She was shocked at first at seeing how much garbage was accumulated in empty fields, and the dogs and white donkeys scavenging for food. She prayed to any deity that might hear her that she wouldn't see a rat, or she'd surely die from the shock. Praying paid off, because she was spared. Her horse trotted like he was on tiptoes, and instinctively, her core tightened as she kept the pace.

She wished her mom could see her so Stevie could say, "See? The lessons weren't wasted on me. I can ride a horse in Cairo and look good without embarrassing myself."

Not that any of the others were embarrassed, but she was definitely the most confident one in the group. Ahmed had stayed behind this round, too. He'd fallen off a horse once, and he'd had enough riding to last him a lifetime. However, their guide, Mohammed, couldn't have been older than twenty, and he took them to all the best spots around the pyramids to take the best pictures.

Cristian offered his phone every time, and the guide took

202 • *Yamile Saied Méndez*

professional-quality photos. He had the eye of an artist, and he looked so free, like he was doing what he'd been born to do instead of living another person's expectations of him. What did she know, though? Other than a few smiles and looks, the universal language, Stevie hadn't exchanged a word with him. It wasn't until they reached the top of a dune that the boy challenged her to a race.

"I'm not even wearing a helmet!" she yelled, half laughing, totally horrified at the idea of falling from the horse and cracking her head on the ground.

She looked at Cristian for support. He'd suffered that in the flesh in his accident, but he shrugged and said, "I'm not going to do it. But you have to, because you're a freaking awesome horse rider."

She protested again, and the whole group yelled at her, "YOLO!"

She laughed and had no choice but to give in to peer pressure. The boy showed her where he'd be waiting with the camera.

"You're sure Jack can do this? Look at his super flimsy legs!"

The horse was a lot slighter than the cowboy horses she'd ridden as a kid.

It didn't help when the boy looked confused. "Jack?"

"The horse! Isn't his name Jack?" Stevie asked.

His face lit up, and he laughed. "I just call them horse. I forget their names."

When she shook her head, and started wanting to turn back, he stopped her gently but firmly, and said, "Trust me. Everything will be okay. Trust yourself. You know how to do this."

What was it about Egyptian people and their deep, bottomless eyes? How could they speak as if they knew her? But this boy was right. She knew what to do, and the horse did, too. They'd been working really well together.

So, she galloped down the dune. She leaned forward and held on to the reins for dear life. Then, seeing Cristian and the rest waiting for her at the bottom of the dune, she got brave. She sat

All Roads Lead to Rome • 203

up and loosened her grip on the reins. Carefully, she let them go. She felt the horse acknowledge that she was giving him permission to unleash. Literally.

The horse sped up.

Against her instincts, Stevie opened her arms and lifted her head. Her legs tightened around the horse. The sound of his hooves matched the rhythm of her heart. Around her, she felt people stop by to watch her and the horse run as if they were one creature. She laughed, feeling free for the first time since she could remember. Grains of sand hit her face, and her braid came undone. Her hair swirled around her, but she didn't slow down until she reached the bottom of the hill. The horse knew how to stop without sending her over his head, and she was so grateful. She was breathing hard, as if she had been the one running. And when she dismounted, she whirled around and fell into Cristian's arms.

That night, back at the hotel, the concierge informed them that the water issue had been fixed, and they could return to their former rooms, or stay in the suite. Cristian and Stevie glanced at each other. She saw him grasp the strap of his backpack, as if to stop himself from doing something stupid.

So she behaved stupidly for the both of them. "We'll keep the suite," she said, and took his hand as she led him to the elevator.

Chapter 21

Liam had been her first everything. Her first crush in middle school. Her first love. Her first kiss. The first boy who asked her to a school dance.

There were so many memories of milestone moments that featured him as the star of her show. She had been a supporting character for him until Tristan was born. Then she became the villain, the obstacle in his journey. Liam had tossed her aside like she didn't matter. She might have forgiven him this, but the fact that he had never reached out after Tristan died still hurt her deeply.

They had created a remarkable tiny human being together, and then when the baby died, it was like he had been relieved. He started posting on social media again, always with a new girl by his side, showing off all his accomplishments as an athlete. Ten years later, and he still behaved like he was the prom king in high school.

It took Stevie a while to not only date other guys, but also be intimate with them. There had been Austin; then Brady; and

All Roads Lead to Rome • 205

Edward, the doctor; but none of these relationships had lasted longer than three months. Now, she stood in the room in front of Cristian, all dusty and sweaty after a life-changing day, and although she still felt invincible, like a mythological Amazonian, riding a horse in the desert, she felt unmoored. It was as if she had to perform this act to show commitment to a guy. The desire and attraction she'd felt downstairs in the lobby, and the bravado going upstairs, kissing in the elevator, left her breathless.

All of sudden, she wasn't sure she could go through with it.

Cristian stood and watched her, as if he were trying to understand what had happened to bring on this change. He took a step toward her, and she shivered with anticipation, but she closed her eyes instead of meeting his gaze dead-on. He gently cupped her face, which she'd turned up to kiss him. And he did kiss her, softly, like butterfly wings. Then he stopped.

She opened her eyes, and in his, she saw a well of compassion. "What's wrong?" she asked. She hated how soft her voice was.

The corner of his mouth twitched, but he didn't tease her or dilute the moment with a joke. "Are you okay? Something changed, and I don't know what it is."

A knot formed in her throat. She wanted to hide, to look away, but he sounded earnest, like he really wanted to know.

"I . . . I don't know what's wrong with me," she said.

"What can be wrong with you?" he asked, sitting on the armrest of a chair so they were more level.

She sighed. "So many things, Cristian. There are so many things you don't know about me."

"Like what? Tell me. It can't be that bad."

Her heart thundered in her ears. She really wanted to tell him about Tristan, and Elise, who'd stolen her business at the worst time in her life, and her mom getting married without involving her at all. But if he heard all the drama she had in her life, he might change his mind about being a friend, even virtually, long-distance, and she couldn't lose him.

206 • *Yamile Saied Méndez*

"It's too complicated," she said.

"Is it something I did? I know moving on to . . . sex. . . ." He blushed. The dork actually blushed. ". . . is a lot, a big step. I, too, grew up in a super conservative home, and I feel weird even talking about it."

"It's a little bit that," she said. "Also, like, I haven't had the best experiences."

His face fell, but before he misunderstood and thought something terrible but wrong, she added, "I never did anything I didn't want to. It's just that I've never had the best experiences after *the act*, and I'm afraid about ruining this friendship we have." She was practically heaving when she was done.

He cocked his head to the side. "We take it slowly, then. I'll go back to the concierge and tell him I'll need my room after all."

She rushed to his side. "No! That's so embarrassing. No. You can stay. We can kiss, maybe?"

He ruffled his hair. He must have been tired after a long day. In Stevie's experience, jet lag hit with a force on the second night.

"Or I can sleep in the little room again. Really, it's no problem," Cristian offered sincerely.

Stevie was shaking, and she didn't understand why. "Or you can sleep with me? I just want someone to hold me."

He looked at her, and this time, she did look away. Stevie didn't want him to see that she was on the verge of crying. He opened his arms, and she rushed to them and nestled her face against his chest. His blood rushed in her ears. He was warm and felt so familiar. How was she ever going to give this up? After this trip, she wouldn't see him again, and she'd be back to her lonely life. How could she do it? But she told herself to enjoy the now for now. There was no danger in just hugging, was there?

"Before I get into bed, I'd love to shower, though. Is that okay?" he asked.

All Roads Lead to Rome • 207

She looked at him then. His eyes were misty, too. "Just don't put that cologne on."

He pointed his index finger at her and, smiling, said, "Gotcha."

After he was done, she took a long, luxurious bath that left her feeling refreshed and sleepy at the same time. While she'd been in the bathroom, Cristian had ordered room service and put the TV on.

Gingerly, feeling more self-conscious than if she'd been naked, she walked back into the room and sat on the bed. He scooted to the side to make room for her, but there was no need. The bed was immense.

"I think the others are going to get the wrong impression of this," she said.

He shrugged. "The girls know me, and they might think this is way serious than I'm telling them. The guys, meaning Santiago and Franco, won't care. And Lucho is secretly relieved I've moved on after Veronica. He's not the jealous kind, but he's not an idiot, either."

"I understand him, you know?" she said, munching on a garlic French fry. "She had you, and now she's with a good guy. The first chance, she might decide to go back with you."

He ate a fry, too, but he dipped in ketchup instead of mayo like Stevie did. *Who was more American than who?* she wondered.

"Once I make up my mind, that's it. I said I don't want to settle down now, and that's what I intend to do," Cristian said point-blank.

The silence between them was heavy.

"Unless someone shows up that changes your mind," she said, repeating the vow they'd made to each other in Rome.

"Except for that," he said, and turned away to the TV.

They watched TV together in languages that Stevie didn't understand, and that he knew a little of. Then they made up a game where she guessed what the show was about just by

208 • *Yamile Saied Méndez*

observing the characters' body language. She shocked him and herself by how accurate her guesses were.

Eventually, they fell asleep, and when Stevie woke up in the middle of night, they were hugging. He was breathing softly, like someone who has no secrets, and she felt the safest that she'd been in her entire life.

The next few days were a whirlwind. They were visiting different ruins and landmarks, and one morning, they went on hot-air balloons over the ancient royal city of Luxor.

While Stevie never had a fear of heights or flying, she was afraid of not being in control. Flying in a hot-air balloon had to be one of the biggest shows of faith as a human. After all, there was no rudder, no wings to ride the air if anything went wrong. It was fire and air and a giant basket containing twenty people or so, including their group. But the view of the Valley of the Kings and the Valley of the Queens, and the River Nile giving life to the land, was something worth fighting her fears for.

Stevie was so fascinated by the beauty of the early morning air shimmering in different shades, and the balloons so high above the one she was in and others so far below. One flew so low, it even seemed to brush the spire of a mosque.

"Open your eyes," Cristian said, hugging her against him. "Everything is okay."

She didn't want anyone around them to hear the conversation, but she knew she'd feel better if she talked her fears out. "What if the balloon explodes? What if there's a sudden gust of wind? Or. . . ."

Cristian placed a finger on her lips. "Everything will be okay. Don't worry about it. This activity fuels the economy of this whole area. They don't want any bad publicity. They don't want anything to go wrong. And if it's not ninety-nine percent safe, they won't let the balloons leave the field. You saw how long it took them to light them up."

It was true. They had arrived at the field before dawn, and they'd gotten the okay from the airport around seven a.m.

All Roads Lead to Rome • 209

Ahmed had told them that in the summer, it was even earlier. It had to be the right temperature for this to work out.

And it had.

It felt like a miracle.

The Egyptian Empire had been around for millennia, and yet, she was one of the few privileged ones who had seen the valley from above. When it was time to land, she braced herself for the impact, but it was as smooth as a butterfly landing on a flower. When the balloon started descending, pickup trucks headed in its direction to help the operator land. Little kids also followed the balloons, riding white donkeys.

Stevie's heart softened every time she looked into a child's deep eyes, and after one let her go on a ride on the donkey named Tina he led with a rope, she gave him a generous tip. She knew a little money wouldn't help much, but it was the least she could do. When she was done riding, she turned around to see Cristian taking pictures of her.

"I can't believe I didn't take any pictures in the balloon!" she exclaimed, sad. "They would've made for the best posts on social." She could imagine her mom's eyes popping out of her head when she saw where Stevie was and what she was doing.

"I'll send them to you," he said. "I took a lot."

She was confused, and he added, "You were too busy looking at the landscape."

She leaned against him. She was so much shorter than him wearing sneakers, but she loved how mismatched they were.

They still had a few more days to enjoy. After Luxor, they headed to Aswan to catch a boat that would sail the Nile for three days. They each had a cabin, and while Connie and Aldana spent a lot of time reading Agatha Christie's books in the little library, and the guys slept in or went on canoe excursions, Stevie spent a lot of time talking to the sailors, about their days and their jobs, the families they only saw once a week. She especially loved to talk with Samir, the cook. He was in his thirties but looked much older, and he smoked like a chimney. But

210 • *Yamile Saied Méndez*

he was so skilled, cooking for the fifteen guests onboard and the crew of ten, in a little stove and a few pans. He showed her how to make rice the Egyptian way and different sauces. Eggplants and tomatoes, and fish. So much fresh fish. Looking at him cook, Stevie realized she kept waiting to have an industrial-sized kitchen before she launched her catering service, but all she needed was the courage to start.

The cruise came to an end, and soon, they were all at the airport, ready to head back to their destinations. Connie, Santiago, and Franco back to Buenos Aires. Aldana to Munich, and Lucho back to Córdoba, where he lived with Veronica. Cristian would be heading to Rosario, via Buenos Aires. And Stevie back to Utah to start recruiting season once again.

The thought of going back to the snow depressed her. Then she realized that it wasn't as much the snow, as the loneliness. Nadia had her fiancé. Madi was doing her yoga certification, and Stevie had to start training fresh salesguys for the summer.

One by one, all the flights left, until the last two remaining from their group were Cristian and Stevie. "We couldn't have planned it better," he said.

"You planned it all," she corrected him.

Cristian shrugged. "Not the flights."

"But the experience. You're good at this, Cristian. Everything went perfectly. Thanks for inviting me."

His eyes were Mediterranean blue today.

"This sounds like a goodbye, and I hate goodbyes," he said, looking away from her.

"Believe me, *not* being able to say goodbye is the worst."

"I know," he whispered. "Being apart just sucks."

Stevie leaned against him again. If only the two of them could have one more day together. Surely that would be enough to give her the motivation she needed to face real life.

He sighed. "That's what Ross said, too, when I was in a coma. She said that if I died without waking up at least for a second so she could say goodbye, she would've killed me."

Stevie laughed, but again, a knot formed in her throat as she thought of her dad. Of Tristan. "So, let's just say *see you later*," she said. "I hope we don't wait a whole year to see each other again." Then she had an idea and said, "Wait, why don't you come see Ross in Las Vegas? I can meet you there! It's only an hour away from me, by plane, I mean. In a car, it's like six hours from Salt Lake."

But he looked serious, and she thought that maybe he didn't want to introduce her to his family. The thought hurt, but she understood where he was coming from. After all, she hadn't even told her family about him yet, at least not the whole story.

"You don't have to introduce me to your grandma or the rest of your family," she said, trying to sound reassuring. "We can just meet for dinner somewhere. To catch up."

"I'd like that very much."

He hugged her so tight, it kind of hurt, but she didn't want him to let go. Finally, she picked up her rolling case and her backpack. "I'll see you around, fiancé. Unless you find the love of your life. In that case, just let me know. I'll be happy for you."

"You, too," he said.

The airline attendant started calling for passengers heading to Paris, her layover. She started walking toward the gate, and Cristian called, "Estefanía!"

She felt her insides vibrate with his voice. She turned around, and he was there beside her again. He leaned over and kissed her on the lips. She wished she could stop time forever.

Why had she been such an idiot? Why hadn't she slept with him every night they had, even if they never saw each other again? There was no time for *what if*s now. Just regrets. So many regrets.

"It's not that I don't want you to meet my grandma. It's just that I don't like going to the States. Not the best memories, you see?"

The flight attendant called again, and Stevie sighed. She was so tempted to stay, to miss the flight. She was about to say this

212 • *Yamile Saied Méndez*

when Cristian, who must have read her intentions in her eyes, stopped her with a kiss again. "You have to go now. Let's talk later."

And she left. A part of her heart stayed in Cairo forever with the boy she'd met in Rome.

Chapter 22

It's not that Stevie was a bitch with a rock for a heart, like many of the guys said; in reality, she was scared of dwelling on her feelings too long for fear of not coming back from that journey alive. The older she got, the farther away her dream of becoming a chef seemed. She was too invested in this sales industry. If she left now, the vice president of the company had said, she would lose her residual, the hard-earned money she'd acquired through years of leaving her feelings aside, lowering her head, and working.

During her flight to Paris, and then to Salt Lake, she and Cristian chatted the whole time. It was still easier for her, at least, to bare her real self on text. When she was face-to-face with him, she was too self-conscious. She couldn't string along more than two sentences together without getting choked up or embarrassing herself. Like the time she said she'd come see him in Las Vegas. What had she been thinking? Of course he'd freak out. Like she would if he had suggested to visit her in Utah.

The people they were when together were too different from

214 • *Yamile Saied Méndez*

their everyday personas. The older she got, the wider the gap between these two parts of her soul became.

When her flight landed, she got a barrage of pictures from Cristian. She was great at taking pictures of landscapes, and she had quite her share of selfies, but real candids? Those were rare. The only others she had were the ones she took with Madi and Nadia, and only because they always insisted on documenting the passing of time on their friendship.

She smiled so wide looking at pictures of her riding Tina, the donkey, or cooking side by side with Samir, or sewing the sails with the crew at the end of the day. If she'd been born a man, she'd move to Egypt to sail the Nile with them.

But how could she complain? At least compared to other women, especially those her age, Stevie had all the freedom in the world. Too much, even. She felt unmoored, un-homed. And then she saw her mom's text.

I miss you, it read. She'd attached a picture of a baby. Stevie felt a jolt. At first, she thought it was one of Tristan's she had never seen before. Then her mom sent her another, this time of a young Ana María holding that baby—Stevie.

Stevie had never thought she and her mom looked anything alike. Maybe they weren't so similar in their features, but the way Ana María had looked at baby. Stevie had the same intensity with which she'd looked at Tristan. For a second, she was mad that her mom would send this to her out of the blue. Didn't she know how it rattled a person to see this when they were unprepared? But maybe she had known, which was why she had sent it.

Stevie usually preferred text over voice calls, but with her mom, it was best to hear her voice. That way, she could understand the current of emotions neither one would have ever put into words. As she headed to baggage check, she dialed her mom's number. Her heart started racing.

Her mom picked up at the first ring.

"Hi!" they both said at the same time, and then there was an awkward silence.

All Roads Lead to Rome • 215

"Thanks for the picture," Stevie said, knowing that it was always her job to breach the distance. Her mom had texted her first, though. Now they were even. "At first I thought it was Tristan."

There were so many things they could never talk about, like what Ana María and Federico had been arguing about when he died. But Stevie could only talk about Tristan with her mom, and she never wasted the chance.

"It reminded me of him, too," Ana María said softly. "I . . . I knew you were coming home today. Do you want to stop by for lunch?"

She'd never say it aloud, but Stevie had been waiting for an invitation, an olive branch of peace. "I'd love to. I'm grabbing my luggage, and I'll come right over. Or whenever you want to if now doesn't work out. It's up to you."

"Now is okay," Ana María said.

There was nothing to add, but Stevie asked, "How did you know I'd be back today?"

"Maximo told me," Ana María replied, and there was the glow of pride in her voice. "He said you two spoke on New Year's."

As if they'd called him with their thoughts, Stevie's phone vibrated again with an incoming text.

Welcome home, Titi Stevie, read the caption of a picture of Jonah, her nephew. Other than the eyes, he looked nothing like Max. He was all Erin, red hair and all. He was adorable.

"He just texted me a picture of Jonah," Stevie said. "Okay, I'll see you soon."

She hung up and grabbed her suitcase.

True to her tradition, Stevie had come back from her travels with plenty of presents. Small little trinkets. She had evil-eye bracelets for her friends, and for Erin, Max, and Ana María. Perfume for her Abuela Yoli, and a little woolen camel for Jonah.

As she arrived at her mom's house—her childhood home, af-

216 • *Yamile Saied Méndez*

ter all—she saw Frank's car parked in the driveway and realized she didn't have anything for him. She kept forgetting he existed, that technically, he was part of her family, although she'd never be part of his. Funny how these things worked.

She swore under her breath and resolved to give him a carving of the Sphinx that she'd intended to place in her office at work. She hated to part with it, but after her mom's grand gesture, she couldn't show up empty-handed.

She stood at the door and hesitated. She found the spare key under the rock that had the painted handprints of little Stevie and Max and held it in her hand for a heartbeat before she put it away. There were so many things to consider when she came back to the house where she'd grown up. With Frank living here, and after what had happened last Christmas, she didn't feel like she could walk in. But she was nervous that if she rang the bell, her mom would be offended. But she was used to her mom finding offense over anything.

Stevie opted for ringing the doorbell. Immediately, she noticed that her mom had a different security system, and told herself it didn't matter, that she could do whatever she wanted.

"Coming," her mom said, and Stevie exhaled forcefully when she realized she could've texted her mom and let her know she was walking in, or that she was at the door.

Her brain wasn't working properly for the nerves and the lack of sleep.

Ana María opened the door, and it seemed that it took her a couple of seconds to process that the woman at the door was her daughter.

"Hi, Mami," Stevie said.

Her mom had a fresh pixie cut that made her look even more like a doll. And also, as with ninety percent of the white women in their area, her hair was also heavily highlighted, pretty much all blond. She was so pale, and her foundation made her look even paler, but Stevie really didn't have it in her heart to judge her mom for wanting to blend in with her new family.

All Roads Lead to Rome • 217

"Hi, Stephanie," Ana María said, leaning in to kiss her on the cheek. Even her perfume was different. For years, she'd used Chanel No. 5 that Federico gave her for her birthday every year. Now, Stevie had no idea what she wore, but she couldn't deny it was still elegant and sophisticated.

A gust of wind blew, and Ana María seemed to realize they were still standing at the door. "Come in before the snow blows in and makes a mess," she said.

Stevie did as she was told, wishing that her mom had hugged her, at least briefly. When she walked in, she saw that the house was completely remodeled. It had been gutted and rebuilt from scratch. Even the wall that had separated the sitting room at the entry and the kitchen had been erased, making it a grand room. It was all white and neutrals, clean, modern lines. Really beautiful. Really cold.

Not that there had been a lot of warmth in their home before, but at least she'd been happy, until she grew up. Ana María watched her expectantly. Was this why she wanted Stevie to come over? To show her that everything had changed? If she had hated the house so much, why hadn't she just sold it and moved? Why didn't she and her new husband move to *his* house?

Stevie stood in front of a blown-up family portrait. An impossibly large group of people for being just one family stood in front of Tibble Fork, the lake up in American Fork Canyon. The mountains in the background were majestic, dressed in white and every tone of gold and ochre. It had been taken in the fall. She saw Max, Erin, and Jonah right next to Ana María, and the rest of the people on Frank's side.

Ana María cleared her throat, and when Stevie looked at her, she thought that her mom was blushing, as if she had forgotten about this portrait, and now couldn't come up with an excuse for why Stevie wasn't in it.

"It's nice," Stevie said, pointing to the wall with her head.

"You were out of town, Max said," Ana María whispered.

Stevie was already exhausted, and she couldn't wait to run

218 • *Yamile Saied Méndez*

out of this house that held no traces of her, or Tristan. She was tired of her mom blaming her for the sorrow, and now using Max as an excuse for the distance between them. She walked to the kitchen island. There was a tea set laid out, and sandwiches and soup. Two tiny cupcakes with the logo of *Twins' Treats* sat on the table.

Stevie froze.

"Come eat before it gets cold," Ana María said, waving her over.

Stevie felt like she was in a dream. She sat on the stool, while her mom fussed around her, serving her soup and a half sandwich.

"Where did you find this stuff?" Stevie asked, but her voice sounded distant, like she wasn't the one who was speaking.

Ana María beamed. "You like it? I thought it was lovely. It reminded me of the little baby meals you made when you were younger."

How to tell her? How to explain to Ana María how much it hurt to see the actual proof of her having failed in front of her? No. Not failing. It was worse than that. It was being taken advantage of. It was being kicked when she was already on the ground. She almost didn't say anything, but she couldn't contain the words.

"Remember that client I had in Park City? The first one I ever had?" she asked, rubbing her thumb and index on the velour tag.

Ana María thought for a second, as if unsure of where the conversation was going. "Yes. . . . Why?"

Stevie scoffed. "That woman stole my recipes and my idea. She even used the logo I had of Tristan's profile and put the one of her twins."

Ana María gasped, and her hand flew to her mouth. In that moment, her new husband came downstairs. Stevie should've noticed there were three teacups, that he had planned on joining them. Of course. Why did it bother her so much if he did, though? He was the man of the house now. He was her mother's husband. Ana María and Stevie didn't even share the same last name anymore.

When Frank looked at Ana María and saw her distraught face, he stomped the remaining of the steps like a charging bull. Standing next to Ana María, he held her by the shoulders and yelled at Stevie, "What have you told her to upset her now? Why can't you stop being so selfish? When will you grow up?"

No one, and certainly no man, had ever yelled at Stevie this way. And under other circumstances, she would've yelled back. Now, after confessing to her mother what had been done to her, she had no more energy to defend herself. She just looked at her mom, begging to step up for her, yes, even if it was to her new husband.

But Frank was on a roll. "She's been waiting for you like a child waiting for her birthday. Why! She hasn't slept in two nights. But every time, you manage to make her cry. Maybe that was allowed before in your family, but this is my home now, and I won't allow for my wife to be so disrespected."

Stevie's face was impassive as she looked at the man and then at her mom, who didn't seem to find any words.

"I'm not staying for this," she said.

Frank tried to bar her way, and for the fraction of a second, Stevie was scared that he'd hit her.

But she was a grown woman, and if he dared touch her, she'd press charges.

Ana María, still speechless, stood in between them. Why didn't she explain that she had been upset not because Stevie had offended her? Stevie didn't understand why she stayed silent. But she wasn't going to stay here to be verbally abused by this guy. She walked toward the door.

"No, don't go, Stephanie!" Ana María cried.

But the man held her back, and Stevie somehow got into her car, drove away to her apartment, and got into bed, with the same clothes she'd been wearing on the flight.

Chapter 23

Her mom called her hours later, and Stevie let the calls go to voicemail. Eventually she just went ahead and blocked her mom's number. It was for the best, to cut all bonds like this. Maybe she'd move to Florida after all, start in a new office, or even better, start her catering business. But she was too tired to even think right now.

She saw Madi and Nadia, who loved the presents she brought them, and this time, they insisted on her telling them every detail about Cristian.

"There's really not a lot to tell," she said. "I met him at Brady's wedding."

"You told us that already. What else can you give us?" asked Madi, frustrated.

Stevie shrugged. "There's not much more to give. I told you guys he was my Plan B fiancé."

"But you didn't tell us you've been talking this whole time!" Nadia exclaimed, outraged.

"We thought it was all a joke."

All Roads Lead to Rome • 221

"And it was—I mean, it is."

"But the ring?" Madi said.

"It's nothing," she said, shrugging. Even as she said it, she hated herself. Because the ring and Cristian meant everything. So why wasn't she telling the girls that she'd caught feelings for him?

"Show us some more pictures, then. The one we saw was so perfect, it looked like AI," Madi said, trying to grab Stevie's phone from her hand. But Stevie was faster and blocked her.

"Okay, I hate that you're forcing me to share stuff with you," she said, scrolling through her photo gallery. But she couldn't help smiling as she realized that his looks weren't even the best part about him. No. The best was that he was kind, understanding, resourceful, and talented—a well-read athlete. Practically a unicorn among men. Stevie couldn't have dreamed up a more perfect guy. If only he didn't live so far away.

Finally, she found a shot of him walking in Cairo, the long scarf hanging from his neck, and smiling crookedly at the camera. The sun hit his face just the right way and made him look like a Roman god. A flesh-and-bone golden god. Maybe he wasn't even real. Maybe she was living inside a paranormal book like the ones the three of them were obsessed with in high school.

"Here he is. This is my favorite picture I took of him," she said, showing them the phone, still holding it, because she didn't trust that they'd keep scrolling at the remaining pictures. There was one of him sleeping next to her that she absolutely didn't want them to see.

When she was sixteen, one of the worst things about being pregnant in public was that now everyone knew she'd had sex. There was no denying it. Even when she didn't put makeup on or wore the biggest, baggiest outfits she could find, the disgusting looks some men sent her way still gave her nightmares. The women hadn't been much better, either. The pity. The judgyness. The condescending pats on her belly without her consent.

222 • *Yamile Saied Méndez*

No. That had been terrible. It had messed with her head. Although her friends had lost their virginity in high school, neither one had been so stupid as to end up pregnant. It was obvious she'd done it with other people after Liam, but she was never going to discuss this with anyone, not even her soul sisters.

No. She didn't want them to see that picture. It wasn't necessary, after all, because the moment her friends saw Cristian, they went speechless. She smiled, smugly. Finally, she had found someone worth showing off.

Madi and Nadia stared at the screen and then exchanged a look. "What?" she said, feeling protective of Cristian. "What does your look mean?"

"You were behind the camera," Nadia said.

"Which means he was looking right at you," Madi added. "And he looked like he wanted to eat you with his eyes."

Nadia slapped the table like she was a judge in a TV show. "Exactly!"

Stevie pulled the phone away from them, and said, "Stop it, you perverts! You're being weird!" But she was laughing. She looked at the phone and hugged it, blushing beet red.

Madi covered her mouth with her hand, but Nadia said, "You're in love."

"I'm not in love." Stevie practically spat out the words. "I, too, think he's extremely hot. But that's not even the point."

"So, you never finished the story," Madi said. "What happened in Egypt? What aren't you telling us, bandida?"

Stevie smiled like a loon, and of course, her friends' minds went there.

"Did you do the delicious?" Madi asked, wagging her eyebrows.

Nadia scoffed. "Come on! It's not a matter of if they did, it's how many times, and how was it. What happens next?"

"You're so dirty-minded," she said, rolling her eyes. "We didn't do anything. We just kissed."

"Where?" Madi asked. "Give us some details!"

"On the lips, where else?"

The silence was deafening.

"But why?" Madi asked. "Are you like, okay?"

Stevie nodded. Other than her fight with her mom—well, her mom's husband—she was all right. Talking about Cristian made her feel elated, actually. But she wasn't going to get out of this argument without giving them something. She sighed. "The first couple of nights, we shared the room because there was water damage." Even as she recounted the whole thing, she realized how silly she had been.

"And?" Nadia asked, making a motion with her hand for Stevie to continue.

"Nothing. We just slept. In our respective beds, okay? We were tired."

Madi's eyebrows now were bordering her hairline. "Listen, you lived in person the first trope of romance and you mean to tell me you didn't sleep in the same bed?"

"We did sleep in the same bed, the second night."

"And?" the two asked, impatient.

Stevie shrugged. "And we cuddled, and talked and went to sleep. That's all."

Nadia and Madi were looking kind of angry at her.

"Poor guy! Are you that much of a tease?" Madi asked, and Stevie was kind of offended.

"What do you mean?"

Nadia swallowed. She might be all correct and prudish in public, but her fiancé boasted all the time that she was a freak in the sheets, according to his disgusting words. "Well, Stevie. Like, is he gay? Or not into women? Because it would take any guy enormous amounts of self-control not to do anything when they're sleeping next to a goddess like you."

"A woman might have a hard time, too," Madi said, fanning herself. "I can say it now that I'm older and have embraced my sexuality, but although I'm straight, I had . . . stirrings sleeping next to you when we were in high school."

224 • *Yamile Saied Méndez*

Stevie hid her face with her scarf. "You guys are the worst," she groaned, laughing.

"It's the truth," Nadia said.

There was a pause, and Stevie finally decided to be clear with them. "I wanted to, okay? I really wanted to . . . do the delicious, or is it make the delicious? I never know! Anyway." She swallowed. "When it came to it, I froze. I had . . . too many flashbacks. Too many bad memories of prom. . . ."

They knew what had happened during prom, and they were all silent for a second.

Nadia's eyes brimmed with tears, but she didn't interrupt her. She just let her talk.

"He noticed right away, and before he thought it was him that was turning me off or giving me the ick, I told him the truth."

"The whole truth?" Madi asked.

Stevie bit her lip. Big, fat tears fell on her shirt. "Not about Tristan . . . I just can't, yet. But I might soon. He's a friend, more than anything, and I've only met him in fun places, but maybe, by the time we're older, we'll know each other so well that getting married won't be because we made a promise in Rome. It will be the only logical thing to do, right?" she said.

"When you're old? Why?" Nadia asked, seething.

Madi caressed Stevie's cheek and said, "You need to go to therapy, bebé."

Stevie let herself fall back on the cushion, but she didn't cover her face this time. "I know," she said. "I need to figure out how not to freak out so next time I have the chance, I won't freeze up like that again."

"Well, I can't wait to meet him," Madi said. "Does he have a brother?"

"And a cousin?" Nadia chimed in.

Both turned toward Nadia with surprise. "And your fiancé?" asked Madi.

Stevie guessed that things between Nadia and her fiancé were

All Roads Lead to Rome • 225

not going exactly great, which made her glad, not because she was envious of her friends, but because she wanted Nadia to be happy, and Brandon was too little boy for so much woman.

"I'm not sure if he has a cousin. I don't think so. His sister and his parents died in the same accident he was in a coma for."

"So much tragedy," Nadia said.

"And so much love to heal it all," Madi added, always the optimist.

Stevie sighed. She knew that her friends would approve of Cristian. Now, for the more difficult part of everything, what to do next? Nadia thought that she should take things slowly. Process everything that had happened—and not happened—in Egypt, and then with a clear mind, reassess how to proceed.

"The most important part is deciding how to be together, Stevie," Nadia said. "You need to get to know him, and not only on vacation, but in everyday settings, and you can't do that until you're within driving distance of each other."

Madi pursed her lips. "Listen," she said. "I wish we could get his information to do his whole birth chart and see what the signs say, you know? Do you think you can ask him what time and the exact place where he was born?"

"That won't be suspicious at all," said Stevie, knowing there was no way Cristian wouldn't think there was something going on if she asked that.

Madi shrugged. "It doesn't really matter, though. We know you're both due for your Saturn returns this year."

Nadia and Stevie exchanged a look. When Madi went all new age on them, they usually went along, because what was the harm? Besides, she was adorable.

"Remind me what a Saturn return is?" Stevie asked, scratching her head.

Madi took a long breath as if to prepare for a lecture, and Nadia said, "The short version, please. We still need to eat, you know?"

Stevie winked at Nadia in gratitude. She was always so dip-

226 • *Yamile Saied Méndez*

lomatic and said the right thing, trying not to hurt anyone's feelings.

"Okay," Madi replied, a tiny bit deflated. "I won't go into a lot of detail. Suffice it to say—"

"Suffice it?" Stevie exclaimed, and they all laughed a little.

"Stop it!" Madi slapped Stevie's knee playfully. "I've been studying for my yoga accreditation, and I've learned lots of new words. Remember, Nadia and I are having our Saturn returns right now, too."

"Which is?" Stevie said.

"A moment in which you reassess your life, Stephanie."

"Things got serious," said Nadia with a smile, but Stevie had chills running up and down her spine. She loved it when Madi went all oracle mode.

"It is serious, girls. It's when you finally become a real adult, and you decide how to lead the next part of your life. Every time Saturn moves in its orbit, there are changes that take your life in every direction. With the return, it's a little like a death, and a rebirth. You get to spin the wheel of life one more time. We all go through this, but if you can be intentional, then, it's much better." Madi had run out of steam and took a sip of her drink, rosé, her favorite.

"So, the choice that I make now can change my life forever?" Stevie said, her heart pounding.

Madi shrugged. "Yes and no. Your life will change no matter what, because life is all about change, love. The thing is that sometimes we come into our identity right around this time in our lives."

"And how long does this thing last?" Nadia asked.

Madi said, "Anytime from your twenty-eighth to your thirtieth birthday. Why?"

Nadia shrugged; she looked both worried and wistful. "It's just that I told Brandon that we're getting married next year no matter what. I want to have a huge celebration, you know? I might make partner. It would be nice to start a family." She paused briefly and glanced at Stevie. "And, I don't know . . . see what the next part of your life takes us."

"See?" Madi exclaimed like a proud teacher. "You're already moving instinctively into the vibes of Saturn. I love it."

"And you?" Stevie asked. "What do you think your next part of your life will bring you?"

Madi lit up like a sparkler. "I want to have my own yoga place. Maybe go to Puerto Rico." She glanced at Stevie. "Travel on my own like you do! Maybe I'll finally meet J.R."

J.R. were the initials of supposedly the love of her life, the soul that she'd been with in different incarnations, and that she'd meet on this earth during a snowstorm.

Stevie loved how romantic Madi was. She wished she had an ounce of her sunny outlook of life, but she was too much of a Capricorn moon, to speak in Madi terms. She had her hooves—or rather, her feet—firmly planted on the ground, and she never had good results when she went all spontaneous.

"I was thinking that I could go to Argentina," Stevie said. "I have enough money to support myself and start my food business."

"A restaurant?" Nadia asked, her eyes shining.

Stevie shrugged modestly. "I want to be a private chef," she said. "I . . . I know it's not the most glamorous job, and probably I'll be cooking for terrible people, but I like cooking for big groups, and unless I have three sets of triplets in three years, I don't think a big family is in the cards for me."

Nadia and Madi clasped her hands.

"You don't need nine kids to be a mother," Madi said.

"Besides, instead of kids, think of the guy first. . . ." Nadia said. She, too, was an earth sign, a Virgo, and had her feet on the ground. "What are you going to do with Cristian?"

Stevie wasn't sure.

Finally, she decided that instead of letting things flow like always, she'd move the course in the direction she saw herself

228 • *Yamile Saied Méndez*

in a few years. She promised them that she'd let Brady and the higher-ups know she wasn't going back for another summer.

"You always say that, and you always come back, Stevie," Brady told her the next day. "I'll see you at the doors."

"Asshole," Stevie said, and stuck out her tongue at him.

He and Céline were expecting their first child, and Céline's attitude toward Stevie had softened a little. She'd even invited her to have dinner together. The only condition had been to bring a date, and Stevie had asked Miguel, a guy she'd met at the farmers' market one day, if he'd like to come along.

Miguel was from Costa Rica, and in every sense, he was the mirror of Stevie. He was hardworking and down-to-earth, but a dark reputation followed him like a shadow. Stevie had never had any issues with him being overtly flirty, so she felt safe with him. They had mutual respect. And because people's minds were permanently in the gutter, they made up stories about them, which left Stevie free of anyone else's advances. She thought that in other circumstances, going out with Miguel would make perfect sense. Besides, he was right there all the time. But, in her mind, she always compared him with Cristian. They were both good-looking and charming, but Cristian had a softness he wasn't afraid to show, while Miguel always felt like a mystery she'd never be able to decipher.

He was a good friend, though.

Miguel agreed to go to dinner at Brady's and Céline's with her, so she didn't have to be alone. He, too, was thinking about not going back to the doors next summer and kept postponing because of one thing or the other. He had been a surfer, and in Utah, he felt landlocked. His only sister and her kids lived in Salt Lake, though. It was just the two of them, so like Stevie, he had an anchor too heavy to lift.

"I've been thinking of working at Lake Powell," Miguel said.

"Doing what?" asked Céline, drinking a glass of red wine, which horrified Stevie, but Céline had assured her that in Eu-

All Roads Lead to Rome • 229

rope, all women had a glass of wine at dinner, even, or especially during pregnancy.

"Helping out the rich people with their houseboats."

Brady nodded, but Céline pursed her lips. "There's a market for that?"

Miguel scoffed. "You bet! Some people hire entire crews, including chefs and cleaning staff. It transforms the lake into a luxury experience."

The dinner moved on to other topics, but Stevie's mind mulled over what Miguel had said. She remembered that one roommate, Mireya, back in the day. As a cook assistant, she hadn't been that well-paid, but maybe things had changed.

Maybe Stevie could try a chef service, and maybe she wouldn't have to move to Argentina to try it out. Didn't Cristian say his grandma had a houseboat in Lake Powell? Maybe he could give her some ideas.

She didn't have to wait long to ask him. Stevie and Cristian talked and texted all the time. She told him about her plans to quit her summer sales job, because she figured the more people she told, the more obligated to follow through she'd feel.

"And what are you going to do for work, then?" he asked.

Stevie's heart started pounding. This was the moment when she could tell him she'd love to travel to see him. To see if they could work it out, be together. Now. Or that maybe he could try Lake Powell with her for a while. But she never gathered the courage to even start telling him, and instead said, "I'm not sure yet. Miguel's plan of working in Lake Powell seems attractive, but . . . I don't know if there's anything else I might do."

"Miguel?"

"Yes, remember I told you about him? He went to Brady and Céline's with me."

There was a silence, like he was considering something but didn't dare say it. Finally he asked, "Are you two dating?"

230 • *Yamile Saied Méndez*

She swallowed the knot in her throat when she suddenly saw things from his perspective. She and Miguel had been doing things together, but just as friends. But wouldn't that be seen as dating by some people?

"We're not dating. We spend time together, but . . . but there's nothing really going on."

He didn't say anything.

She couldn't stand the tension, so she asked, "Have *you* been dating?" She hadn't even considered that he might be seeing anyone, and now she saw how stupid she'd been.

The long pause that followed made her itch.

"Are you, Cristian? You can tell me. After all, I'm really invested in your love life, too."

"Actually. Yes. I have been seeing someone," he said, in a grave voice that made her shiver.

"Really?"

"Yes, like you've been dating Miguel, whether you want to call it that or not," he said. "You post him in all your stories."

Stevie sighed in relief. He sounded jealous. "Miguel is a friend. He went with me to Brady's and Céline's because seeing me with a date was the only way she felt safe around me. Silly, huh? But she's pregnant. I didn't want to upset her."

Cristian didn't reply.

"Why are you mad?" she asked. "Wasn't that the whole point of our experiment? Exploring, dating around to see if we found our other half?"

"I don't need another half," Cristian said, in that infuriatingly calm tone of voice of his. "I'm not looking for someone to complete me, Estefi. I'm complete as I am."

She hated when he got in this better-than-thou mood. "You sound so full of yourself, Cristian," she shot back. "What is a partner but a complement?"

"A partner should be that companion in life who already knows what they want. I know what *I* want."

All Roads Lead to Rome • 231

Stevie knew what she wanted, too. *Who* she wanted. But she couldn't say it. Not upfront. It had never gone right when she did.

"So, tell me about this girl?"

"Woman. I date women, Estefi. I'm not a boy," he answered curtly.

"Listen, stop acting like this self-enlightened being. I hate it when you get like that. Are you going to tell me about her or not?"

"Fine!" he exclaimed.

Stevie's ears rang. He hadn't yelled, but he'd never been upset at her before, either. Like she always did when she felt threatened, she closed up like a clam.

"Sorry," Cristian said after a couple of seconds. "I just have too much on my mind right now. She's great. I like being with her. It's just . . . complicated."

"Did you sleep with her already?" she asked, although she had no right.

She heard him swallow.

"It's none of your business."

"Did you?"

"I'm a man, and as far as I know, you and I never made promises to each other. That . . . that night? You don't understand how hard it was to be rejected like that, but I knew you were going through something. The whole time, I gave you space, and you know? We never have to move on and get intimate. We're friends. But that doesn't give you the right to even think that I'm not seeing other people or sleeping with them, if it comes to that."

She felt like he was breaking up with her, which was ridiculous. He was doing exactly what she had expected him do, to let her be free the rest of her life.

"You told me multiple times you're not ready to settle down. Ever," he said. "And I wasn't when we met, but I'm tired of

232 • *Yamile Saied Méndez*

drifting like fluff. Is that wrong? If I find someone, you won't have to even joke about ending up with me anymore like I'm the worst-case scenario."

She'd never meant it like that. She'd always been joking. But she saw now how she'd hurt his feelings. She had known that he had feelings for her, which was why she had felt safe sleeping in the same bed with him that night. And she appreciated that he'd given her time and space. She'd just taken too long and lived too far.

"So, are you going steady with her? Is it Veronica?"

He laughed. "It's not Veronica. Her name's Delfina. She's a little older than me, than us."

Stevie felt like she had lost him already. When he talked about this woman, Delfina, it sounded like he was smiling. And she didn't want to ruin this for him. He deserved someone who loved him unconditionally.

Once, he'd told her he loved rain, and Stevie was a storm. Just too much. Nice at first, just what he'd wanted, but then she became a destructive force that blew apart everything in her path.

She couldn't do this to him. She had to let him go. "Are you happy with her?"

"I'm happy with myself, Stevie," he replied, and she rolled her eyes. How could he say that? "She's . . . one in a million."

Stevie had waited too long. She'd thought he'd always be there in the background, the backup shoulder to cry on. The guy who never expected anything from her. And now he, too, had found a person who was better than her in every way.

"I'm glad for you," she said, hoping he couldn't tell she was crying.

He didn't say anything, and it was obvious the call was over.

She was putting off hanging up, because she knew the moment she did, that might be the last time she spoke with Cristian. But someone spoke in the background—a woman's voice. Delfina was there with him, and Stevie imagined he couldn't wait to hang up so he could be with the woman of his dreams.

All Roads Lead to Rome • 233

After all, Madi had warned her that this moment in life was a turning point. She should've listened and done something instead of waiting for things to fall into place.

"We can still be friends, like we have been all this time," he said. "It's not like you have to erase me from your life."

But she couldn't be the friend again like she was with Brady. The wild card every wife and girlfriend was scared of. She didn't want that anymore. Especially not with Cristian.

"I'm not going to erase you," she said. "But I think it's best if we don't talk for a while."

Silence again.

"Let me know when the big day arrives. Maybe I can come to your wedding, meet another fake fiancé, and start the cycle all over again."

Like always, watering down her feelings with a cheap joke.

"Bye, Stevie," he said. "Ti amo sempre."

Chapter 24

Five Years Later

After the conversation with Cristian, Stevie went through a period of intense anger. At him, herself, but mostly destiny. She was angry that the moment she had shown interest in their relationship moving forward, he'd pulled this surprise on her. That he was seeing someone.

It wasn't fair that she'd realized she wanted to take a leap of faith, when his feelings had changed.

Maybe her mom had been right. Maybe she didn't deserve to be loved like she wanted to be. Every time she opened up her heart to love, terrible things happened. Her heart broke in ways she'd never imagined were possible. But she couldn't help herself, either. She had a loving nature, and to those around her, she was devoted. She showed it by cooking, at least for special occasions.

Madi had told her that her Saturn return would bring life-changing events in her life. She had imagined her life with Cristian was starting out. Instead, she changed careers, finally. It didn't happen all at once.

All Roads Lead to Rome • 235

Although she'd announced that she wasn't going back to the doors, when Max called to tell her their mom had breast cancer and the medical treatment was astronomical, she put her plans and dreams for her catering business on hold. Max helped, when he could. But he and Erin had another baby, a girl this time. They named her Penny. Max was stretched out to the limit, so Stevie stepped up.

Her mom never knew it was Stevie who sent a check for her mortgage and treatments every month. After that time Frank had yelled at her, Stevie had never gone back to the house. She'd never reached out to her mom. Every time she did, she ended up losing. She wouldn't put herself in that position again, but that didn't mean she wasn't going to help in a moment like this.

If there was one thing that Madi had predicted, it was that Saturn would wreak havoc in their lives. Nadia broke up with her fiancé and instead threw herself a double quinceañera to celebrate her birthday. In the process, she reconnected with the only other person she'd dated in college, Marcos, and was living a fairy-tale romance with him. She'd even gotten a tattoo. Who would've thought that down-to-earth Nadia would have it in her to completely reinvent her life?

And Madi? Madi had eventually found her J.R., in Puerto Rico, of all places, and had moved there. She visited Utah once in a while, but she was happily settled in Culebra, a tiny island that didn't appear in most maps.

Stevie was sure she wouldn't have a romantic happy ending like her friends, although Miguel was always hinting that they could work something out. He was kind, considerate, and hard-working. Most importantly, he was there, all the time.

After Cristian had broken her heart, she'd considered getting her revenge and hooking up with Miguel, just to spite him. But she found that it was too much effort, too complicated. It was actually impossible. Even if Cristian had broken her heart by doing exactly what she'd been telling him to do for years—finding a girlfriend—no one matched up to him.

236 • *Yamile Saied Méndez*

At first, Stevie stalked his social media posts, trying to make sense of the random pictures he never captioned. A rainy day was surely about her. The cheap gold ring was obvious. But then he disappeared from all platforms. When she unblocked his number and sent him a New Year's message, he never replied. She imagined he'd changed his to make sure he avoided Stevie.

At least she and Miguel were still friends. They worked well together. He went ahead and opened up a company that provided labor in Lake Power: a captain for a houseboat, housekeeping, lifeguards, people who'd drive speedboats and surfboards, and chefs. Miguel was usually gone all summer, but this time, he was living his best life in the water, teaching people how to surf, and manning enormous houseboats for different wealthy families the whole season.

One time, one of the chefs on his team got sick, and when he called Stevie to fill in, she didn't even hesitate. She was lonelier than ever. How bad could it be? It turned out not to be bad at all. She assisted the main chef, who had provided the menus and bought all the groceries. After the food prep, serving, and cleaning were done four times a day (for the three meals and a snack), she was free to explore the lake.

She'd only ever been to Lake Powell on reward trips with her team. The one woman in a pack of guys. A few times, the wives or girlfriends would be invited, but even then, she had a hard time socializing with them. They didn't have much in common.

She preferred being a chef. She got her dose of seeing other people and feeding them in the most beautiful place in the world. The best was seeing their reactions when they tried one of her meals inspired by the delicious food she'd had in Egypt, or a dessert infused with Italian gelato. Seeing the kids have fun and enjoy themselves was her favorite part of it. Then she got to go home for a few days at a time, until it was time to prepare a banquet for a baby shower or wedding.

One time, she was at a wedding, setting up Peruvian-inspired appetizers, when someone tapped her on the shoulder.

All Roads Lead to Rome • 237

Stevie turned, but she didn't recognize the woman with four kids clinging to her.

"I'm Frank's daughter, Tiffany," the woman said. "Remember me?"

Stevie thought for far too long to be polite.

"Our parents are married?" the woman said, shrugging like she was embarrassed.

"Oh, of course I remember you," Stevie said, and because she was so flustered, she leaned in to hug her. Tiffany was surprised but hugged her back. Stevie glanced at the crowd, half-hoping, half-fearing her mom would be among the guests, but she didn't see Ana María.

Everything would've ended there, until Tiffany said to one of her kids, "This is Abuela Ana María's daughter, Stephanie."

The oldest boy looked at Stevie with surprise. "Really? I love Abuela. She's teaching me Spanish."

Stevie was stunned. She was embarrassed at how she'd never reached out to her mom. Why did she keep putting off even texting her to let her know Stevie thought of her, in spite of everything? She didn't know.

"How is she?" Stevie asked, retying her apron around her waist just so she'd have something to do instead of feeling like the worst human in the world.

Tiffany seemed to perk up a little. "She's doing a lot better. But I'm sure she'd be better if she got to see you once in a while."

Stevie felt her cheeks burn. "I doubt it, but thanks for saying that anyway." She sighed.

The music started for the bride and groom to dance their first dance. One of Tiffany's kids, the oldest—Tysin—rushed forward to get on the dance floor.

"You should stop by their house sometime," Tiffany said, and turned to catch her flock of kids.

That night, Stevie missed Cristian more than ever. She imagined how she'd finally open up, tell him the whole story, even the part about Tristan, and he'd hug her and tell her everything

238 • *Yamile Saied Méndez*

would be okay. He'd tell her to call her mom, forget and forgive, and let everything go. Some anchors keep us steady and alive, but others, when they're too heavy, can drown us. She imagined his voice against her ear, the depth of his eyes when they were the blue of a summer sky. But she had too many bruises in her heart for a memory to heal.

But she couldn't ignore the pain much longer.

Finally, before the end of the summer, she took the plunge and went out as a caterer and private chef on her own instead of working for Miguel. She called her business Fontana di Trevi, all her thoughts leading to that night in Rome, when she'd wished for Cristian to find happiness, and for her to find something that would at least dull the sharpness of Tristan's loss in her life. He'd be almost the age she'd been when he was born, sixteen. She still felt that age in her heart.

What kind of person would he be if he'd had the chance to grow up? He would've been a junior in high school, with a driver's license; maybe he'd have a girlfriend. Stevie would have raised him to be genuinely nice to girls and women, to always love and protect them. Maybe at sixteen, Tristan would also get in trouble. Not as much as his mother had, but the usual things for a high school kid. She didn't feel his ghost haunting from the grave, but he was everywhere. When she looked at her nephew Jonah from just the right angle, she could see a glimpse of Tristan. The ache was still in her heart, but it didn't cripple her anymore. Now it made her appreciate her family. Tristan lived in them.

One day, on his birthday, she went to the cemetery to leave flowers. She saw someone had been there earlier in the day and had left a bouquet and a teddy bear. As an offering, Stevie had brought flowers and a pack of chewing gum. It had been her mom who visited earlier, that much was obvious. It was the only thing they'd ever shared, the unconditional love for that baby who had only lived five months. She was grateful her mom was healthy enough to come by the cemetery, and again, she promised herself she'd stop and visit before it was too late.

All Roads Lead to Rome • 239

But she didn't.

Making Fontana di Trevi a success occupied her every thought and took every second of her day. This time, she was careful with her business. She never gave out her recipes, no matter what people promised for them, and she paid her employees fairly, employing mainly older teenage girls and single moms she met at Planned Parenthood when she went volunteering.

When she wasn't working in her kitchen, she was volunteering at the group home where Laurie Boer, the social worker from when Tristan was born, now worked. Stevie taught girls how to open a bank account, make a budget, and be financially independent. Between work and volunteering, her life was full. Still, she had a hole in her heart that nothing and no one seemed to fill but had a name and the face of a blue-eyed Roman god.

She'd been lonely for too long, until Miguel called her with a job opportunity. "Wanna come to the lake and cook for a family?"

Stevie got excited just thinking about it.

"Are you going to be there as a captain, too?" she asked, getting excited about seeing his friend.

Miguel clicked his tongue. "Not this time around. I did captain for them a couple of years ago, but they have someone from the family who can drive the surfboard and stuff. They just need a chef."

"Should I bring an assistant?" she asked, thinking of Samuela, a girl from El Salvador she had met the previous year at one of her night classes at the group home. Samuela had aged out of the system, and Stevie had become a sort of godmother to her. She'd given her a loan so she could rent her first apartment and a glowing recommendation at the restaurant that she now managed, Cancún Querido.

"That might be a good idea," he said. "They have a large group of people, all family."

"What's their name? Do I know them?" she asked. A lot of the guys she'd started summer sales with had gone on to open

240 • *Yamile Saied Méndez*

their own marketing companies and made bank. So much so that several, including Brady, had their houseboats, although it was pretty much impossible to get a docking slip at the Antelope marina, the most prestigious of all.

"They're not the typical Utah valley family, in fact," he said. "They're not from here at all. They're from Nevada, I think. So, what should I tell them? Can I give them your contact?"

"Sure. What's their name so I don't send the call to voice-mail?"

He laughed. He knew how much she hated to talk on the phone. "The lady's name is Rossana Allegri."

It didn't ring a bell.

"Oh, a lady? So, she's the boss, not her husband?" she asked, immediately curious about this person. "She must be rich!"

"Yes, she's the boss. Loaded, Stevie. You don't know how much money she has. Loaded!"

She was definitely interested. "Thanks for the referral, Miguel," she said. "I owe you."

"Come skiing with me in the winter, please," he said. "I don't know anyone crazy enough to keep up with me."

She laughed. "Okay! It's a deal. I'll take you skiing this winter."

"With my luck, now that you agreed to go with me, we won't get snow, but thanks," he said.

They hung up, and she got busy with an order for a quinces that had come through Nadia and Marcos's venue, Enchanted Orchard. She'd finished making the empanadas, when her phone rang. She saw the Nevada number and got nervous all of a sudden.

"Hello?" she said.

"Oh, hi," a woman's voice said. "Is this Fontana di Trevi?" She had a perfect Italian accent.

"Yes," Stevie replied. "This is Chef Stephanie Choi." She'd started using her full name professionally.

"Great! I spoke with Miguel, the captain, and he gave me glowing recommendations about you. He tells me you're inter-

All Roads Lead to Rome • 241

ested in helping us with meals at the lake? We haven't been there in a couple of years, and I'm not up to cooking like I used to. There's too many of us now."

Stevie already adored her. The warmth in her voice was like wrapping yourself in a luxurious blanket.

"I need some help making my favorite foods for my family. I have a few traditional recipes that we must have for the kids, and I'll bring some ingredients, but most others you should be able to get at any store."

Stevie's mind was already calculating and planning. "And the rest of the meals?"

"The rest you can provide me a few options, and I can approve? Nothing too spicy, for the kids, you know? We have a vegetarian teen and a vegan one."

Stevie was taking notes. "No problem." She loved challenges.

"Snacks, drinks, but most of all? Things need to be made with love," the lady said.

"Of course," Stevie replied. "For how many people?"

"There's twenty of us," she said. "Ten adults, and the rest are kids and teens."

"Any special occasions?"

"Yes, in fact. We have Cairo's fourth birthday."

"Cairo?" Stevie asked. "I love that name! Boy or girl?"

"A little boy. He loves football, I mean, soccer, you know. So, anything Argentina related will be welcome."

"Of course," Stevie said, already thinking of the cake-decorating store that would have fun things to make a soccer-field cake. She didn't even know the kid, and she was already invested in him having the best birthday ever.

"What are the dates?" she asked. "I want to say yes right away, but I want to make sure everything's in order."

"It's the last week in July. Does that work?"

Stevie gazed at her calendar, but she already knew that if she had something, she'd move it. A week in Lake Powell with a big family of Latines, celebrating a birthday party? She was all in.

242 • *Yamile Saied Méndez*

"I'm free. What's your email? I can send you menu options, rates, and a list of things I might need. Do you keep your boat fully equipped all summer, or are you bringing the stuff then?"

She knew of houseboats that were owned by multiple families. Sometimes they also shared all the bedding and kitchen stuff. But most times, the only thing they shared was the actual houseboat, with the furniture, of course, and then she'd definitely need help to load everything before the family showed up.

"It's fully equipped, and we don't share with anyone else, but we don't keep the boat open year-round."

Miguel had been right. To have a houseboat that only gets used during one summer week a year! Yes. This family was certainly loaded. Many times she'd had bad experiences with rich people like Mrs. Llewellyn, but Rossana was polite and charming. Stevie hoped her impression held after they met.

"Okay, we'll be in touch," Stevie said.

A few minutes later, Stevie emailed and sent her budget and her rates. Immediately, Rossana sent her approval. Stevie did a happy dance and called Samuela to get ready. The girl wasn't going to believe how lucky they'd gotten with this job.

Chapter 25

Shopping for food was one of Stevie's favorite parts of the process. The first year she'd been on her own, she'd known what it meant to go hungry. Shopping with an unlimited budget for a group of twenty who wanted to spend the best time of their lives was like getting ready for Christmas.

She and Samuela went over the menu, and the plan of action, like what needed to be prepped in advance, and what had to be done in the boat. They were giddy with excitement.

"I think we're going to need a little more help," Stevie said, biting her lip. "It's too many people and too many fresh dishes."

"You're fast," Samuela said. Every time she looked at Stevie, she seemed starstruck, for some reason. She had escaped a criminal gang in El Salvador as a young girl and crossed the border on her own. She ended up staying in a detention center for close to a year until she was transferred to a group home in Utah, where Stevie met her. She was tall and strong and had the blackest hair Stevie had ever seen. It was gorgeous, long, and straight. She had a big birthmark on her left cheek, but she

244 • *Yamile Saied Méndez*

wasn't self-conscious of it. In fact, she'd once told Stevie that the birthmark had saved her from terrible things more than once in her life.

"I'm fast but not that fast," Stevie said. "Do you have a friend who'd want to help out?"

Samuela blushed. "Any friend?"

Stevie elbowed her. "That roommate of yours, Ginny. Would she like to come with us?"

"I'll ask her." Samuela blushed bright red. As red as Ginny's hair. They said they were roommates, but Stevie had known right away there was something more than friendship between the two girls, but never wanted to tease them. They were so protective of each other.

"Okay, ask her, and let her know I pay well. Also, tips are usually amazing, and from what I know of Rossana, I'm sure the rest of the group is as lovely as she is."

"Okay, thank you," Samuela said. Before she left, she looked over her shoulder and mumbled, "Thanks for letting Ginny come along. She'll be good. She's hardworking, and she was worried about staying home by herself."

"Of course," Stevie said, but she was glad she'd thought about this. It was better to have extra hands rather than too little help. Besides, if Samuela didn't worry about Ginny, who was on the spectrum and had a hard time being apart from Samuela overnight, then she'd work happier, which always meant better service.

"We'll be there early tomorrow," Samuela said. "Thanks, Stevie. It means a lot to me."

"Absolutely," Stevie replied.

That night, she had to take medicine to be able to sleep. She was so excited that when Samuela and Ginny arrived with their little duffel bags with their belongings, she'd been up for a couple of hours. If Madi knew she'd even meditated, she'd be so proud of her.

Ginny, short-haired and freckled, was as shy as Samuela was

All Roads Lead to Rome • 245

outgoing and upfront. She always stayed a step behind Samuela, and the way Stevie's heart melted when she saw them exchange a smile here and there!

"Did you bring swimsuits?" Stevie asked.

The girls looked at each other with horror.

"I don't have any," Ginny said. "I . . . don't like wearing them. Can I wear board shorts and a T-shirt? I promise I can wear a sports bra underneath."

"No problem," Stevie said. "And you, Sam?"

Samuela winced. "No. I can stop by Walmart and get one?"

Stevie waved a hand in front of her. "I have plenty of swimsuits. Come take a look."

They walked into Stevie's room. The girls looked around like it was a fantasy land. Her closet was organized by color, and she had her collection of bags and purses on one wall. Nadia had helped her organize it. It was Stevie's pride and joy, and every girl's dream.

Samuela chose two swimsuits—a red one that looked like those the lifeguards wore on *Baywatch*, and a black one. Ginny eyed a tankini set that Stevie didn't even remember owning.

"Maybe I grabbed it from someone else by accident," she said. "You can keep it."

Ginny smiled, glad to have found something that was pretty but that made her feel comfortable.

Gazing around the room, Sam said, "You have everything a woman might need in this house, Stevie. You're goals."

"You are," Ginny echoed.

Stevie felt a glow expand on her chest. She'd never been a role model for anyone. How many times had her mom, people from the church, teachers, and even random strangers told her that she'd be a failure?

She didn't think she'd made it in life (she had wanted a family of her own forever), but she was satisfied with how things were shaping up in her thirties.

246 • *Yamile Saied Méndez*

"Okay," she said, clapping her hands, "let's get going before it gets later, and traffic becomes nightmarish."

"Traffic in southern Utah?" Sam said.

"It's a long weekend. A lot of people heading to Powell, Las Vegas, and the national parks. Even California."

They set out, Stevie at the wheel, and Ginny in charge of the music selection. At first, Ginny played some songs she thought Stevie liked because they were from the early 2000s, like the *High School Musical* soundtrack and Miley Cyrus's songs. But then she started playing some chill rock music that resonated deep in Stevie's soul.

"What's this? It sounds old but new at the same time," Stevie asked.

"It's called shoegazer music. Because the guitarist has to gaze down at the pedals of the guitar throughout the song," Samuela replied.

"I dig it," Stevie said, and the girls laughed at her outdated slang.

Stevie loved road trips, especially seeing the changing landscape from northern Utah to the south. How the snowy mountains (even in July) and luscious green canyons gave way to the red rock that made it seem like they'd driven into an alien world. The beautiful formations in the rocks, the resilient plants clinging for dear life at the side of the cliffs.

The girls, who hadn't been outside of Utah County in years and didn't remember any other place, were struck with awe.

"I never even knew this existed in real life," Ginny said.

"I always wondered why people would come to Utah," Samuela said, "and now I kind of get it."

Stevie was delighted to have given them this chance to see the world, or at least this part of it. For a minute, she remembered the look of pure joy on Cristian's face when someone reluctantly tried a new meal and they ended up liking it, or when they saw a place with new eyes and discovered the treasures hiding in

All Roads Lead to Rome • 247

plain sight. She was delighted to find out that she loved the feeling, too. It was like giving someone a well-thought-out present. That's how it felt making someone's life better.

She and Cristian would have made a good team. She couldn't believe that of all the guys she'd met in her life, he'd be her one who got away. But her melancholy passed quickly. They stopped in a small town in the middle of nowhere to get gas and use the bathroom, and Ginny was surprised at how diverse the people in the gas station looked.

"I've always thought Utah was mostly white people who've been here forever, but I talked to a Hispanic lady who told me she was fifth generation here, that her family had lived in the same house her great-great-grandma had built when this area still belonged to Mexico."

"What?" Samuela asked. "I'd love to read up on that when we get back home."

Stevie felt vindicated that the girls' love of learning and desire to succeed was there, in spite of what the lady at the group house had said. They just needed to be interested in something that applied to their lives to want to read and study on a topic.

They finally arrived at the lake, a serpentine blue ribbon cutting through an orange and ochre canyon.

"It seems unreal," Ginny said. "How does this exist?"

Stevie felt the awe in the girl's voice. She'd felt the same way the first time she'd seen the lake. "It's actually a man-made reservoir, one of the largest in the country."

"What do you mean it's man-made? Like humans dug out the area and put water in it? How?" Samuela asked.

"They didn't actually dig up the canyon. Glen Canyon has existed for thousands, maybe millions of years. Kind of like Arches, the national park. But they dammed it and brought water from the Colorado River," Stevie explained.

"A dam?" Samuela asked.

"Yes, they built these enormous walls at each end of the can-

248 • *Yamile Saied Méndez*

yon to contain the water, and then for years, the water rose until it became Lake Powell. Kind of like Tahoe, in California," Stevie continued.

"It's amazing," Ginny said. "What happened with the people who lived here? With the animals? Didn't that wreck the ecosystem?"

Stevie was impressed with her questions. She'd never wondered about that kind of thing at that age.

"Yes, it destroyed the habitat of a lot of animals and plants. This is actually reservation land, so when we're out in the lake, we're actually in the Diné Nation. There are specific rules to follow. And that's why you'll see in the marina that most of the employees, from those in the gift shop to the housekeeping company, and the captains that take the boats out to the docking places, are members of the Diné Nation. If we're lucky, we can stop by Navajo Canyon on the way back and take pictures there. A famous photographer's shot is a famous screensaver that I'm sure you've seen, even if you didn't know that it was an actual shot of an actual place and not a painting or an AI-produced image."

The girls listened in silence, taking in all the info.

"You think being here is ethical, then?" Ginny asked.

Stevie thought before she replied, "I know that tourism helps the nation. And there are talks about draining Lake Powell to restore Glen Canyon to what it once was. But I think doing that would hurt more than it helped. After all, the water from this reservoir keeps thousands of communities thriving."

"I think that as long we treat it with respect, then we won't be contributing to the exploitation the nation has suffered through the years, you know?" Samuela said.

Stevie wasn't sure what to tell them, but she was impressed by them. They parked the truck and the trailer, and Stevie texted Rossana and let her know that they had arrived.

A minute later, Rossana replied, "I'm so excited. We'll be

All Roads Lead to Rome • 249

there tonight. Head to our slip and contact Mr. Russell. He's our pilot, and he'll take you and your assistants to our spot on the lake in the speedboat."

"Getting there is like an odyssey," Ginny said, smiling excitedly.

"It is," Stevie replied, as she texted her contact. They'd need help, loading the speedboat with the food and other supplies they'd brought, like a portable pizza oven for one of the most important meals Rossana had requested.

Mr. Russell insisted they called him Doug. He was a Diné man with a laugh as large as he was. He shook hands with the three of them, and laughed when Samuela called him Dog.

"I'm sorry," she said, shrugging and blushing deep red. "I have a hard time pronouncing that name."

"Don't worry, amiga," he said good-naturedly. "My wife's family is from El Salvador, and they all call me Big Dog. I love it."

"I'm from El Salvador!" Samuela said, excited.

As they talked, they loaded up the fancy speedboat. By the time they were done, they were all sweating bullets, and every inch, the little bathroom, and the actual boat was filled with boxes, coolers, and crates.

"We did well," he said, appraisingly. "This is a lot of food!"

Stevie nodded and sighed. "I'll need to make a couple of runs back to the grocery store in the middle of the week. How far are we from the houseboat?"

"About an hour back, in the speedboat. It's more like six in the houseboat."

"Six hours!" Ginny replied. "How big is this lake?"

Big Dog's eyebrows went up all the way to his cap. "It's enormous. Which is why you need to learn the number of your marker, in case you're out and about by yourselves. I anchored it by a clear landmark out of the main canal, but if you go out, it's easy to get lost."

250 • *Yamile Saied Méndez*

"I'm never going out on my own," said Samuela.

"That's what everyone says until the water calls you," Stevie replied.

Big Dog signaled for them to jump into the boat and take a seat. When the two girls sat in front, he noted, "It gets jumpy up there. Put vests on."

The girls exchanged a worried look that made Stevie's heart bloom with tenderness.

"Will we fall overboard?" Sam asked.

"No, but we can't ever be too careful," she said.

"But how deep can this lake be? Utah Lake is like six feet deep in some parts."

"Utah Lake is disgusting," Stevie replied.

"And Powell gets to about six hundred feet in some parts."

Ginny went even paler than she already was. "Six hundred!"

"Depth doesn't really matter," Stevie said, trying to calm her. "You can drown in five feet if you don't know how to swim and can't keep your head over water."

"The danger is that when you're not ready to be submerged, the body can enter in panic mode, and you forget how to swim. Also, this boat will be going at seventy miles per hour. If you fall from it at that rate, you could end up unconscious," Big Dog said seriously.

"Or break your neck, like some people did trying to keep up with that social media challenge," Stevie said.

"Idiots," replied Big Dog.

Sam and Ginny looked terrified.

"When I signed up for this job, I didn't know what I was getting myself into," Samuela said, gazing back to the dock and the exit from the marina. All around them was a mayhem of activity as families arrived, others left, and service golf carts zipped up and down the narrow plankway.

"You'll be okay, chicas," Stevie said, laughing and winking at Doug. "Now, buckle up and enjoy the view." She sat next to Big Dog in the cabin, and he turned on the engine.

All Roads Lead to Rome • 251

At first, he navigated the boat slowly through the main canal. There weren't only speedboats there, but also cruise ships that took people sightseeing, Jet Skis, and even automatic surfboards that hovered over water. At both sides of the main canal rose two enormous walls of smooth-looking red stone. There were lines where the water had reached in previous years. Stevie remembered how small she had felt the first time she'd seen this gargantuan canyon.

Once they passed the line of buoys, Big Dog asked, "Ready?"

"Ready," the girls and Stevie said at once.

The wind snatched the sound of shrieking from their lips, and Big Dog laughed. Stevie had tied her green scarf around her head, knowing that when the girls arrived at their destinations, their hair would resemble nests. She laughed, too, as she played the girls' favorite music.

They drove for what seemed an eternity. The sun was bright, and the blue sky seemed painted in vivid acrylics. The water glinted as Big Dog sped through the lake toward the destination where the houseboat was anchored.

The temperature was perfect, and Stevie thought she'd had to remind Ginny to put sunscreen on regularly, or she wouldn't last the day before she fried like calamari. They passed houseboats of all sizes. Some were docked on the beaches, and some on the rocks. She tried to memorize the turns he took, but lost track soon enough. She hoped that he'd be the one driving her to the store come Wednesday, or that the person in charge actually knew how to drive the speedboat. The ride just seemed to take forever, but it was only about an hour.

Finally, Big Dog took a turn into a cove. Stevie smiled at the perfect location. There was a distinct mesa right behind it. There was a little half-moon beach connected to a tiny peninsula, and space to stretch your legs in the expanse behind the boat. The most stunning thing was the boat.

She'd been in luxury houseboats before, but this one was something else. She guessed it was three floors plus a helipad.

252 • *Yamile Saied Méndez*

It had two enormous decks where people would hang out. She guessed it had at least two kitchen areas. Big Dog slowed down as he approached the boat.

A man who looked related to him waved at them.

"That's my cousin Alfonso," he said. "He's in charge of all things electric, heavy lifting, and any other help you might need."

Alfonso helped them get out of the boat. Samuela and Ginny were stunned by how beautiful it looked inside the houseboat. Six Jet Skis were attached to a line going from the houseboat to an anchor on the beach. A surfboat was attached to the houseboat on the right. The speedboat was parked on the left.

"Welcome," said Alfonso. "It's great to see the rest of the team."

They all shook hands, and right away, they started unloading all the food and putting things in fridges and a pantry in the downstairs kitchen.

While the girls filled up a small fridge with drinks, Stevie inspected the rest of the boat. It was a dream. There was a regular-sized kitchen downstairs and an industrial-sized one on the second floor. There was a full bathroom right next to it, and a master bedroom with en suite bathroom. She guessed Rossana would stay there.

The third floor was an open area with hammocks and daybeds all around the perimeter. She went up to the helipad and saw that the view from up there was breathtaking.

When she went down, Alonso asked, "What do you think?"

"It's lovely," she said. "Where will the girls and I sleep? The hammocks upstairs?"

Alfonso shook his head. "No. There's a room for you. It's the other master suite that has a queen-size bed and a set of bunkbeds."

It was perfect. They had their own bathroom, and they'd have privacy to rest, away from the guests. She was delighted with how considerate Rossana had been with her. She imagined

All Roads Lead to Rome • 253

her as an imposing Amazonian kind of woman, blonde, with long acrylic nails.

"When's Mrs. Rossana arriving?" she asked.

"The whole family arrives in stages starting at six tonight, with the last group coming in at ten or eleven tomorrow morning. I think Rossana said she'd be in the last group tonight."

"Sounds great!" she said, clapping. "Why don't I prepare a lunch, and then we start getting dinner ready?"

"What's on the menu?" Big Dog asked.

"I'll make veggie sandwich wraps now, and for tonight, we have grilled chicken, garlic mashed potatoes, salad, and tres leches for the dessert," Stevie said. "I'll add the menu on a board every day."

"I love it," Alfonso replied.

The men set out to work making sure the rooms were in order while the girls got settled in. Stevie made lunch, and then they all took a break to eat and share stories on how they met Rossana. After they cleaned up, it was time to set up a candy and snack table in the downstairs kitchen, which was the girls' job. Stevie was in her paradise, setting up a meal for a huge family she was going to spend seven days with.

Alfonso went back to the marina to pick up the first group. When all was done, she took a quick shower, always mindful of the water usage, and got dressed in her black scrubs. The girls followed suit. Soon enough, the first boat arrived.

It was an American family, the Parkers, with three kids and an elderly grandma, Louise, who introduced herself as Rossana's oldest friend. The kids wasted no time in jumping into the lake. Ginny looked panicked.

"Don't worry so much," Stevie told her. "As long as they're wearing swim vests, they're okay."

"Is the water cold like Utah Lake?" she asked.

"Stop going on about Utah Lake," Samuela teased her. "Nothing is colder than that disgusting lake."

"Is that right?" Ginny asked.

254 • *Yamile Saied Méndez*

"That's right," Stevie said. "Tomorrow, either early before breakfast or after lunch before we prepare for dinner, we can go for a swim."

"I don't know how," said Ginny.

"I'll teach you," said Samuela, with a mischievous smile that made even Stevie blush.

Alfonso headed to the marina for the last trip of the day. "I want to be done well before the nighttime," he said.

"Why?" Samuela asked. "Doesn't the boat have lights?"

"Yes, our boat does, but not other people's. I don't love going on the speedboat after dark, because there are always people on paddleboards or canoes, or people who run out of gas and have to wait to be rescued without lights on. Too much risk. After dark, we stay put," he said, and left.

"This lake sounds more and more like a horror movie waiting to happen," Ginny murmured, and Stevie chuckled.

"Everything's going to be perfect. You'll see," she said.

"Well, to be honest, every year there are horror stories of freak accidents at Powell. People drown. People fall from cliffs or break their necks when they go cliff jumping. Or a houseboat that sinks, or catches on fire." Samuela kept enumerating with her fingers.

Stevie laughed. "Girls, nothing will go wrong. Things happen, but you only hear of them because they're so out there."

She grilled the chicken and made the garlic potatoes while the girls set up the serving area. The little kids had razed through the snacks and soft-serve ice-cream machine, but Stevie knew from experience that by the time dinner was served, they'd be ready to eat again. Water and sun and a stunning view had the power to open people's appetites.

Suddenly, one of the kids announced, "Grandma Ross is coming! I see the boat!"

They all ran to the lower deck to greet the newcomers. Unlike the first trip, when it had only been the girls and all the food,

All Roads Lead to Rome • 255

and the second, which had brought the Parkers, this time the boat was filled to the brim with adults, teens, and children.

Stevie smiled at the girls, as they washed their hands and got ready to welcome their host. Downstairs, cheers exploded as everyone chanted, "Nonna, Nonna!"

Stevie's eyes got misty thinking that this woman didn't only have everything material a person could want, but also had the most important thing of all—a family who loved her. This was success. Would she ever have that? She felt worry gnaw at her stomach. Did she deserve this?

Everyone deserves this, she thought.

The teens rushed to the first level to quickly wave at her and the girls, and then jumped from the diving board to everyone's cheers. Then some small kids rushed upstairs to get ice cream, clearly informed by the Parker's triplets, two boys and a girl, that the soft ice cream was unlimited, and delicious.

And then the adults followed.

Stevie smiled, each girl at her side, but then her smile faltered. She saw a man she thought was Lucho, the guy from the trip in Egypt, the one who had gone even though his girlfriend was recovering from appendicitis. She blinked, thinking it was just her imagination. But then she saw Connie and Aldana, and Santiago and Franco. They stopped short at seeing her, their eyes wide in surprise.

"Stevie?" Connie was the first one to exclaim and rush to her with open arms. "Is that really you?"

Before she had time to answer, she saw him—Cristian. He carried a boy that must have been around four or five. Behind her was a woman, no taller than Stevie, hunched over with age and hair white as snow, but dressed in pink from head to toe. She walked toward Stevie, a glowing smile on her face, and said, "Hello, Ms. Choi. I'm Rossana Allegri, so nice to meet you. Thanks for agreeing to come feed my family."

She hugged Stevie with such tenderness, Stevie felt herself

melt into her arms, and realized that although small and frail in appearance, Rossana had the soul and strength of a giant.

"Hi, Rossana," she said, and her voice sounded alien to her ears, so soft and sweet it was. "Nice to meet you. These are Samuela and Ginny, my assistants."

"Rossi!" Aldana exclaimed. "We know this girl. She was with us on the trip to Egypt we all went on a few years ago, remember?"

"Were you?" Rossana asked, and she sounded so innocent, but Stevie didn't miss the glance she sent at the tall, blond man who was still rooted in place at the top of the stairs.

Cristian.

All the others came to hug her, all except a woman with curly hair and an accusing look in her eyes, as if she hated Stevie. She wondered if she was Delfina, and wished there would be a tidal wave that took Stevie away.

But then Lucho came up, holding the woman by the hand, and said, "Stevie, this is Veronica. My wife. We have two kids, Lucas and Milo."

Stevie glanced at Cristian. He looked the same but so different at the same time. He was tall and bronzed by the sun, and his blond hair, bleached, was severely short. She could see a long scar on top of his ear, from his surgery, she guessed. But his eyes were the same—intense and bottomless. Except that now they were guarded, as he clutched the kid closer to him.

But the kid squirmed out of his arms, and Cristian had to put him down so he wouldn't fall.

"Careful, Cairo," he said in Spanish.

Cairo still had that baby-rounded tummy and chubby cheeks. A look of determination on his face as he walked toward Stevie. When he reached her, he smiled.

"I like you," he said, in a tiny voice that resonated deep inside her.

Cristian sighed and started walking toward them, as if he

All Roads Lead to Rome • 257

were afraid that Stevie was going to reject Cairo, which made her angry. She wasn't a baby whisperer, but she wasn't an ogre, either! She knelt down to Cairo's height and hugged him.

"You smell nice," he said. "I'm hungry."

The scent on his black hair was intoxicating. She closed her eyes so tears wouldn't escape them. "You smell nice, too," she said. He smelled of sunshine and baby boy sweat. "And you arrived just in time for dinner."

Those seemed to be the magic words, because everyone was hungry. While Rossana headed to her suite to change, everyone else got their food and ate around an enormous table and along the wraparound kitchen counter.

"Tonight, Santiago's family is in charge of dishwashing duty," Cristian bellowed.

There were a few groans and mutters, but then Aldana said, "We all have different shifts. So don't protest that much."

Kids and adults talked in a mixture of English, Spanish, and Italian as they ate.

"This is delectable," said Connie. "Stevie, you finally did it! You opened your chef business!"

As she refilled a tray with garlic mashed potatoes, Stevie felt Cristian's eyes on her. Out of everyone, he was the only one who hadn't come up to her to even say hi.

"Thanks," she said. "I finally did it."

"What's the name of your company?" asked Aldana. She'd aged well. She looked like the best mom in the world.

Stevie swallowed. She didn't want to answer, since she was sure Cristian was listening in on the conversation, but she didn't know how to get off the hook.

"Fontana di Trevi," she said.

"Like the fountain in Italy?" asked Veronica. She'd slithered up to Stevie's side without being noticed. Stevie felt a chill go all over her.

"Yes," she replied, lowering her gaze with the excuse she had

258 • *Yamile Saied Méndez*

to tend the chicken, but she looked up in time to see Veronica make a gesture to Cristian, who went bright red, as if he was embarrassed.

"So," Veronica said. "You're the famous Stevie—the one who replaced me."

It hadn't been a question, but Stevie felt she was being drilled. "I don't know how I replaced you on anything," she said.

"The trip to Egypt, of course," Veronica said, and laughed, but the sound made Stevie's stomach hurt.

Other than the veggie wrap at lunch, she'd eaten nothing, telling herself she'd eat at the end of the day once everything was done. Usually, when she'd been on other trips, she and the rest of the crew had hung out with the guests, or played games with them; a favorite one for big groups was Mafia. But now, she wanted nothing more than to go to her room and hide there.

In that moment, though, Rossana walked into the kitchen, and Ginny hurried to prepare a plate for her. Everyone fawned over the lady, but she kept looking at Stevie and smiling at her.

"This all looks and smells delicious. I'm so glad Miguel referred you to me," she said.

So it seemed that the old lady hadn't moved the strings in the background to bring her and Cristian together, as Stevie had feared. It had only been an honest coincidence. Madi would say that there's no such thing as coincidences. How many times had she said that everything happens for a reason? Cristian had said that once, too. Madi also added that once we wanted something, the universe always works in mysterious ways so everyone can have what they desire the most.

Stevie wasn't sure what the universe wanted her to learn now. She only hoped to survive the week. "Thank you," said Stevie. "Here's the updated menu. I hope you'll be happy with all the selections."

She gave Rossana a printout with the meals she'd added at the last minute. A melon slushie for dessert, an eggplant dip like

All Roads Lead to Rome • 259

the one she'd tried in Egypt. Mini milanesa sandwiches for one day, and butter croissants for another breakfast.

Cristian peeked over his grandma's shoulder, and there was a hint of a smile on his face.

"Mint chimichurri?" he asked, and this time, Stevie was the one blushing.

Her mint chimichurri had been inspired on that night she and Cristian had slept on the same bed, snuggling like they were longtime lovers who didn't need sex to connect. They'd had room service, and Cristian had mixed a mint chutney with the chimichurri, his best invention ever, and she'd made it her own.

Cairo came up to Stevie and tugged at her shirt. She smiled at the way he looked at her. He had beautiful bright eyes that reminded her of Tristan, like every little boy did.

"What's up, friend?" she asked.

"Can I have another ice cream?" he asked in a loud whisper.

Stevie was about to start getting him one when Cristian intervened. She was still trying to make sense of which kid belonged to which set of parents, but it had been a long day, and she couldn't figure it out.

"Actually," he said, "no more sugar for Cairo tonight."

"Why not?" Cairo asked, his hands on his waist, and stomping a foot.

Cristian cocked his head to the side and said, "Because of this attitude."

The little boy narrowed his eyes as if he had lasers that he was shooting at Cristian and said, "It's not fair, Papi! Why can't I have one? Lucas said he already ate ten!"

"Ten?" exclaimed Rossana, and then laughed.

But Stevie felt like the floor had vanished under her feet and she was falling into six hundred feet of cold, dark water.

Papi? Had Cairo called Cristian *papi*?

As if to answer her question, he said, "This is my son, Cairo."

Stevie smiled, although inside she felt she was breaking into a million pieces. "We met already, but nice to meet you, Cairo. I have everything ready for your birthday party at the end of the week. Maybe you can save all your points for sugar until that day?"

Cairo's little face got all lit up as he considered his options, and then he smiled. "Deal," he said, and ran downstairs to watch a pirate movie with his many cousins.

"Thanks," said Cristian. "He has a sweet tooth."

"I can't imagine who he takes after," she replied, and then regretted it. She shouldn't act all familiar with her boss's grandson. She'd just found out Cristian had a son. That baby had to have been born of someone, and she imagined it was the woman Cristian had been seeing when they stopped talking, Delfina. Maybe she would be in the next group arriving the next day.

Stevie had endured nightmarish situations in her life, like her mom's new husband yelling at her over a misunderstanding, or Mrs. Llewellyn's husband threatening to call the police on her. But she didn't want Cristian's baby's mama or whatever she was to set up a scene if she found out she'd had something with Cristian. She'd been so careful at building her reputation, at growing her company. Was everything going to crumble because of being in the wrong place at the wrong time again?

She started cleaning the kitchen, until Santiago and his kids came up to help and insisted on doing their part of the chores as they had all planned before.

Samuela and Ginny had eaten, and they were playing with the little kids who weren't watching a movie. The little girls wanted to have a manicure session, and they'd lined up nail polishes on the coffee table.

Cristian looked at her and made an imperceptible motion with his head that she understood too well meant he wanted to talk. But she wasn't going to ruin her career for a man, not even for the one guy she'd been in love with since she first saw him when she was twenty-seven.

She turned around and headed to her room.

Chapter 26

The long cry in the shower helped clear her head and lighten her heart. But she couldn't hide in the room forever, although it would make sense for her to go to bed early, since she had to wake up before the rest of the guests to make breakfast.

From her room on the first level, there was a back door to a balcony, and from there, to the back entrance of the houseboat. There was a type of plank connecting the entrance to solid ground.

Stevie took the chance to grab the garbage bags that they'd collected in the back and took them far from the boat until they would take them to the marina on Wednesday, when she went back for supplies. There were rats and other rodents in Glen Canyon, which is why they left the garbage far from their camp. It was pitch black, and she took a flashlight. She hadn't smoked since her early twenties, but the urge to smoke a cigarette was overwhelming now. She was still so tense thinking of Cristian's partner arriving the next day that she felt she was going to throw up.

262 • *Yamile Saied Méndez*

She had no one to blame but herself. After all, when they broke up, her wish had been for him to be happy. And wasn't he happy? He had a son. Why had he named him Cairo?

And where was Armando, Ross's love? Had he perhaps died?

She wished she'd never agreed to this trip. She wanted to run away. She wanted to swim back to the marina and run back home. She would've if it weren't for Samuela and Ginny.

Stevie swung the garbage bag to the stacked boxes, and climbed to a ledge in the red rock formation from which she could see the whole cove. The houseboat shone like a Christmas tree, but the Milky Way was still bright in the sky. She lay on her back on the ground. The red rock wasn't as smooth up close but had the texture of sandstone. It still held the heat of the day, and it soothed her. She closed her eyes to steady herself, and then realized someone, or something huge, was breathing next to her. She sat up with a bolt.

"Ouch," Cristian said, rubbing his forehead.

Stevie rubbed hers. When she'd sat up, they'd hit their heads against each other.

"What are you doing here?"

He sat next to her. He'd put on that cologne that still drove her insane. She wrapped her arms around herself to avoid doing something stupid like brush the back of his head to see if it was as soft as it looked.

"I've been wanting to talk to you since I arrived. I saw you taking the garbage out, and heading over here, but then the light went out. Didn't you hear me calling for you?"

She shook her head. "The wind is blowing toward the water."

"I thought you had fallen off a cliff or something. Or that you'd set out away from here on foot."

She shook her head. How could it be that the one person in the world who knew her the best was someone who'd only seen her on vacation? Someone who was a father and had commitments?

"I almost did," she said, looking up at the stars.

All Roads Lead to Rome • 263

He sighed. He understood the gravity of the situation. There was no easy way out.

"You're a good cook," she said. "I got all the supplies, and I know I can trust you with my recipes. You can cook for your family. Or rotate, like you do the chores? Maybe Sam and Ginny can stay. They're young but responsible, although they've never cooked for so many people on their own. And fancy people at that."

"What are you talking about, Estefi?" he asked, turning her face toward him.

She slapped his hand away, and he took a sharp inhale. "That I can't be here when your wife arrives tomorrow."

"My wife?"

"Your long-term partner?"

"Estefi, I don't—"

"Cairo's mother? You can't tell me he was born in a cabbage patch."

Cristian looked at her. His eyes were brighter than the stars. "You think Cairo's mom is going to come tomorrow, and that's why you want to run away?"

"Of course!"

"Cairo's mom isn't arriving tomorrow."

Stevie clapped a hand over her mouth. All her fears were confirmed. "You're going to tell me Veronica, your ex, is your son's mother?"

Cristian started laughing. "What? You're making zero sense!"

"Tell me, then! Who is his mom, and why didn't you ever reach out to me and tell me you're a father!" She shoved him and regretted it immediately. She'd accidentally touched his naked skin, since his fancy gauze shirt was open. Like every time they touched, she felt a current go from one to the other. How could she be so attracted to someone whose love she didn't deserve? She covered her face with her hands. She couldn't let him see her crying.

264 • *Yamile Saied Méndez*

"Hey, I think it's time for me to explain," he said. "Don't be upset, please."

Why did he have that smooth voice that was worse than a drug? She had missed him so much. And now he was sitting right next to her, so close, and yet so far. So unreachable.

"I'm not with Cairo's mother at all," he said. "She left us a couple of months after he was born."

Stevie's breath caught in her throat. Music and laughter reached her from the boat, clashing with the storm raging inside her.

"What?"

"I mean . . . she and I had a one-night stand, and we were both careless. A couple of months later, she came to tell me that she was pregnant and asked me if I wanted to parent the baby, and I said yes. So, I did. And after that, Romina walked out of our lives. I never saw her again."

"Romina?"

"Yes, she was a master's student from Peru, can you believe it? What can I say? I have a type."

"But you don't do one-night stands," she said.

Cristian sighed and shrugged. "I did that one time. It was irresponsible, I know. And from that terrible mistake came the person I love the most in the world."

Stevie's eyes filled with tears at the intensity in his voice.

"Why didn't you ever tell me?"

He leaned away from her, as if to see her better. "You blocked me, Stevie. When I told you I was seeing Delfina, you erased me from your life."

"But I unblocked you a year later, and you weren't on social media anymore," she said.

"Someone stole my phone and hacked all my accounts. I had to start from scratch, and you know I wasn't really good at them anyway, so I didn't open new ones."

"You have an answer for everything," she said, petulantly, but relieved that no one was coming to claim him tomorrow.

All Roads Lead to Rome • 265

Relieved that they were still friends, that their banter was still as fun as the first day.

"We moved to Nevada, to be closer to Rossana," he said. "And one day, I came up to Utah and saw Brady."

"He never said anything," said Stevie.

"Well, he thought you were going out with that Miguel guy, and he said that if I ruined that for you, he was going to wreck my face, so I'm sure that's why he never mentioned anything."

"Brady said that?"

Cristian nodded. "By the way, how is it going with Miguel?"

"Miguel is great," she said, a little too harshly.

"I'm glad to hear," he said, a little too quickly, too.

They sat in silence, and then Stevie said, "We're not together, just so you know."

"You're not? But Brady and his wife seemed so sure you guys liked each other."

"Well, sorry to say that Brady and Céline maybe have the emotional intuition of gnats, because granted, Miguel and I might have kissed, once or twice, but it never went beyond that."

"Oh," he said, understanding falling on him.

"We're not together, Miguel and I. We've never been." And then she asked the question that had really been torturing her all this time. "What happened to Armando? Why isn't he here today?"

Cristian's eyes filled with tears, and she knew. She knew.

"Their love didn't end when he died, you know?" he said.

"Life's so short."

"It's so unpredictable."

"I don't want to have any regrets," she said, tears falling down her face. "When I die, I don't want to regret not spending it with the people I love."

Cristian looked into her eyes for seconds that stretched into eternity. "I've missed you, Stevie." He sighed and leaned into her.

Stevie couldn't help it. The inches away from him were torture. She leaned into him, too, her heart jumping out of her mouth. She turned toward him and saw a shooting star, bright blue, streaking through the sky. She didn't know if she deserved him, but she wanted him, so she finally put her hand over his neck and gently brought him closer to her mouth.

"I've missed you, too, fiancé."

Chapter 27

The next day, three more families arrived. They were bursting at the seams, but with so many things to do in the lake all day, the only time everyone was together was at meals. And every time, Stevie and her dishes were the star of the show. Everyone raved about her food, and treated her, and her girls, like family members. And not just at meals. The kids wanted Ginny and Sam to swim with them, to watch movies, and asked them to join Mafia at night. One afternoon, Ginny braved her fear and went paddleboarding with Samuela, and by the way they were smiling when they came back to help prep for dinner, things had gone well between them.

The next day, Stevie left them in charge of the afternoon snack, and she went Jet Skiing with Cristian, racing each other to the Narrows. The lake was a never-ending playground, and it seemed like their group explored every nook and cranny. On the last night, they got ready to celebrate Cairo's birthday. The whole group had helped set out an area out on the rocks, where they could all fit. It was a plateau with a beautiful view of the

268 • *Yamile Saied Méndez*

lake and the moon. She was a little worried about how sharp the drop was to the lake, but Samuela and Ginny had staked a garland of lights to keep the little ones away from the cliff.

Stevie had just finished putting the finishing touches on the soccer-field cake, when she heard the little patter of tiny sandaled feet and felt a little hand tugging at her shirt. She was ready for him. She took a candy out of her pocket and gave it to Cairo. "Last candy before dinner, or I'll get in trouble with your dad, okay?"

"Okay, Stevie," he said, rubbing his temples with pudgy hands. When he put his hand down, Stevie felt something was wrong with him. He was so pale, his lips were blue, and the hand that held the candy was shaking.

"Bud, are you okay—"

She didn't get to finish her question. He fainted and started falling. She threw the spatula covered with green icing and caught Cairo right before he hit the ground, his little body convulsing in her arms. His skin was clammy, but the worst was his lightness, as if his soul had left his body, and without it, he weighed no more than a feather. Until the shaking turned into thrashing, and she was scared they'd both tumble to the edge. They weren't that close to the water, but she didn't want to take any chances.

Stevie didn't know what to do, but a voice in her mind told her to make sure his airways were clear while his body shook.

"Help us!" she screamed, her voice trembling. "Cristian!" Her voice echoed against the red rock.

A second later, the sound of someone running toward her reached her. When she saw it was Cristian, tears burned her eyes. He'd know what to do.

Cristian only had eyes for his son. "Bring me the red backpack I have in my room. It's on the side table," he told her.

Full of adrenaline, she ran barefoot on the hot stone, her feet screaming in agony. But she would've run on fire if that would help Cairo. She ran through the kitchen, not really seeing the

All Roads Lead to Rome • 269

looks of worry in the others' eyes but feeling them burn behind her back. She snatched the backpack and ran back out.

On her way out of the room, Veronica crossed her path. "Is it Cairo?"

Stevie didn't stop, but yelled over her shoulder, "Yes! He's having a seizure or something!"

Veronica started calling everyone out to help, while Stevie ran back to where Cristian was with Cairo. He'd stopped shaking. His stillness was scarier than the convulsing. "Is he okay?" Stevie asked, trying not to take Cristian's attention from the little boy.

Veronica and the others were running from the houseboat. She reached Cristian first and gave him a bottle of water. They all huddled around the little boy. Stevie went back to the boat, leaving bloody footprints on her wake. She sat on her bed and cried until she thought she would have no more tears.

A little while later, someone knocked on the door. She thought it would be one of the girls. "Come in," she said.

It was Cristian, looking pale, his sweaty curls plastered to his forehead.

She got ready to explain that it had been her fault. Something in the food must have made him sick. He should know she could never be trusted around a little kid.

But Cristian knelt in front of her and kissed her hands. Tears brimmed in his eyes. "Thanks for saving my son," he said, and swallowed. "If you hadn't caught him, I don't know what could've happened. He would've rolled from the plateau and silently fallen to the lake. He would've died, and we wouldn't have known for hours."

"Is he okay?" She wanted to see him, but she didn't know how to ask.

Cristian sighed. "He will be. He's with Ross in her room."

"What happened to him? It was terrible!"

He nodded, his face stony, as if his memory were conjuring similar episodes that were too hard to put into words. "Cairo's

270 • *Yamile Saied Méndez*

had seizures since he was two years old, but it never gets easier seeing him go through them." Guessing the question in her eyes, he added, "The doctors don't really know what causes them or how to avoid them forever. His medicine helps, and he took it this morning, but too much sugar and dehydration can make his symptoms worse. This whole week, he's had a lot of sugar and not too much water."

"It's my fault." She cried, hiding behind her hands, but the image of Cairo shaking was imprinted in her mind.

"Why do you keep saying it's your fault?" he asked, softly pulling her hands from her face.

"I gave him a candy. . . ." She swallowed. "The food that I cooked made Tristan sick. . . ."

There was a pause in which the fact that she'd called Cairo the wrong name sank in.

"Estefanía, Cairo's not Tristan, darling." He paused. "And Cairo, who adores you, is alive because you saved his life."

She gasped and clasped a hand over her mouth. She stared into his eyes, afraid she'd find judgment in them, or worse, pity. But there was only compassion, and so much love.

"How do you know about Tristan?"

Cristian lowered his head and took a couple of breaths, as if he were trying to decide what to tell her. Finally, he looked up at her again and said, "In Egypt, you, too, talked in your sleep. You kept saying his name." He scoffed. "I was jealous. I thought it was a boyfriend that you couldn't forget. But then you called him your baby, and I guessed you'd placed him for adoption or something like that. Brady told me he'd died in his sleep."

Her heart thundered in her ears.

Cristian sat on the bed, shoulder to shoulder with her. "When he told me, I felt terrible for having asked him. I had no right to pry. I was worried, but I should've asked you, or just respected that you had never told me. I understand if you're angry at me. I'm sorry."

All Roads Lead to Rome • 271

Stevie's mind was a whirlwind, but she wasn't mad at him, Brady, or even herself.

"Speaking about Tristan always destroyed me, but not having anyone to speak with about him has been even worse." She held Cristian's hand, the one on which he still wore the cheap ring she'd given him that night so long ago. "But I'm ready to tell you about him now; that is, if you want to hear about him."

"I do," he said.

Stevie told him the whole story, about Tristan, and how she'd lost him although he'd been sleeping right next to her, and all the heartache she'd kept silent for so long.

When she was done, she leaned into Cristian, and he hugged her tightly against him. "I'm sorry you went through that, amore. I'm sorry you've hurt so much."

She cried on his shoulder. Contrary to what she'd thought a little while ago, she did have tears left, after all.

"What are you thinking?" she asked, sniffing when she realized the shoulder of his T-shirt was soaked with her tears and snot.

"I'm thinking that I should've married you right there in Rome, that same night. I should've been brave and kept you with me always."

"But then you wouldn't have Cairo, and I wouldn't have the girls," she said. Had her life gone differently, perhaps she'd have never started her business or volunteered in the group home. She loved Samuela and Ginny as if they were hers.

She didn't know why so many terrible things had happened to her, why she'd have to suffer so much, but in the warmth of Cristian's arms, she realized the best things in her life started happening that night in Rome, that all the shortcuts, dead ends, and roads she'd taken throughout her life had led to him and this moment.

Cristian, holding her hand and kneeling in front of her again. "I don't want to wait until we're seventy to be your husband, and I know that this might not be the ideal moment, after what just happened, and that things are more complex since I know I have a child. But I can't contain myself anymore," he said so softly, she had to lean forward to hear the next words. "Estefanía, will you marry me?"

The familiar panic made her tremble. She stared into his eyes that were the color of the lake at midday. She would never tire of seeing herself reflected in his lovely gaze. She didn't want to spend one more day without him.

And she knew he felt the same way. That she was his person, and that once you find that person, you can stop running and live.

"Before I answer, I have a question of my own," she said, and smiled seeing the alarm flash in his eyes. "Is a certain little boy included in this deal?"

He nodded, and she beamed at him. "Then yes, a thousand times yes."

She held his face in her hands and kissed him like she'd been dreaming for years.

Epilogue

One Year Later

Stevie didn't want to be late, so she left the house with plenty of time, in case an emergency popped up and complicated her day. Just as she'd feared, she got delayed, and not necessarily because of an emergency. It was the Fourth of July weekend, though, and with all the chaos and excitement of the preparations, she'd forgotten her town did a patriotic parade across Main Street. She was about to take the detour that the big orange signs indicated, when from his booster seat, Cairo exclaimed, "Fire truck!"

When her kid wanted to wave at a fire truck, or any big truck for that matter, Stevie paused everything, even life-changing events, and waved at the truck with him. The group of cheerleaders walking beside it threw candy at them, which Stevie expertly caught, like in her best years as a softball catcher. Even though she was worried that by the time they arrived at their destination, Cairo's smart little linen suit would be a mess, she couldn't say no to that adorable face.

When she and Cairo finally arrived at the restaurant, the sidewalk was already teeming with friends, family, and neigh-

274 • *Yamile Saied Méndez*

bors, but not a single parking spot could be had for a one-mile radius. But not for nothing had Madi told her this was the ideal date to start a venture. Stevie didn't understand all the astrological graphs her friend had drawn for her. All she got was that the planets and stars aligned to make this one of Stevie's most auspicious days of her life. She hadn't always been the universe's favorite, but she trusted the signs, and her effort didn't go unnoticed. Just when she was about to call Cristian, she saw him waving at her from the door of the restaurant. Then he guided her to a parking place he'd saved for her.

Nadia beamed at Stevie, gave her a thumbs-up, and mouthed, "He's a keeper," as if Stevie didn't already know it. In her midthirties, there were still so many things she wasn't sure about or didn't understand. However, she was certain of a few: Cristian loved her; she deserved that love; and she had to enjoy every second of the present, because that's all one got. She was going to enjoy the heck out of the inauguration of her restaurant, her dream come true.

"Abuela Ana María!" Cairo squealed.

A second later, Stevie's mom was unbuckling him from his car seat. Stevie's heart expanded as she watched them hug like they hadn't seen each other in ages, even though he'd been staying with her all week while Cristian and Stevie finished the last-minute details for the grand opening. Theirs had been love at first sight. Nothing and no one would replace Tristan, but his memory didn't slash across her soul anymore. Not that she didn't cry sometimes when she thought about him—grief is a treacherous beast—but the memories now were also comforting and sweet. She hadn't noticed when the change had happened— whether it was Cairo, or finally sitting down with her mom to repair their relationship.

"You look like a butterfly," Cairo said with adoration. His two obsessions were bugs and trucks, so this was one of the highest compliments a person could receive from him.

"I'm wearing your mama's favorite color," she said, winking

at Stevie, whose eyes prickled with gratitude at seeing that indeed. Her mom was wearing green, as Madi had advised.

Not that things with Ana María were perfect now, but at least the love between them didn't hurt. If there was anything else Stevie had learned, it was that love is always worth fighting for.

She followed her mom and her son to the sidewalk, and the crowd parted for her, but she wanted to say hi and hug each of the people who'd come to celebrate this achievement with her. Brady and Céline with their two kids; Nadia's whole family; Madi's mom and stepdad; the girls she mentored at the group home; people from all the sales teams she'd managed; even Tiffany, Frank's daughter, Stevie's stepsister.

Max and his family had flown in from New York, where he worked as an editor for a publisher, and they were running toward the restaurant. But it wasn't necessary, because there was no way anything would start without them.

The scent of Cristian's cologne announced his presence. Stevie inhaled deeply, and then she felt his arm draped around her waist. She turned around and stood on tiptoes to kiss Cristian on the mouth. It was a dance they perfected day by day.

"Thanks for saving me a spot," she said. "We got trapped at the Mountainville parade, and you know how it is."

He chuckled and lowered his head to kiss her again. He then signaled with his puckered lips to the front of the restaurant. "So? What do you think? Did it turn out okay?"

She realized he was talking about the marquee that read STEVIE'S KITCHEN. When she'd left to go shower earlier this morning, the sign was getting installed. When she was seventeen, making baby food from her kitchen, she hadn't dared to imagine that one day, she'd have her own restaurant. But the vision had been there, and she'd been fighting to make it a reality ever since.

"It's perfect," she said, pressing herself against Cristian. "Are the girls inside?"

276 • *Yamile Saied Méndez*

He nodded. "Yes, they and Ross said they'd take out the tarts from the oven and come out for the ribbon cutting."

Right as the words were out of his mouth, Samuela, Ginny, and Ross walked out of the door, and sent her a thumbs-up.

"I guess it's time," she said, gazing around to make sure all the most important people had made it.

"Olivia has a microphone for you," Cristian said, pointing at Nadia's niece, who was waiting behind a DJ table decorated with intricate emerald green and gold balloons, the colors Stevie had chosen for the restaurant.

It was a short distance, but those few steps seemed like a giant leap for Stevie. She took the microphone, turned around, and smiled. The crowd broke into applause. They were all there for her. She wanted to encapsulate the feeling bubbling inside her for the moments of doubt she knew would come back. She wanted to remember all the faces, the applause, all the happiness forever.

"Thank you all for coming today. My thing isn't words, or I'd be a writer," she said, and people chuckled. Stevie continued, "The main thing I wanted to express is my gratitude. Thanks to my family: Mamá and Frank, Max and Erin and the kids, Nadia and Marcos, Madi and Peter, Samuela and Ginny, Tiffany, Ross, Cristian and Cairo." Cairo cheered when he heard his name. "And also, Papá, Tristan, and young Stevie, for not giving up." She paused then and counted to ten. "All I ever wanted was a big table where I could feed my family. And I'm grateful that's what I got. I hope you enjoy. Buon appetito!"

While everyone cheered, Nadia and Madi handed her a pair of giant scissors, and Stevie cut the ribbon. People went inside the restaurant, and for a second, she stood on the sidewalk, flanked by her Nadia and Madi, savoring the moment.

Nadia's eyes glistened with tears. Good thing she had lash extensions, or her mascara would already be ruined by now. Madi sniffled. "It all turned out perfect, chicas."

"Sisters," Nadia chimed in.

"Hermanas," said Stevie, and the other two nodded, impressed at how her accent in Spanish was already so much better now that Cairo personally tutored her.

In those wedding planning binders, the last page had contained a sign that said: AND THEY LIVED HAPPILY EVER AFTER. Stevie knew there was no way to warrant happiness or avoid heartache. There was only enjoying the now, the present moment with the people she loved.

Life wasn't perfect. Who knew what challenges the future would bring to the tres amigas? But for now, they were together, celebrating love, and that was all that mattered.

Acknowledgments

I'm so proud of this book! In spite of its imperfections, I tried to do Stevie justice, and I'm honored to have written her love story, not only with Cristian, but also with herself and her two best friends!

Thanks to my agent Linda Camacho and the Gallt & Zacker Literary family.

To Leticia Gomez, Norma Perez-Hernandez, and all the Kensington team.

To my family and friends, especially Karina and Anedia.

And to you, readers. It's an honor to share these stories with you.

Discussion Questions

1. At first sight, Stevie seems like a very unconventional protagonist, but what are her fears and desires that make her a classic heroine?

2. Food and drink are intrinsic elements in Stevie's story, not only for her, but for all the characters. How does the characters' relation to food show their emotional journey?

3. How do blame and guilt affect Stevie's relationship with her mom and brother?

4. How are Stevie's and Cristian's views on second chances, love, and commitment similar or different?

5. How are Stevie's relationships to other women crucial to her growth as a character? How do these relationships affect her relationship with Cristian?

6. Grief is a recurring theme in the story. How do Stevie and Cristian deal with grief? What about the other characters?

7. Although Stevie is so talented and has many plans for her future, in what ways does she self-sabotage? What is the turning point for her?

8. Who are the villains in the story? Why?

9. What's something Rome, Cairo, and Lake Powell have in common?

10. Where do you see the characters five years after the story ends?

Visit our website at
KensingtonBooks.com
to sign up for our newsletters, read more from your favorite authors, see books by series, view reading group guides, and more!

Become a Part of Our
Between the Chapters Book Club
Community and Join the Conversation

Submit your book review for a chance to win exclusive Between the Chapters swag you can't get anywhere else!
https://www.kensingtonbooks.com/pages/review/